Ga|

Murder of Ravens

Mouse Trail Ends

Rattlesnake Brother

Chattering Blue Jay

Fox Goes Hunting

Turkey's Fiery Demise

Stolen Butterfly

Churlish Badger

Owl's Silent Strike

Bear Stalker

Damning Firefly

Cougar's Cache

A Gabriel Hawke Novel
Book 12

Paty Jager

Windtree Press
Corvallis, OR

COUGAR'S CACHE

Contact Information: info@windtreepress.com

Windtree Press
Hillsboro, Oregon
http://windtreepress.com

Cover Art by Covers by Karen

PUBLISHING HISTORY
Published in the United States of America

ISBN 978-1-962065-48-1

Author Comments

While this book is set in Wallowa County, Oregon, I have changed the town names to old forgotten towns that were in the county at one time. I also took the liberty of changing the towns up and populating the county with my own characters, none of which are in any way a representation of anyone who is or has ever lived in Wallowa County. Other than the towns, I have tried to use the real names of all the geographical locations.

Special Thanks

I would like to thank everyone who answered questions and enlightened me about subjects I needed to know to write this book. D.P. Lyle, Steve Rush, Wesley Harris of the Crime Scene online group. Family members Dan Conner, Mandy Dillman, and Tim Norman. Most importantly, Oregon State Trooper Mark Knapp of the Fish and Wildlife for giving me the information I needed to make Hawke's trip on the Snake River as factual as I could and still tell a good story.

Chapter One

Hawke sat on the bench seat of the Oregon State Police Fish and Wildlife jet boat, admiring the rugged scenery of the Hells Canyon. It had been a year since his last assignment to patrol the Snake River. He preferred riding his horse in the mountains and traveling the dusty forest service roads to the fast-moving river and its rapids.

Luckily, he'd been teamed with fellow Fish and Wildlife Officer Mac Cuperman. Mac patrolled the Snake a couple times a month and knew how to handle the jet boat and the numerous rapids.

Hawke shouted above the boat's twin engines and the water slapping against the hull as they pushed upriver. "Are you looking for anything particular this trip?"

Mac had both hands busy. The one on the right was on the throttle and the left was on the stick that steered the watercraft. He shouted over his shoulder. "Just making sure everyone is being law-abiding and safe. I like to pop down here at different times of the month and days. It keeps the illegal people on their toes." He wiggled his red bushy eyebrows which looked like two caterpillars moving across his forehead between his sunglasses and ball cap brim.

Hawke laughed and leaned back against the plexiglass that stretched along half the length of the boat and kept the bridge, or cabin area, and long benches dry. Their gear and food were stored under the seats along with safety and first aid gear and their weapons. He scratched Dog's head and stared out at the wall of rock that started under the water and rose to the sky on both sides of the river.

Dog liked going along whenever he could. This trip, Hawke hadn't seen any reason to leave him home. The animal had proven useful on many of Hawke's trips in the mountains and Dog was good company when it was just the two of them and the horse and mule.

It was July which meant the temperature the next few days could reach one hundred or more. Other than the heat, Hawke didn't expect to run into much trouble out here this time of year. Usually, a fisherman without a license or someone not being safe on a raft.

They'd put in at Lewiston, Idaho, heading upriver at 8 am. After an hour of fighting the current and several rapids, they were now in their jurisdiction on the Oregon side of the Snake River.

It was the time of the year for guided jet boat adventures, rafters, kayakers, and fishing trips on the river. Hawke wished one of the times he had this assignment it would be when there were fewer sightseers and more hunters. Then the river wouldn't be so full of jet boats, kayaks, and rafts going up and down the river as busy as a highway. The farther upriver they went, the more traffic they encountered.

Mac cut the engine and Hawke twisted his neck to see what the other man had noticed. A raft was tied up on the Idaho side of the river. Several teenagers were jumping off the raft into the water. Without life jackets.

Mac idled, keeping the jet boat moving against the current but getting close enough to the group he could be heard.

"It would be safer to have a life vest on any time you're in this river. It could mean the difference between you going home with your friends or going home in a body bag. That is if we find your body."

Hawke watched the teenagers look at one another. A boy on the raft handed life jackets down to the ones hanging onto the side as he said, "I told you it wasn't a good idea to jump in without a life jacket."

Mac waved and revved the throttle, pushing the jet boat back out into the faster-running middle of the river. They moved through several small rapids and around Eureka Bar.

Before they went too far, Mac eased back on the throttle and sized up the Imnaha Rapids.

Hawke studied the roiling water and points of rocks sticking out of the spray. It was one of the class 3 rapids on the river.

"Grab your dog, we're going in," Mac called over his shoulder as he shoved the throttle and they lurched toward the surging, roiling water.

Hawke caught Dog by the collar and pulled him up on the seat beside him. Wrapping an arm around Dog,

Paty Jager

they both flinched as water hit the plexiglass beside them and the boat tipped to the left and popped back upright as a wave hit the opposite side of the boat.

Several intense seconds passed as Mac maneuvered the boat through the choppy water and they were back moving upstream in a loping motion. They barely started moving and Mac pulled up to a boat tied to China Bar.

Downstream from the boat were four men in their thirties drinking beer and holding fishing poles.

"I have this," Hawke said, hopping out of the boat behind Dog. Dog bounded over to a bush and peed, while Hawke continued toward the fishermen.

"Morning," he said, stopping about six feet from the group. "Beautiful day to be fishing."

"It sure is, or was until you showed up," said one of the men farthest from him.

"Larry, shut up," the man closest to Hawke said. "Ignore Larry, he's been drinking ever since we got here."

"When was that?" Hawke asked, pulling out his notepad.

Larry pointed at him. "We're doing nothing wrong, why you pullin' that book out?"

Hawke held it up. "I have to make notes of all the people I talk with and learn about the fishing conditions. I'm just jotting down four men about thirty years of age, fishing near China Bar." He turned his attention to the man closest. "How long have you been fishing and have you caught anything?"

"We came here last night and set up camp and went to bed. We were up at first light to catch fish for breakfast." He tipped the creole toward Hawke, it was empty. "So far no luck."

"I hope you brought some eggs and bacon with you." Hawke grinned. "Just out of protocol, can I see your fishing licenses?"

They all handed them over, including Larry. Hawke wrote down their names and handed them back. "When are you headed back home?"

"Thursday. We have to be back to work on Friday."

"Good luck." Hawke put the pad in his pocket and pivoted to walk back to the boat.

Dog bounded toward the boat and leaped on.

Hawke waited for Mac to edge the boat a little closer and then grabbed the railing and hauled himself over onto the deck as Mac backed the boat out into the current.

"Everything check out?" Mac asked.

"Yeah. One's drunk already so we may need to keep an eye on them."

Mac nodded and sped the boat up as they continued upriver. They slipped through Warm Springs Rapids without any trouble and were soon cruising by Dug Bar and the flight strip that ran parallel to the river.

They continued upstream, stopping and visiting with the fishermen they saw along the way and waving to the jet boat tour guides. Mac knew most of them from their cheerful waves and shouts.

At Pittsburgh Landing, on the Idaho side, there were two tour jet boats tied up and people standing along the loading ramp.

Hawke walked up to stand beside Mac. "This is where the water gets busier with boats."

Mac nodded. "And where the public thinks because they are on a tour, they can wander wherever they want.

I hauled four people out of here last month with rattlesnake bites."

Hawke shook his head and sat back down on the bench. It always amazed him how city people paid for adventures into the outdoors and then didn't use caution when it came to wildlife.

From here on the water got rougher with more upper-level rapids and more boats and rafts to watch out for. Not just the large tour guide rafts but the individual rafts and kayaks. He was glad that Mac was running the jetboat.

There were kayaks and a tour boat at the Kirby Creek Lodge. Hawke had used that lodge as a base of sorts while tracking an escaped convict in Idaho. He was happy to see the place seemed to be thriving.

They passed a tour boat and he counted two boats tied up to the dock at the Kirkwood Ranch. Hawke's stomach growled as they continued through two more small rapids. At a sand bar on the Oregon side, they pulled up beside a boat and both Mac and Hawke talked to the fishermen sitting in chairs, enjoying the sunshine and fishing. The group consisted of two families. The kids were playing in the sand and the shallow water not far from where the moms sunbathed.

Returning to the boat, Hawke commented, "This has been a pretty good start to the trip."

Mac nodded. "Some trips are like this the whole time and others I feel like I'm playing referee." He backed the boat away from the sand bar and headed upriver.

Nearly every bar along the Oregon side and Idaho side of the river had families or fishermen camping or enjoying the day. They stopped and talked to all the ones on the Oregon side.

It was nearing noon when they arrived at the Sand Creek cabin where they would be staying the next two nights. Mac eased back on the throttle, turned the boat with the stern to the land, and Hawke hopped out the back to tie the boat to a large rock. Dog leaped off the side and paddled to the bank. He lapped at the water before walking out and shaking all over Hawke.

"You think I need to cool off?" Hawke asked his friend.

Mac placed their gear on the platform at the back of the boat and Hawke carried it up on the bar away from the water. When it was all unloaded, including the food, they hauled it a little over two hundred feet to the cabin used by Idaho and Oregon fish and wildlife agencies and Oregon State Police.

The building was large enough for four bunk beds, a cook stove, and a table and chairs. Just enough amenities to make a three-day stay comfortable for up to eight people. They were lucky to be the only ones using the cabin right now.

Hawke stowed his gear under one of the bunks and pulled out the lunch he'd packed for today. He and Dog sat outside on a bench eating while Mac stowed his stuff and found his lunch.

"You don't come out here much," Mac said, emerging from the cabin with a sandwich in one hand and a bottle of water in the other.

"I prefer my feet on the ground or in stirrups," Hawke said.

Mac nodded. "Fair enough. I feel safer in a level four rapid than I do on a horse."

Hawke chuckled. "I'm the opposite. A horse even

when they are scared or crazy can be jumped off of and you don't drown. When a boat goes out of control, you have only one option."

"True. But I'll take handling a rapid over a crazy horse any day."

Hawke held up his water bottle. "We each have our own path to follow."

Mac nodded and finished off his sandwich. "Ready to keep going? I'd like to get to the dam and back here early enough to do some hiking."

"I like that idea. Dog and I like to hike." Hawke reached down and scratched the coarse hair on Dog's head. The animal's tongue hung out of his mouth and he appeared to be smiling.

They cleaned up their lunch garbage, putting it in the container they would take back with them when they left, and climbed back onto the boat.

They made it through Sheep Creek Rapids without any trouble. As they approached Rush Creek Rapids, a level four rapid, Mac said, "Get strapped into the seat beside me and bring your dog with you. The water is rising today and this rapid is going to be wild."

Hawke had noticed several kayaks and smaller rafts pulled to the banks on the upriver side of the rapid. They had all pulled over to discuss the best way to get through the churning white caps. He grabbed Dog and strapped into the seat to Mac's right, holding Dog on his lap with both arms.

"We're going in!" Mac shouted and gunned the boat.

Hawke felt his stomach lurch as the boat shot into the boiling water and they pinged around in the waves like a ball in a pinball machine.

Dog whimpered when they came out above the rapid, making Hawke relax his grip. Dog jumped down and went to the side of the boat, whining as if he wanted out.

"Any chance we can pull over somewhere? I might have squeezed the pee out of Dog," Hawke said.

Mac laughed and said, "Probably a good idea. Let's get through the next small rapid and we can stop at Sluice Creek."

The jetboat easily navigated through the smaller rapid and Mac eased the boat up to the shoreline. As soon as the boat hull scraped sand, Dog leaped over the edge, lunged through the water, and took off into the brush and trees.

Shaking his head, Hawke exited the boat a lot slower and with more grace, before he headed to the nearest hawthorn tree. He made sure not to touch any of the poison ivy growing near the tree. When he finished, Hawke walked around a rose bush with wilting petals and found Mac already back in the boat.

Hawke whistled for Dog. He hadn't witnessed what direction the animal had headed when he'd leaped out of the boat. Scanning the brown grass on the side of the hill, his gaze traveled to the makeshift airstrip with rocks marking the ends and rocks placed as arrows to show which way to land and take off.

Bringing his gaze back to the bushes and trees along Sluice Creek, Hawke whistled again. He heard the sound of something coming through the brush toward him. Dog appeared with a large white bone in his mouth.

"Come," Hawke said and Dog ran over, dropping to his haunches.

Hawke extracted the bone from Dog's mouth and muttered, "I hope you didn't dig up one of my ancestors."

Hawke held what looked like a human femur and studied it.

"What did he bring you?" Mac asked from behind Hawke.

That's when he registered the boat motor no longer rumbled in the canyon. Hawke glanced up at Mac. "It looks like a human bone that has been out in the weather a long time."

Mac looked at it and jogged back to the boat. He returned with two evidence bags. "I'll notify Forest Service and they can get an anthropologist out here as well as someone from the Nez Perce tribe."

Hawke nodded and stared at the green bushes and trees cascading down the side of the canyon along Sluice Creek. "Dog and I could find where the body is if you want to keep to your patrol."

"Sorry, you know we have to have two people in the patrol boat for safety. It's been there this long it won't hurt for it to be hidden for a few more days. By the time your patrol with me is over, they will have rounded up everyone necessary for finding the remains." Mac carried the double-bagged bone back to the boat.

Hawke took one last look up the green line of brush that followed the creek up a ravine and returned to the boat. Dog trotted along at his side as if he hadn't just dug up what might be an archeological find.

Chapter Two

They finished the day making a full trip up to Hells Canyon Dam and back down to Sand Creek. The bone in the evidence bags kept creeping into Hawke's thoughts as Mac eased the boat up to the landing at Sand Creek. While they were at the dam, Mac had reported what they'd found to the proper authorities.

He'd wanted to ask Mac to let him and Dog out to scout around at Sluice Creek on the way back to the cabin but knew it would be dark soon and they wouldn't be able to see where they were going without more moon than would be available tonight.

"You're itching to go back and look for the rest of the remains, aren't you?" Mac asked, as they tied the boat up for the night.

"Yeah, I don't like unfinished business. Finding a bone that looks old makes me want to see if it could be an ancestor, or if it is a rancher or sheepherder who was hurt and died waiting for someone to help him, or if it's a lone hiker who was bitten by a snake. There are so many possibilities that my mind won't rest until I know the truth." Hawke shrugged. It had been his curse ever since his father deposited Hawke and his mother on her parent's porch in Nixyáawii and drove off. He never really learned why his father left them there or what happened to him afterward. It was a puzzle he had never been able to solve, but he could solve the other mysteries like homicides and trouble in other people's lives, just not his own.

Mac opened the cabin and a gust of hot air swirled out into the slightly cooler evening air. "Shit, we forgot to open the windows when we were here. I usually never forget to do that."

"That's okay, Dog and I sleep out under the stars a good deal of the time during the summer." Hawke scratched the dog's head, studying the area for a good spot to place his sleeping bag.

"If you sleep out there you could end up with a rattlesnake for a bed partner," Mac said from inside the cabin. "What do you want for dinner?"

Hawke entered the hot cabin and immediately took off his ballcap and wiped at sweat on his brow. "I'm not picky. Make what you like. I'll eat it." He continued to the bed where he'd stashed his belongings and pulled out a sealed bag of dog food and a collapsible bowl. Dog trotted over at the sound of the bag being opened. His eyes were bright at the prospect of dinner.

Hawke dumped food in the bowl. "That's all you get so we have plenty for the trip."

Dog eyed him skeptically before lowering his head and crunching.

"How long have you had Dog?" Mac asked.

"Long enough to know I'll probably only have a

couple more years of him coming with me. When he's too old to go in the mountains, I'll retire." He'd been thinking about retiring more and more lately. If he was retired, he could be up in the Eagle Cap Mountains with Dani helping her run the lodge. Instead, this time of the year, they were lucky to see each other when she flew down to Alder to deliver and pick up clients.

Although she had promised to fly down and go to the Tamkaliks Powwow in Eagle with him in two weeks. He hadn't been to a powwow since leaving home and joining the Army. That was almost forty years. That was a long time to stray from his upbringing and heritage. While he'd been contemplating spending more time at Nixyáawii with his mom to get back to his roots, it was his sister moving back and returning to dancing at powwows that made him think harder about revisiting the world he'd known as a child.

"How long have you been with OSP?" Mac asked, stirring something on the propane burner that smelled delicious.

"Thirty-three years. For the first fifteen, I was on patrol. As soon as an opening came up in Wallowa County for a Fish and Wildlife officer, I applied." Hawke smiled. He loved what he did. Not only did he keep the people of Wallowa County safe, but he also protected the wildlife and first foods of his ancestors' homeland.

"Wow, that's a long time. Ever feel burnt out?" Mac handed him a plate heaped with spaghetti.

Hawke inhaled the herbal and tomato aroma. "Not yet. You didn't get this out of a can."

"My wife made it and put it in a jar. I've found it makes hauling the garbage easier if I bring food in reusable containers like jars and Ziplock bags. And the food my wife makes tastes a whole lot better."

"I agree! This is delicious. Tell her I appreciate her efforts." Hawke took another bite and savored the garlicky sauce and noodles. It was as good as he'd had at a fancy Italian restaurant. He and Dani weren't much for cooking. They ate too many meals at restaurants or out of cans. They should eat healthier but neither one wanted to cook.

Dog sat at his knees staring up, a bit of drool slipped out at the corner of his mouth.

"You can lick the plate," Hawke said. As promised when he finished off the food on his plate, he set it on the floor for Dog and turned his attention to Mac. "When do you think an anthropologist and search team will show up?"

Mac shrugged. "Maybe tomorrow or the day after."

Hawke picked up the paper plate Dog had nearly licked a hole through, folded it up as small as he could get it, and shoved it in the garbage bag by the small counter. He'd made up his mind to help find the remains. "I have two days off when I finish here. I'm staying on until I have to return to work. I want to help them find the remains."

"I don't have a problem with that but you might need to talk to Spruel and Titus." Mac put his empty plate on the floor for Dog and walked over to his bunk. He picked up a toiletry bag and headed outside.

Hawke wanted to help find the remains as soon as there were people here looking. But he would need to have another OSP Fish and Wildlife member come in and replace him as Mac's partner. When he called Sergeant Spruel and Lieutenant Titus to get the okay to help with the search he'd ask if they could send someone in to take over with Mac.

Grabbing his small day pack, Hawke walked out of the cabin and down to the river to wash up and get ready for bed. The last of the sun's glow barely lit the top of the rocky canyon on the Idaho side. The moon was a thin curved, white slash in the darkening sky. When the sun went down there would be very little light to navigate by.

He stripped to just his boxers and walked out into the water up to his knees. The cold was welcome after being in that sauna of a cabin while eating his dinner. He quickly splashed his sweaty upper body, cooling his skin and washing away the sweat. Walking out of the water to his daypack, Hawke pulled a t-shirt over his head, slipped his feet into his boots, and walked back to the cabin, Swatting at mosquitoes on his legs every third step.

Dog ran up to him from the direction of Sand Creek and joined him at the cabin door.

"Do you want to chance sleeping with snakes and mosquitoes or sleep inside?" Hawke asked, holding the screen door open.

Dog pushed by him and into the cabin, curling up on the floor next to the bed Hawke had stored his things under.

"It looks like you'll be in here," Mac commented from a lower bunk across from Hawke's.

"I guess so. I'm not sure if it's the river water or the cabin has cooled." He drew in a breath that didn't feel suffocating.

"With the windows and the door open, there is a good airflow. Another hour and it will be comfortable in

21

here." Mac had an electronic device in his hand.

"You reading or playing a game?" Hawke asked.

"Reading. It helps me wind down." Mac glanced over at him. "Does the light bother you?"

"No. I'm fine." Hawke turned on his side with his back to Mac. Sleep was slow coming as he thought of all the scenarios that could account for the bone Dog found.

《》《》《》

The next morning Hawke asked Mac to run him to a spot where he could call both Spruel and Titus. He stood on the parking lot at Pittsburgh Landing on the Idaho side making his calls.

"Hawke, I don't mind you using your days off to help, but summer is when we need everyone," Spruel said.

"I know. But it just feels like I need to help find the remains. Dog started the whole thing and I need to finish it." He sighed. "It could be an ancestor. If we find out it is a Nez Perce body or burial ground, then I think it would be fitting if I'm one of the searchers."

"This is more than just remains to you, isn't it?" Spruel asked.

"Yeah. I feel like Dog found the bone for a reason. My head says that's ridiculous but my gut…"

Spruel blew out air, and Hawke heard papers shuffling. "I'll see who we can spare to take over for you. But you have to stay with Mac until your relief arrives. And I'll see what I can do about covering for you until you discover what Dog found."

"Thank you. I'll work extra days to make up for it." Relief that Spruel was willing to allow him the time to help with the search eased his guilty conscience.

"There's no need for that. You never take all your vacation time anyway. Keep me posted."

"I will. Do I need to call Lieutenant Titus and tell him what I'm doing?" Hawke asked.

"I'll talk to him. It would be good P.R. to have you working with the search efforts if it does turn out to be Indigenous remains." Spruel ended the call.

Hawke smiled. If he was lucky, his replacement would be here by tonight.

"That call must have gone well," Mac said when Hawke climbed into the boat.

"When a replacement gets here for me, I can start searching for the remains." Hawke patted Dog's head and stared up the river.

"I learned the anthropologist and tribal representative will be here tomorrow morning. Sheriff Lindsey and a deputy will be here this afternoon along with the USFS Officer. We're to meet them at Sluice Creek."

"Sounds good. Let's get to work." Hawke sat on the bench seat looking toward Oregon and enjoyed the ride as they once again stopped and talked to boaters, rafters, and fishermen as they worked their way back upriver to the dam and back down to Sluice Creek by mid-afternoon.

A boat was tied up to the beach at Sluice Creek when they arrived. Hawke hopped out and tied the jetboat as Mac dropped an anchor off the front of the boat.

Hawke shook hands with Sheriff Rafe Lindsey and Deputy Dave Alden. He hadn't met the USFS Officer wearing the beige green shirt and dark pants of the Forest Service employees. Out of the back of her ball cap hung a long red braid.

"Hawke, this is Meghan Odam of the Forest Service," Rafe said, by way of introduction.

Hawke held out his hand and Meghan shook, giving his hand a good squeeze as if to say I can do my job. *Not a chip on her shoulder.* "Pleased to meet you. What region are you from?"

She peered at him with dark green eyes. "Region six. I've helped with this type of search before."

Again, she was trying too hard to prove to him she knew her job. Not a good sign. He preferred that a person let their work show they could do the job.

"Good. I've looked for people or recently dead bodies before but not human remains." He held out his hand to Dave. "Good to have you in on this."

"Thanks. Though I'm not sure I want to be digging through that brush looking for bones. I'm not a fan of rattlesnakes or poison ivy." Dave shuddered.

Hawke, Rafe, and Mac laughed.

Meghan stared at them. "Rattlesnakes are not a laughing matter. We'll have to use sticks to disturb the ground and flush the snakes out ahead of us as we search."

"Where exactly did you find the bone?" Rafe asked.

Hawke grinned and then said, "I didn't." He pointed to Dog who sat a few feet away from them scratching his ear.

"Do you have any idea where he found it?" Meghan asked, studying Dog as if he were a rodent.

"Mac, did you bring the bone with us?" Hawke asked.

"I did. I figured someone would like to make sure

it is human before we start this adventure." Mac walked back to the jetboat and came back with the evidence bags they'd placed over each end of the bone.

He handed it to Rafe, who handed it to Meghan.

She in turn pulled off one of the bags and then the other. She turned the bone over in her hands. Nodding, Meghan said, "It is human. This is a femur. By the dryness and cracking, I'd say it's been here a while." She glanced at Rafe. "You said an anthropologist is coming as well as someone from a tribe?"

"Yes. They'll be here tomorrow," Rafe answered.

"Then we better see if we can find more than this bone." Meghan put the bone back in the evidence bags and shoved it into her backpack. She scanned the side of the canyon before looking over her shoulder at Hawke. "Any suggestions?"

"If you give me the bone, I can see if Dog will go to where he found it." Hawke held out his hand palm up.

She pivoted and stared at his outstretched hand, then at Dog. "What makes you think he can find another bone?"

"I've used him before to track people. Once he realizes I want to know where he found the bone, he should take us to the spot." Hawke continued to hold out his hand, waiting for the woman to decide he knew what he was talking about.

"I can vouch for Dog. I've been on some of the searches where Hawke used him," Dave added.

"Me, too," Rafe said, nodding to Dog. "He might not look like much but he's got a nose on him and he's smart."

Dog peered up at the woman and danged if Hawke

didn't think the animal was smiling.

Meghan reluctantly opened her pack and held the evidence bag out to Hawke. "I hope that dog is as good as you all think he is. It's not protocol, but if we can find the location to start sooner, I'm all for it. This heat is getting to me."

Rafe handed her a bottle of water as Hawke knelt in front of Dog and pulled the bone out of the bag, allowing Dog to sniff it all over.

Hawke pointed to the creek bed and said, "Find."

Dog looked at the Hawke, the bone, and pointed his nose toward the creek. He stood up and trotted toward the trees and bushes. Hawke shoved the bone and bag at Meghan and jogged after Dog.

The animal wove in and out of the wild rose bushes, poison ivy, hawthorn, and even some Osage orange trees until about a hundred yards upstream in a grove of cottonwoods, he stopped and dug at the ground.

Chapter Three

Hawke quickly pushed through the thorny brush, pulled on leather gloves, and squatted near the spot where Dog was digging. "Sit," he commanded the animal. Dog sat and stared at the ground.

Using his gloved hands, Hawke scrapped at the dirt and felt his fingers touch something hard. It was another bone. This one appeared to be a rib. "He found it!" Hawke called out to the others standing outside the green strip of vegetation along the nearly dry creek.

Scrapping and cracking limbs drowned out the buzz of flies and mosquitoes.

"Don't come much closer. It looks like the bones are scattered. Too many people walking could break them," Hawke said, halting the procession.

"He's right," Meghan said. "If you two want to make a clear path from the hillside to me that would make it easier to find this spot when the anthropologist gets here."

Hawke moved aside dirt and discovered more

bones.

"Stop! That's the job of the anthropologist not someone uneducated in digging up remains."

He glanced at the woman. Her glare would have made him laugh anywhere else. But he could see she was adamant about making sure no one touched anything. He rose and walked toward her making sure he set his feet gently.

"Come on, Hawke. We need to finish up our patrol for the day," Mac said, still standing beyond the brush Rafe and Dave were clearing.

He passed the two men. "I'll be back tomorrow when my replacement arrives."

Rafe nodded. "Nathan told me you were taking time off to help with this project. Do you think it's an ancestor?"

"I don't know. The bones don't look that decomposed. But it is someone who has been here a while." Hawke walked out of the trees, brushing the sleeves of his shirt to make sure he didn't have any ticks or spiders clinging to his clothing. There were days like this, and the ones coming up, when he wished he could take a pill like he gave Dog that would ward off ticks.

《》《》《》

When they returned to the cabin for the night, Ward Dillon, another OSP Fish and Wildlife Trooper, was waiting for them.

"How did you get here so fast?" Hawke asked, wishing he'd known this before they'd made a last pass by Sluice Creek. He could have had Mac drop him off there.

28

"Caught a ride down here with Idaho Fish and Wildlife. Spruel said you found a body? Jeez, Hawke, you can't go anywhere that you don't find a body." The trooper had a smile on his face as he handed them both ice cold bottles of water.

"It's the remains of someone who died a while back." Hawke settled in a lawn chair that sat outside the cabin.

"How long ago?" Ward asked.

Hawke shrugged. "Your guess is as good as mine. Not recent by the dryness and cracks in the bones but not ancient either." He chugged down half the bottle and felt his body temperature lowering.

Dog lay at his feet panting.

"You want me to fire the boat back up and take you to Sluice Creek?" Mac asked.

Hawke studied the man he'd been riding in the boat with the last two days. Even though Hawke hadn't mentioned taking him back to the creek, Mac had figured out it had been on his mind.

"I wouldn't mind going there tonight but if you want to just rest, I can wait until morning. The bones aren't going anywhere overnight and that Forest Service LEO made it clear no one but the anthropologist could dig them up." Hawke downed the rest of the water. "But Dog and I could snoop around beyond the area she's not allowing anyone in and see if we find anything interesting."

"Grab your gear. I'll run you up there before I make dinner." Mac finished off his water bottle and he and Ward walked down to the jetboat.

Hawke sprang to his feet and entered the cabin, gathering up his stuff, and shoving it into his backpack.

"Come on, Dog. We won't be on the water tomorrow."

They jogged down to the shoreline and hopped on the jetboat as Mac revved the engine. Once aboard, the boat headed upriver, easily dancing through the first set of rapids.

At Sluice Creek, Hawke and Dog unloaded, thanked Mac and Ward, and walked toward two tents set up in the clearing at the south end of the airstrip. He and Dog would definitely be sleeping outside tonight since he hadn't brought a tent. He thought about making a hammock in the trees. He wouldn't have to worry about snakes but there would be ticks and the mosquitoes were worse closer to the water.

Rafe and Dave sat on foldable stools outside of their tent.

"I win," Rafe said, as Dave handed him a bill.

Hawke glanced between them. "You were betting on when I'd be back?"

"Yep," Dave said. "I lost. I didn't think they'd get a replacement to you this quick."

Hawke laughed. "I didn't think so either. But they did. Dog and I will sleep out here between the tents." He dropped his backpack and other belongings on the ground beside the tent.

"We do have an extra cot. We brought it in case we need another deputy up here," Rafe said. "But the quarters inside are tight."

"Dog and I don't mind sleeping out here. But a cot would be nice. Less chance of snuggling up with a snake."

Rafe and Dave laughed and Dave rose from his stool. "I'll get the cot." He disappeared into the tent.

"How's it working with Ms. Odam?" Hawke asked

quietly.

"She's worried about making sure we know she knows what she's doing." Rafe raised an eyebrow. "Which makes me think she doesn't know what she's doing."

"I had the same thought earlier." Hawke took the cot from Dave as he carried it out of the tent. Opening the cot, Hawke placed it in front of the two stools and sat where he could talk quietly with the two county officers.

"We managed to clear a decent trail into the area where you found more bones," Rafe said. "Odam isn't going to let us do anything else until the anthropologist gets here."

Hawke nodded. "That works for me. I plan on scouting the whole area for anything interesting. If it's an ancestor, I shouldn't come up with anything. It will also give me a better idea of where the bones might have scattered to."

Rafe nodded. "It can't hurt."

"That's what I think." The sun's fading glow gave Hawke just enough light to move his cot to the side of the tent and unroll his sleeping bag before darkness settled over the canyon. The river was farther away tonight. Even though he was sticky with sweat, he didn't feel the energy to walk down to the river to wash off. He'd do that in the morning at first light before Ms. Odam was out and about.

《》《》《》

A low growl next to his ear, ripped Hawke awake. Dog lay across his body staring toward the creek. Dog's throaty growl vibrated his body as his gaze remained riveted on the trees.

31

"What's up?" Hawke whispered and turned to his side, sliding Dog down onto the cot. He peered in the same direction as Dog.

The sun shone bright, high above the eastern canyon rim, but it wasn't high enough in the sky to shine down the slopes. A deer bolted from the brush. The flash of a cougar followed.

Hawke felt Dog tense to take off in pursuit and grabbed his collar, holding him on the cot. "You don't want to get between a cougar and its breakfast," Hawke said softly. "It is the way of things."

When the cougar and deer were out of sight, Hawke released Dog and grabbed the clothing he'd draped over his pack the night before. He slid his feet into his boots, tossed the clothing and a towel over his shoulder, grabbed his toiletry bag, and headed down the slope to the river.

"Come, Dog," he said only loud enough for the animal to hear.

They wandered down to the river where Hawke washed up and donned his clothing. He was shoving his sock-clad foot into a boot when Dog's tail started swishing back and forth across the rocks where he sat staring up toward the tents.

Hawke figured it was one of the county officers and continued to put on his other boot.

"Oh! I'm sorry," Ms. Odam said, backing up when Hawke glanced up at her.

"I'm finished. The river is all yours." He noticed the towel and uniform over her bare arm and her bare legs below the items she carried. Standing, he donned his hat, picked up his toiletry bag, and walked past her, all the way up to the tents.

From this distance, he could have watched her and not seen anything he shouldn't. But in case she was watching to see if was looking, Hawke busied himself rolling up his sleeping bag and shoving his belongings into his backpack. He left it all sitting on the cot, except for a canteen of water, a handful of jerky, and a granola bar.

"Come," he said to Dog and they headed off toward the creek. They were halfway to the creek when he heard a shout.

Hawke whipped around and spotted Ms. Odam running toward him. He stopped and crossed his arms, waiting for her to get close enough he could hear her garbled words.

"Don't go near the bones?" she hollered.

Rafe popped out of his tent half-dressed. When the sheriff saw she was shouting at Hawke, he raised a hand and returned to his tent.

Hawke grinned. At least Rafe was ready to keep the site clear of people who didn't belong.

"I'm not going to the bones. I'm going to take a look around above the site," Hawke called back to the woman.

She stopped about thirty feet from him, panting. Her hands were on her knees as she bent, drawing in breath.

Hawke closed the distance between them and said, "I know to not bother the remains. I'm going to see if there is any sign of either more bones or something that will give us a clue to who that is."

She finally caught her breath and glanced up at him. "You don't think it's Indigenous?"

As much as he hoped they were, he'd seen enough

bones out in the forest and digging around in his pasture to know they weren't old enough to be one of his ancestors. He'd thought about it long and hard last night. Comparing memories of bones he'd found over the years. They had been in the weather a while, but they weren't brittle enough to have been lying so close to the top of the ground for over a hundred years.

He shook his head. "I think someone had an accident and they are a missing person."

Ms. Odam took that in and stared at the trees in the ravine. "I'd guess the same thing."

"Have someone whistle when the anthropologist shows up, please." He spun around and continued on his path toward the creek without waiting for her reply.

Chapter Four

A shrill whistle drew Hawke's attention from a nasty patch of poison ivy he was trying to move with a stick. He'd seen something flash inside a hawthorn tree beyond the poison ivy. He'd thought about coming at the tree from the backside but he'd found the ivy growing all around the tree. It was less aggressive on this side.

He rammed the stick into the ground, pulled his red bandana out of his back pocket, and tied it to the top of the stick. It was rare he couldn't find his way back to a place he'd been, but just in case, he marked the spot. "Let's go meet the anthropologist," he said to Dog, who had stopped digging when the whistle penetrated the trees where they were.

Following the path he'd stomped down on their way into the creek, Hawke and Dog exited the green growth along the creek and headed toward the tents. He figured they would drop off the anthropologist's gear at the camp before they went to the bone site.

He spotted the group walking slowly toward the camp, everyone carrying gear. It was the woman toward the back of the group that intrigued him. She wore a plaid long-sleeved shirt, jeans, knee-high moccasins, and a straw cowboy hat with sunglasses. That had to be the Nez Perce tribal member.

He reached the camp only minutes before the rest of the group.

A man in his fifties with graying close-cropped hair, wearing a straw hat and dressed properly for digging around in this area, set his things down and held out a hand. "Dr. Phillip Galler."

"Oregon State Police Fish and Wildlife Officer Hawke." He shook hands with the anthropologist and heard someone gasp.

"Gabriel Hawke?" a female voice asked.

He faced the woman who had just arrived. "Yes, Ma'am."

A smile spread across her lips and she pulled off her sunglasses. "That's no way to greet your auntie." She stepped forward and wrapped her arms around him.

Hawke's mind flashed through the few memories he had of living on the Lapwai Reservation before his father dumped them at Nixyáawii. He didn't remember this woman. He eased out of her hold out of embarrassment and because he was covered with poison ivy sap.

"I'm sorry, how are we related?" he asked, forgetting they were there for work. His heart beat rapidly inside his chest as he stared into the woman's face. One that wasn't familiar. Could he finally learn what happened between his parents and where his father was?

"We'll talk about that tonight when the work is done," the woman said.

"What's your name?" he asked.

"Florence Bright." She smiled and piled her pack and things on his cot.

"Where is the bone that was found?" Dr. Galler asked.

"Here." Ms. Odam held out the femur for the anthropologist to examine.

"I think we brought you out here under false pretenses, Flo," Dr. Galler said to Hawke's auntie.

"How so?" she asked, stepping up beside him.

"This bone isn't over fifty years old. I doubt that it will be found to be Indigenous. But we need to dig up all we can find of this person and see if we can piece together the story." Dr. Galler handed the femur back to Ms. Odam and picked up the smaller of his packs. "Lead me to where you found this bone."

Hawke fell in behind the Forest Service Officer, the anthropologist, Rafe, and Dave. His auntie fell in step with him.

"You were small when you left Lapwai. I'm not surprised you don't remember me. I babysat you when your parents were fighting." She put a hand on his arm and stopped him. "I know you didn't realize how much they fought. Your mother pleaded with your father to move back with her people. Your father liked the company of other women. It was not a marriage of love. I don't blame either of them. Except for the fact you were kept from our family." She smiled. "But you are grown up now and can make your own decisions." She squeezed his arm. "It is so good to see you." Auntie continued walking.

Hawke lagged behind studying the woman's back. Was that why he couldn't understand why his father had left them in Nixyáawii? Because he hadn't realized they didn't get along?

When they reached the bushes and trees, Dr. Galler told them to wait until he could discern where the bones might be scattered.

They had stood not saying a word for nearly twenty minutes when he returned. "We'll need to bring in some of my students to help grid and dig for the bones. I have a feeling they could be scattered all up and down this creek bed. However, I do think, since there are ribs, that what you found is the spot where the body landed." He glanced at Rafe. "Can you call in more help to uncover the bones?"

"I can contact the patrol boat and have them call in more help. Until then, you have all of us but Hawke. He hasn't helped with this type of search before and his skills are better at finding more bones along the creek." Rafe gave Hawke a nod.

"Yeah, I already have something tagged I'm trying to get to in a tree." Hawke whistled for Dog and turned to go back to the task he'd been working on when they'd notified him of the newcomers' arrival.

"Trooper Hawke, this death was decades old. How on earth do you think you'll find anything of significance?" Galler asked.

Hawke spun back to the group. "I may not. But if I can find all the things in this ravine that don't belong here, then there might be something that will help identify this person." Hawke glanced at his auntie. She was grinning and winked at him.

It was unsettling to have a person know him and he

didn't have a clue about them. He strode up the hill toward the path he'd made into the tree where he'd been hacking away at the poison ivy. Now that the others were here, he could concentrate on what he saw in the hawthorn tree.

Dog sat on a rock that didn't have any poison ivy growing over it and watched as Hawke used the stick he'd jammed in the ground to try and reach what now looked like a scrap of clothing hooked on several thorns of the tree.

There was no way he'd be able to climb up and get the fabric, but he might be able to work it out of the grasp of the thorns if he had patience. Normally, he had patience. So much so, that it frustrated Dani. But today, his mind was on two things. Finding evidence to help solve the identity and possibly the reason the person died here and how the woman, who called herself his auntie, knew so much about him and he knew nothing of her.

He said her name over and over again as he held the stick up toward the piece of fabric. Finally, the cloth caught on the tip of the stick and Hawke lowered it down for inspection. The glint he'd seen in the sunlight was a short piece of metal zipper. The fabric attached to the zipper was brittle and faded. But it resembled fabric used by sportsmen.

Hawke pulled an evidence bag out of his daypack, slid the fragile item in, and wrote where he found it along with the date and time. He put the bag into his pack and dug around the base of the tree a bit. He found small bones that resembled parts of a hand. Jamming the stick into the ground a foot away, he re-tied his bandana to the top.

"How would a piece of clothing get up in the tree and the bones on the ground?" Hawke asked Dog. Then he peered up beyond the foliage of the hawthorn at a cottonwood. Almost directly over the smaller tree, in the limbs of the cottonwood, was a large nest. He wasn't an ornithologist but he had a suspicion the nest would belong to an eagle. Judging by the size and because there were bones on the ground below it. Eagles were known to eat dead animals. In this case, he surmised that a wild animal, wolf, bear, or cougar had come across the body or killed the person and tore it into pieces. The eagle came by and saw a chance to grab a meal and grasped an arm.

If an eagle carried off an arm, what other pieces could be strung up this creek bed? He wondered if Dr. Galler would have his team work their way up or down the creek.

Hawke glanced at Dog whose ears were straight up as if he were listening to something. "What is it, Dog?" He peered in the direction Dog was staring and caught a glimpse of a tan body. "That's the cougar from this morning, I bet." He glanced down at Dog and back up the ravine. "Think we can find that cat's home?"

Dog whined.

"I won't let anything happen to you. Let's go see what that cougar's been storing in his home."

《》《》《》

An hour later, Hawke stood on the side of the canyon drinking from his canteen as he stared at the small cave opening he and Dog found. The cougar had run farther up the hill as they approached the cave. Hawke didn't like the fact he would have to crawl in on his hands and knees. That meant if the animal came back to protect his home, Hawke would be easy to attack and kill.

His first thought was to have Dog stand guard. But neither scenario would keep them both safe. The correct thing would be to bring Dave back up here to stand guard while he skulked around in the cave. But that would mean walking back down to where they were digging for the bones and back up to here after getting Rafe to allow Dave to come up with him. By then it would be dark and they might as well wait until tomorrow.

He offered a drink to Dog by pouring water into his hand from the canteen. The animal lapped at the liquid until the container was empty. "We could make something to keep the cougar out." Peering around at the brush, rocks, and dead tree limbs scattered about, he started hauling limbs and cutting brush that he carried to the opening.

"Okay, let's let this critter know we don't want him around." Hawke unzipped his pants and made a line across in front of the cave with his urine. Dog raised a leg and peed on the side of the entrance.

Hawke could have sworn the dog winked at him. "Okay, in you go." He pointed to the cave. Dog studied him for a few seconds and walked into the four-foot-high opening.

Backing into the hole, Hawke stopped just inside and pulled a couple of limbs up close, crossing them in front of the opening and then dragging the brush up against the poles. Covering the opening made it even darker inside the small area.

Turning around, to face into the cave, Hawke pulled a flashlight out of his daypack and turned it on.

The cave remained four feet high and four feet wide fifteen feet into the side of the canyon wall. A large rock was the back wall. Before he moved forward, Hawke caught the sound he'd feared more than the cougar coming back.

Dog backed into Hawke as the distinctive sound of a rattler filled the small space. "Behind me." Hawke shoved Dog behind him and swept the beam of the flashlight across the dirt floor, looking for the snake.

The reptile's eyes and tongue came into view in a back corner near a pile of bones.

Hawke's Glock was in his right boot, but the sound would deafen him and Dog in this small area. Not to mention possibly causing the ground above him to collapse and bring out more of the snake's buddies.

Holding the light on the snake, Hawke debated what to do. The creature was still tasting the air with a twitching tail, but it hadn't coiled into a striking position yet. A slow scan of the bone pile with the flashlight didn't reveal any more eyes, but he couldn't be too careful when it came to dealing with a rattlesnake. He'd heard stories of his ancestors catching the snakes, and then easing them with liver to get them to strike. After the snakes had put venom in the organ, the warriors would smear it on their arrowheads and go into battle with their enemies.

Right now, he didn't need or want any venom coming his way. He backed to the opening and grabbed one of the limbs he'd put up as a deterrent for the cougar. If he couldn't get the snake to go back into the crack in the rocks behind the creature, they would have to abort this try and come back tomorrow.

He took a deep breath, gripped the stick, and gently

tapped it up and down on the ground a foot in front of the snake. The creature slithered back a few inches, its tongue continually tasting, probably trying to figure out what was approaching.

Tapping and moving the stick toward the snake until the snake turned and slithered into the crevice, Hawke grabbed a rock on the side of the cave and stuffed it in the hole. As long as there wasn't another snake in the bones, they should accomplish what he'd come to do.

Now that the threat was taken care of, Hawke shined the light around the end of the cave, studying the pile of bones. He used the stick he'd retrieved to push the bones around. Most of them appeared to be from animals. There were a couple he wasn't sure about and decided to take them with him. At the bottom, he found a larger scrape of the fabric he'd found in the tree.

Using the stick, he pulled it out of the pile of bones. It appeared to be the back of a fishing vest with the pocket still intact. Holding up the fabric, he noticed it listed to one side as if something were in the pocket. He reached in and pulled out a small plastic film canister.

He smiled. If this belonged to the body, they could possibly identify him.

Chapter Five

Hawke was in a good mood as he walked down the side of the canyon toward the makeshift camp. About an hour of daylight was left. He wanted to get down to the river's edge and find out when Mac would be leaving the following day. He'd catch a ride back to Winslow with him and then take the film canister to the OSP lab in Pendleton.

He and Dog arrived at the camp as everyone else wandered up from the creek. They drooped and their feet dragged as if the heat had gotten the better of them.

"Did you talk to Mac today?" Hawke asked Rafe.

"I did. He was getting the word out that we need more help. Specifically, people who have sifted dirt for bones." Rafe opened an ice chest and pulled out water bottles. He handed one to everyone present.

"I found something that I want to get to the Pendleton lab. Any chance he'll come up here in the morning before he leaves?" Hawke took one of the bottles. "Thanks." He unscrewed the top and drank, watching Rafe quench his thirst.

"Yeah, he was going to check back by here before he leaves in the morning to see if we need anything else."

"Good. I'll be going out with him." Hawke dug into his pack.

"What did you find?" Dave asked.

Hawke told them about finding the piece of fabric and zipper in the tree and then finding the cougar cave and the snake.

"Yikes! You shouldn't have gone into that cave alone," Ms. Odam said.

"I didn't. Dog went with me."

"What kind of a name is that for a…dog?" she asked, crossing her arms as if she were ready to argue.

Hawke shrugged. "I started out calling him Dog trying to come up with a name and he came to it so well, I stuck with it." He patted Dog's head. "And it is what he is."

Flo returned to camp with half a dozen fish. "What do we have to cook with?" she asked, looking from Ms. Odam to Rafe.

"A two-burner propane camp stove," Rafe said.

"A frying pan?" Flo asked.

"I'll show her what we have," Dave said, motioning for Flo to follow him to a smaller tent that was set up behind the first two tents.

Rafe faced Hawke. "What did you find in the cave?"

Hawke first pulled out the evidence bag with the bones he thought might be human. "These." He handed them to Dr. Galler. "They looked like they might be from a person."

Dr. Galler opened up the evidence bag and pulled out the first bone. He studied it. "Yes, this is a scapula." He set it down and pulled out the next bone. "And this is a humerus. The upper part of the arm that would be attached to the scapula." He stared at Hawke. "Do you think this is from the person we are digging up?"

"We won't know that until you find most of the bones and see if these two are missing." Hawke shrugged. "I also found what I believe is more of the piece of clothing that was hanging in the tree." He pulled out another evidence bag and opened it, but didn't take the fabric out, just showed it to the group. "It's barely staying together, but it seems to be the back of a fishing vest. The kind with a large pocket in the back to hold your catch. There was a plastic film canister in the pocket. I'm hoping the photos on the film will help us identify the remains." He smiled and peered into the eyes of the skeptical faces.

"Did you open the canister? That would ruin any film, if it isn't ruined already," Rafe said.

"I didn't open it. I just shook it and heard the spool thunk back and forth in the canister." Hawke wasn't going to let anyone talk him out of his belief that this would help them find the identity of the body.

Flo walked around the side of the tent. "Dave and I are making dinner. I hope you're all hungry. Phil, if you and Meghan could set up my cot in her tent, and then Gabriel could help you set up your tent." She disappeared back behind the tents.

Hawke and Dr. Galler exchanged glances and the anthropologist walked over to the stack of belongings he and Flo had dropped to go take a look at the bones. He picked up a bag and asked Ms. Odam, "Which tent is yours?"

She hustled ahead of him saying something about making room for the cot.

Rafe and Hawke were alone. Rafe said in a quiet voice. "Is that woman, Flo, really your aunt?"

Hawke shrugged. "She must be related somehow. But I don't recognize her. Guess I'll find out the connection later tonight."

《》《》《》

After dinner, one by one the members of the camp slipped down to the river to wash up and then went to bed. It was just Hawke and Flo sitting on the folding stools staring into the darkness at the occasional white cap on the river.

"How exactly are you related to me?" Hawke asked in a quiet voice.

"I lived next door to you and your family in Lapwai. I am a cousin to your father which makes you my nephew."

Hawke heard the pride in her voice. Was it because of being his auntie or because she was related to his father? "I remember very little about my father. I only know what my mother would tell me. He liked lots of women and she didn't like that."

"That's true. Your father did have a roving eye and hands. He considered every woman he met as a challenge. Do you know he courted your mother for two years before she finally gave in and married him?"

"And then once he had her, he didn't want her anymore," Hawke said.

"That's pretty much the truth." She sighed. "I missed your mom and you. You were both good company when my husband was away so much."

"Why didn't you try to contact us?" Hawke asked, wondering for the millionth time why no one from his father's side of the family cared enough to come to see them.

"It was your mother's wish. When I first met her, she was so bright and funny. By the time your father took you both to Umatilla, she rarely smiled, and you had become sullen, taking in her hurt. I think it was best for both of you to stay clear of your father."

"Is he still alive? I'd heard rumors he wasn't." Hawke had never resolved if he wanted to meet the man who had dumped him and his mother in Nixyaawii and left her to marry a violent man. Marion's father.

"No. He left this earth nearly ten years ago. He liked to party and did so right up until his death."

Hawke nodded. "If you don't take care of your body there is no one else to do it."

"*Tikú?*." His auntie agreed. "How did you happen to be in Hells Canyon to find the bones?"

Hawke explained how he patrolled the river once a year and that Dog had been the one to find the bones, not him.

"You always gave others credit for your good deeds. Phil doesn't think this is one of our ancestors. He says the bones don't look that old but they have been in the elements for maybe four decades. It is a good find. It will be interesting to see if we can learn how he came to die here."

"You're staying on and helping with the dig? Don't you have to go do other things?" Hawke knew little of this woman or any of his family in Lapwai.

Shaking her head she said, "I am trained as an anthropologist. It is part of my job to advocate for our people when their bones or belongings are dug up. I have nowhere else to be at the moment and will see this through."

"I'm headed back to Wallowa County in the morning. I want to take the film I found to the Oregon State Police lab in Pendleton and then see what I can dig up on missing persons in this area."

"You always were one who needed all circles closed." He heard the smile in her voice. She stood. "*Tá'c cik'éetin.*"

Hawke replied, "Good night." Childhood memories of this woman's voice saying good night to him in Nimiipuu came rushing into his mind. He wandered down to the river to wash off the sweat and dirt he'd accumulated throughout the day. Staring up at the stars glittering in the sky, his mind filled with the Nez Perce or Nimiipuu words he remembered from his childhood. His mother still used some of the words but the Cayuse Nez Perce language had mixed with the Umatilla on the reservation.

As a child, she'd spoken to him in Cayuse because her second husband had never learned enough of his Umatilla language to figure out what Hawke and his mother were talking about. Of course, this only infuriated his stepfather, who was usually drunk and angry. Hawke had pleaded with his mom to not talk to him in their language when his stepfather was around. He didn't like her getting beat up for speaking to him.

She only shook her head and said, "I will speak to my son in our language when I want. To have you know the words of our ancestors is worth the beating."

He still didn't understand why she taunted her husband by speaking to him and Marion in Cayuse.

However, hearing the words spoken by his auntie stirred something in him. What he wasn't sure, but he wanted to reconnect with that side of his family.

Dog lapped at the water as Hawke shoved his outer clothing into a plastic garbage bag to keep from touching his washed skin with clothing that may have poison ivy sap on them. He walked back to camp in his boxers and a clean t-shirt. His backpack was packed and ready to go and his clothes for in the morning sat on top of the pack.

He slipped into his sleeping bag on the cot outside the tent and Dog curled up on the cot beside his feet. Laying on his back, Hawke stared up at the stars and asked forgiveness from the Creator for taking the snake's life today.

Chapter Six

In the morning, Hawke had his backpack down at the river's edge when Mac arrived.

"You heading out today?" Mac asked, as Ward hopped out and tied the jetboat to a large rock.

"I am. I found something I want to take to the lab in Pendleton. Dr. Galler believes the bones have been here no longer than forty years. I'll do a sweep of the missing person's records and see what I can come up with for possible matches for the bones." Hawke tossed his pack and the garbage bag with his dirty clothes up to Mac as Dog leaped into the boat.

"I think you may be looking for a needle in a haystack," Mac said, staring up at the camp. "Anything else they need to send out with me?"

"I have the bones that I found in a cave along with a plastic canister of film. Galler told me to have those bones tested as they haven't been as weathered." Hawke took a seat on one of the benches as Ward untied the boat and hopped in.

"Does this mean you'll be back on duty when we return? You're going to owe me a couple of days for filling in for you on my days off," Ward said with a smile.

"Like riding up and down the Snake River is hard to take on your day off," Hawke joked.

Ward smiled. "Actually, you got me out of painting the house. I told my wife to hire someone with the money I'm making in overtime."

"There it worked out the best for both of us."

"Hang on!" Mac said, and revved the engine, heading downriver to Lewiston.

They stopped along the way to check fishing licenses on the Oregon side until they were out of their jurisdiction.

Pulling up to Hells Canyon Marina near Lewiston, Idaho, Hawke and Ward helped Mac load the patrol boat on the trailer.

"Want to ride back with me?" Ward asked Hawke when the boat was loaded.

"Sure, we'll get there faster than Mac pulling the boat. Not that I don't like your company, Mac," Hawke said, holding out a hand to Mac.

"None taken. I know you want to get to Pendleton today with your finds." They shook hands. "See you around the station."

Hawke nodded and put his backpack and Dog into Ward's SUV. Then he slid into the passenger seat.

Ward started the vehicle and eased out of the parking lot. "You still going to take that evidence over to Pendleton yourself?" he asked.

"Yeah. I want to stop by and see my mom and sister while I'm there. I have some questions to ask them." He'd decided to see if the women in his family wanted to go with him when he made a trip to Lapwai. He knew Dani would go with him. Some of her family lived there. But he wasn't sure how his mom and Marion would feel about it.

"Always good to keep the women folk in the loop," Ward said.

"Yeah, that's one thing I've learned growing up with a mom and a sister."

They both laughed then talked about work and Ward's kids the two-hour drive back to Alder.

"You can drop me off at the parking lot behind the Courthouse. That's where I parked to ride with Mac," Hawke said as they entered Alder city limits.

"Works for me. I don't need to go into the office until tomorrow." Ward drove to the parking lot and pulled up alongside Hawke's pickup.

"Thanks for the ride," Hawke said after loading Dog and his things into the pickup.

"No problem. Keep me updated on what you find. It sounds interesting."

"I will. Thanks again for stepping in for me."

"Any time." Ward drove off and Hawke slid in behind the steering wheel of his vehicle.

He put his phone in the holder on his dash and called Sergeant Spruel as he drove out of Alder.

"Hawke, I guess you found what you were looking for?" Spruel answered.

"Yes and no." Hawke told his superior about the items he'd found and that he was taking them to the lab in Pendleton.

"You know someone could take them for you," Spruel said.

"Yes. But I want to visit my mom. I'll spend the night and be in to work at noon tomorrow." Hawke had a feeling in his gut that the remains didn't die of natural causes and he hoped the film would give them a place to start in reaching out to the person's family.

"Okay. Tell your mom 'hi.'"

"I will, and thank you for sending Ward to finish out my days at the river."

"Just don't do it again," Spruel ended the call.

Hawke smiled. He knew Spruel wasn't being harsh with his comment. Hawke had asked many favors of Spruel and before him Sergeant Titus, who was now Lieutenant Titus. He'd been lucky to have had two men who understood his need to find the truth behind the inconsistencies he came across while doing his job. Lucky for him, he usually found the answer and jailed a murderer.

As he drove through Winslow, he called his mom. He'd have a harder time keeping reception as he drove through Minam Canyon.

"Hello?" she answered.

"Mom, it's Gabriel. I'll be there for dinner and spend the night."

"Oh! This is short notice."

His senses went on alert. "Are you busy?"

"Marion and I have a meeting."

"What time will you be home?" he asked.

"About nine. It's a potluck at the longhouse. You could come if you like." The hopefulness in her voice almost had him agreeing. But he wasn't clean enough to be seen in public with his mom.

"I'll grab something in Pendleton. I'm taking some evidence to the lab. I'll catch up with you at your house around nine."

"Are you sure?"

"I'll be fine. Enjoy your meeting." He ended the call, glad he'd reached out to her before he drove to her house and was dragged to the meeting. It must have something to do with politics on the rez or family. His mother was keen on knowing what was happening on the reservation that could be detrimental to the people. Marion worked for the legal aid office, mostly working with women and children in abusive households.

Two hours after leaving Alder, he pulled into the parking lot at the Oregon State Police lab on the west side of Pendleton. He let Dog out to pee on a few tires before having him get back in the vehicle.

Hawke walked into the lab with the film, bones, and clothing. He encountered a man at the desk in the lobby.

"How may I help you?" he asked, looking Hawke up and down.

He wasn't dressed in his uniform. He'd managed to get both uniforms he'd taken with him covered with poison ivy so he was wearing jeans, a t-shirt, his uniform boots, and an OSP ballcap. Hawke pulled his badge out from under his t-shirt by the chain hanging around his neck.

"OSP Trooper Hawke. I have pieces of evidence to give to a technician."

"I'll take them and give you a case number." The man opened the sliding glass window on the side of the window where he was talking through a metal grate-like opening.

"I'd rather talk with the technician and explain what I have." Hawke kept a grip on the bags.

The man narrowed his eyes. "That isn't protocol."

Hawke pulled out his phone and dialed Lt. Keller. "Hi Lieutenant, it's Hawke. I'm over here at the OSP lab and the person at the desk in the lobby won't let me take my evidence to a technician."

"Hawke, why are you calling me about this? You know the protocol," Carol said.

"This is a special case. I found human bones in Hells Canyon. The state anthropologist they called in has information he wants me to tell the lab tech." He watched the man behind the glass listening to his conversation.

"I want you to hoof it over to my office as soon as you turn the items over to the tech. I'll call and tell whoever is on duty at the desk to let you through."

The call ended and the phone in the small office rang. The man picked it up, answered, and then listened. "Yes, ma'am," he said and put the phone down. "I'll call a tech up to get you," he said, picking the phone back up and pushing a button. He said something into the phone and then replaced it again. "Someone will be out shortly." He indicated a chair along the wall by the door.

Hawke took the seat and waited. At least telling Carol what he'd been up to would take up time until he could go to his mom's house.

Twenty minutes later a door to his right opened. "Sorry I kept you waiting. I had to finish a test I was running." The man appeared to be in his forties, possibly early fifties. His graying hair and thick knuckles were the giveaway. And the fact he walked as if his joints all needed a good dose of oil.

"I know this isn't usual protocol but Dr. Galler,

the—"

The man spun around, his eyes alight with interest. "You brought me something from Phil? Now this is a bright point to my day. I can't wait to hear what he's been up to."

Hawke followed the man down the hall to a room that looked like a high school chemistry lab with more shiny machines and humming noises.

Once inside, the man turned to Hawke with his hand outstretched. "Dick Rowan."

"Trooper Hawke."

They shook hands and Dick asked, "What do you have for me?"

Hawke told him about finding the bones and then the ones in the cave.

"Those will give us a better idea of the time of death than ones that have been out in the elements. So, you say, Phil doesn't believe they are old enough to be Indigenous?"

"Correct." Hawke handed him the bagged bones.

As Dick set the bag down and pulled on gloves, Hawke told him about the film he'd found.

"You'll need to take that to Coralee. She's our expert on working with old film." Dick looked up from the scapula. "This is a very good specimen to date. I should have an answer as to whether they are older than nineteen-forty for you by tomorrow." Dick looked up from pulling the second bone from the bag. "Coralee is down the hall, second door on the left."

"Thank you. Here's my card. If you could call me with the results, I'd appreciate it. I plan on treating it as a missing person."

"I'm sure someone somewhere is missing a loved

one." Dick turned his attention back to the bones and Hawke exited the room.

He found Coralee's lab without any trouble. She was interested in his find.

"You know, not many people use film these days. Which is sad, because being digital their photos can be used by anyone." Coralee reached into the bag and pulled the plastic canister out. She studied it all around the lid. "It appears to have remained tightly sealed. If temperature conditions haven't been too extreme, I should have some photos for you tomorrow."

Hawke thanked her, asking her to call him when she had a set of prints for him. He told her it was for a missing person case. She agreed and he left the building.

He crossed the parking lot to check on Dog and found the animal lying on the floorboards to stay out of the sun, even though the windows were down.

"Come on. I don't think Carol will mind if I bring you into her office." To bypass any objections from someone at the front of the building, Hawke drove his vehicle to the back parking lot of the building and entered through the back door. He knew where Carol's office was and headed straight for it.

He heard her voice as he approached the door.

"No, I've had it up to my chin with sitting through another get-rich-quick presentation. You go if you want, but we are not putting money into anything unless I've checked it out."

Hawke had Dog walk into the room ahead of him so it didn't look like he'd been listening.

"Where did you come from?" Carol said, before, "We'll talk about this tonight," and hung up the phone as Hawke stepped into the room.

"Ahh, you must be the famous Dog I've heard about," Carol said, reaching out and scratching Dog on the head.

"He's famous?" Hawke asked, settling in the chair in front of her desk. He and Carol met at the State Police Academy as recruits and had become friends over the hardships of minorities in the OSP. She being female and Hawke Native American.

"Yes. He's famous for getting your ass out of trouble," she said, smiling.

Hawke grinned. "There is truth to that."

"Tell me about what you brought to the lab." Carol leaned back in her chair as if she didn't have anything else to do.

"Do you have time for dinner? I can tell you while we eat steak at Hamley's." It had been a while since he and Carol had caught up on life. And from the sound of her phone call, her husband was up to his old tricks of trying to make easy money.

She glanced down at her desk calendar and nodded. "Sounds good. I don't want to go home until later tonight. I can have a nice dinner with you and catch up on what you've been doing and then come back and finish up the paperwork before I go home." She picked up her phone, pressed a button, and said, "Stella, I'm going to dinner and will come back and finish those reports at about seven." She nodded and replaced the phone. "I'm ready when you are."

Hawke stood. "No time like the present since I haven't had lunch."

Chapter Seven

Hawke enjoyed catching up with Carol and having someone to share dinner with. After he'd told her about finding the bones and that he and Dani were doing well, she told him about the financial trouble her husband couldn't seem to stay out of. While he couldn't offer any help with that, they had a good visit.

Now he drove toward Mission on the Rez. His mom lived in the same house they'd moved into when she'd found a job two days after his dad had dropped them off on his grandparents' front lawn. It was the only house he remembered. The home had been full of love and full of hate and anger. But the love remained now that his stepfather had died at his own hands while driving intoxicated.

It was only eight o'clock by the time Hawke arrived at the house. He parked on the street in front of the house and let himself and Dog in with the key his mom had given him years ago. The aromas of home cooking brought back memories of the good times when his stepfather was away from home working. Hawke and his mom would bake cookies and Marion, being ten years younger than him, usually licked the spoons and tested the first pan that came out of the oven. The three of them had as many good memories as bad. He needed to make more good ones.

He'd missed out on them the last thirty years, first being in the Army and then moving from Nixyáawii when his wife divorced him. He'd not come home near enough. Neither had Marion. Her corporate lawyer job had kept her away from the family and Nixyáawii until her fiancé was murdered and she was the suspect. Now they were all back together and he needed to make sure he came over more often.

He put his duffel bag in his old room and started the fan that sat in the kitchen window to pull in the cooling outside air and cool off the house. He should get his mom air-conditioning. Every time he brought it up, she said she'd lived this long without it, and she could finish her lifetime the same.

He'd have to use the excuse if she had air conditioning, he'd visit more often. That would get her to change her mind.

Peeking into Marion's old room, he smiled at the photos of her dancing at powwows. Now that she had come back, she had begun dancing again. They were all going to participate at Tamkaliks in Eagle at the end of the month. It surprised him how excited he was to attend and perhaps join in on one dance.

He sat down on the couch in the living room and Dog heaved a sigh as he lay down in the middle of the room. Hawke closed his eyes and inhaled. All the scents of his childhood filled his nostrils and unfurled memories.

《》《》《》

The loud thump of a car door closing shot Hawke's eyelids up and he snorted a little coming awake. The room was a monochrome of grays since he'd fallen asleep before the sun had completely gone down.

"Well, his pickup is here, but why aren't there any lights on?" his mom said, as her voice grew nearer.

Hawke scrubbed a hand over his face and straightened on the couch, reaching for the switch on the table lamp.

The door opened as the light came on.

"There you are," his mom said. "Why were you sitting in the dark?"

"It wasn't dark when I fell asleep," he said, standing and giving his mom and then his sister a hug.

"See, there. I told you there was a reasonable explanation for his vehicle being here and no lights on," Marion said, walking by them carrying a large plastic tote bag.

"How was the potluck?" Hawke asked, following the two into the kitchen.

"Good. We played Bingo and gossiped," his mom said, opening the refrigerator door and pouring a glass of milk. She placed the milk in front of him and then placed the cookie jar on the table. "I see you didn't raid the cookies while I was away."

"No. I had dinner at Hamley's so I was stuffed when I arrived." He plucked a chocolate chip cookie from the jar and took a bite.

"Alone?" Marion asked, sitting down across from him and grabbing the cookie jar.

"No. I had dinner with an OSP lieutenant." Hawke

didn't want his sister making more out of his friendship with Carol than there was. Ever since she and FBI Special Agent Quinn Pierce had locked eyes, she thought everyone should be a couple. Which he was, with Dani. Though Marion didn't understand his and Dani's mutual desire to live together and not get married.

"Was it that nice lady you went through the police academy with?" Mom asked, sitting at the table.

Hawke peered at his mom. Leave it to her to bring up what he didn't want to talk about. "Yes. She is having some concerns about her husband and since I needed to waste time we had a nice visit over dinner." He glared at Marion in an attempt to keep her from making more of it than there was.

"You had dinner with an old flame?" Marion asked, her eyes lighting up.

"No. An old friend and someone I work with from time to time." He downed the milk and stood. "I'm beat. I've been on the Snake River for the last three days. I need a shower and a soft bed."

"What were you doing there?" Marion asked.

"I was on patrol, but Dog found a human bone and they called in an anthropologist and someone from Lapwai." He watched his mom. Her gaze immediately dropped to the table.

"Really? Anyone you knew?" Marion asked.

"As it turns out, yes. My Auntie Florence." He continued to watch his mom.

Her face slowly rose as her gaze met his. "Florence was there?"

"Yes, she is the liaison when there is a chance the remains could be Nimiipuu." Hawke was happy to see his mom was acknowledging the woman who had nothing but kind things to say about her.

"Did you recognize her?" Mom asked.

"No, she told me who she was when she heard my name. Then we visited the first night. She told me about living next door to us and keeping me when you and my father weren't getting along." He saw the hurt and anger that flashed in her eyes. For all her denouncing his father, Hawke could tell she had loved the man, and that made his betrayal all the more agonizing.

As he watched her, she picked at the cookie in her hand. "Did she say if he was still alive?"

"He passed ten years ago."

She nodded her head. "I thought so."

Hawke studied the woman who had brought him into the world. "What made you think so?"

"I no longer felt betrayed." Her gaze rose to his.

She had been deeply in love with him. "I'm going to take a shower," Hawke said, unsure what else to say.

《》《》《》

In the morning, Hawke didn't bring up his father or auntie. He'd do that after his mom had time to think about what he'd told her. Instead, he had a big breakfast cooked by his mom and then headed to Pendleton. Coralee had left a message on his phone that she had a set of photos for him and he'd be surprised by what they revealed.

Hawke presumed the photos would have family pictures and he would be able to give a family the resolution they'd been needing.

At the lab, he walked in and was happy to see a different person at the take-in desk. "I'm here to pick up something from Coralee," he said.

"Trooper Hawke?" the young woman asked.

He showed her his badge and she handed over an envelope thick with photos. "Thank you."

He headed out to his vehicle. Once he was seated behind the steering wheel, he opened the flap and pulled out the photos. The first ten photos were of places along the Oregon side of the Snake River. The next photo showed two men facing one another as if arguing down along the river's edge. Then a photo of a man raising a rifle. The next photo showed that man bashing it against the other man's temple. There was a photo of the man with the rifle bent over toward the river. Another photo showed a body with a pack floating along on the current. The last photo was a rifle aimed at the person taking the photo.

He studied the photos and knew he would need them enlarged to try and make out the face of the man who'd murdered two people.

Chapter Eight

Before driving away from the lab, he walked back in and left a message for Coralee to send him enlarged photos to the Winslow OSP Office. He figured there would be a copy of Dick's results waiting for him in the file when he turned up for work.

Hawke and Dog headed for Wallowa County and two hours later he drove up his driveway between Winslow and Alder to get a clean uniform on and pick up his OSP vehicle. After putting his two poison ivy-coated uniforms in the washing machine, he changed into his uniform and walked out to the barn to check on the horses and mule.

He stopped at the gate leading into the pasture behind the barn. He whistled and three heads popped up from where Jack, Horse, and Dot were eating. Once they spotted him, they came racing across the field. Jack fell behind as his old legs weren't keeping him up with the younger gelding or the mule's long legs.

"What have you rascals been up to?" Hawke asked,

patting their necks and giving them each an alfalfa cube he'd picked up on his way by the barn. "We'll make a trip up in the mountains next week. This week, I'll stay close to home to gather information on something I found on the river."

Dot, or Polka Dot as his young friend Kitree called him, was a six-year-old who was turning into an excellent trail horse. Hawke rubbed his hand up and down the Appaloosa's spotted neck. He was pleased his ex-landlord and now neighbor, Darlene Trembley, had thought this horse would be a good replacement for Jack, his twenty-something gelding he'd been using since he'd become a Fish and Wildlife Officer in Wallowa County.

"I have to go. But I'll be back tonight to give you grain." Hawke turned from the pasture in time to see a four-wheeler coming down the road between this property and his neighbors'.

Herb Trembley was on the ATV. He cut the engine as he rolled to a stop beside Hawke. "We expected you back last night," he said by way of greeting. "Glad I saw you here just now or Darlene would have been calling up your boss to see what happened to you."

Hawke smiled. He'd lived in a one-room apartment above the Trembleys' arena for most of his time here in the county. It was a short two years ago that he and Dani had purchased this property next door. It was good to have someone keeping an eye on things when he and Dani were gone so much of the time.

"I had some things to take to the lab in Pendleton so I spent the night with my mom and sister," Hawke said.

"Oh, that's good you're spending time with your

family." Herb nodded. "You going to be home for a while or do you want me to keep tabs on the water trough and feed your guys some grain?"

"I'll be home for a while and then I'll be headed up in the mountains."

Herb did a nod and said, "I figured you'd be itchin' to get up there with the weather we've been having." He winked. "Not to mention Dani hasn't been home in a while."

Hawke grinned. A trip to the mountains could take him close to the lodge and a night with her. "That has been on my mind," he said.

Herb laughed and said, "I'll let Darlene know everything is fine. Have a good day." He started up the ATV, turned it, and headed back down the road.

Hawke walked to the house, grabbed his work computer and the envelope of photos, and walked out to his work vehicle. "Stay," he said to Dog and patted him on the head. "I'll be home tonight. You keep those boys in line." He pointed to the horses still standing by the gate.

Dog barked and headed to the pasture. He and Jack had been buddies since Hawke brought Dog home.

Hawke slid behind the steering wheel, placed his computer on the console between the seats, and started up the pickup. He'd head to the office and see what he could find about two missing persons in the possible late 80s or early 90s.

《》《》《》

After a short conversation with Spruel, Hawke planted his butt in his chair and turned on his computer. Spruel believed, like Hawke, that they were looking at two homicides. It was clearly evident from the photos that one man struck the other man with the butt of a rifle and then shoved him into the river. The last photo of the same man pointing a rifle at the camera, and the film was found with suspicious bones, made it pretty clear that the man with the camera was also a victim.

He opened up the missing person reports in Wallowa County in the 1980s. The good thing with such a small population, around 7,300 people, in an area of 3,100 square miles, few local people went missing. But if someone visiting went missing there would be a record.

Pulling up all missing person reports, he started sifting through them. In 1987 two people were reported missing. A professor from Oregon State University and a lawyer from Salem. He continued reading. The lawyer had been on a fishing trip with a friend and the friend reported him missing when he didn't show up back at camp one night. A year later his body was found hung up on rocks when the river lowered.

Hawke pulled up the report. He read through it and then pulled up a photo of the man. Typing in the friend, Lucas Brazo, to the Motor Vehicle system, a driver's license came up. The man had a puffy, craggy face, a small amount of stringy hair, and he appeared to be about two hundred pounds overweight. He pulled out the photo of the man holding the stick, trying to find a resemblance between the two. Could the friends have gotten into a fight and one killed the other?

He jotted down Brazo's address. He lived in Wallowa County. That would make talking to him easier.

Next, Hawke pulled up information on the professor, Yu Chang. He'd worked in the history department of OSU. He'd headed to Wallowa County on the Snake River to work on a piece about the massacre of 30 Chinese miners in Hells Canyon in 1887. Hawke had heard about and read about the atrocity. Chinese miners had taken boats up the Snake River and set up two mining sites. A gang of men, mostly from the county, had slaughtered the miners, throwing their bodies in the river and boats, before pilfering their living quarters looking for the gold that the Chinese miners had found. The men who were caught weren't punished.

He shook his head. If Professor Chang was the one who took the photos, it was a pretty good chance he was the body Dog had found. Hawke wrote down the phone number for the professor's next of kin. His wife, Jin Chang. Tapping the pen on the notepad where he'd written the address and name, Hawke wondered if he should wait until they had proof it was the man.

"What are you thinking about so hard?"

Hawke looked up at Ivy Bisset, the newest trooper to the county. "Trying to decide if I should give someone hope or wait until we know for sure."

"This have anything to do with the bones you found in Hells Canyon?" she asked, pulling up a chair.

"Yeah. I think I know whose they might be, but wonder if I shouldn't wait until we can come up with some kind of actual proof."

"I say wait. How long has it been that the person was missing?" Ivy asked.

"Thirty-six years."

"That's longer than I've been alive. A few more days or weeks isn't going to make a difference. I say wait until you have proof." She swiveled the chair and

70

turned on the computer in front of her.

"Yeah, you're right. Thanks." Hawke glanced at his inbox. He had three new messages. Opening the email, he discovered Dick had sent him information on the bones and Coralee had sent the photos so he could enlarge them.

"Are you going out on patrol today?" Spruel asked behind him.

Hawke spun around. "Right after I check out the emails that just came in."

Spruel tipped his head to Ivy. "She's off duty so you need to take up the slack."

"I'll hit the roads in half an hour." Hawke spun back around and read the email from Dick.

Using UV light, I can positively say the bones have not been lying around for 100 years. I ran isotopes and will have results from that in 7-10 days. I would venture to guess this was a male, given the ridges on the humerus. Or a female who did physical work. Bring me more and I'll see what I can do.

All Dick told him was what he already knew. Hawke opened the email from Coralee and opened the photo of the men arguing. He enlarged the photo and held the driver's license photo of Brazo up to the enlarged photo. It could be him but again, it was hard to tell with the image so grainy. He added the emails to the folder of this case and turned off his computer.

"Taking over for me?" Ivy asked, looking up from the computer.

"Yeah." Hawke grabbed his hat off the desk, settled it on his head, and headed out to his vehicle. The first place he was headed was Eagle to talk to Lucas Brazo.

《》《》《》

Hawke drove into Eagle and turned right on Fourth Street. Down at the end was a small mobile home court called Six Pines. Brazo lived in the one in the far back. Knowing there was little parking space inside the fenced-in area around the nine older mobile homes, Hawke parked in front of the manager's trailer and walked through the gate. He walked along the road that ran down the middle of the two rows of four mostly single-wide homes. Six years ago, he'd been called here for a domestic dispute. He'd learned that the couple who'd been throwing knickknacks and trinkets at each other and had since split up.

He walked up to the door of number 9, which sat square in the middle in front of the road and knocked. Several small dogs yapped and he could hear toenails clattering across the floor. Something hit the door on the inside and the yapping grew louder.

"Shut up!" shouted a male voice. A dog yipped and the skittering of claws receded.

"Whose there?" called the male voice, which he figured was Brazo.

"Oregon State Trooper Hawke. I'd like to talk to you."

"What about?" The door knob jiggled a little.

"Your friend who went missing thirty-six years ago." Hawke waited and listened. He could hear the man breathing heavily on the other side of the door.

The knob wiggled back and forth, something clicked, and the door swung out toward him.

An obese man filled the doorway. Hawke knew he was 63, but he looked more like 73. His round, saggy face was unshaven. A sour smell caused Hawke's nostrils to scrunch. The sweat beading the man's furrowed brow proved standing for very long was work. He only had on shorts, which were barely visible under the gelatinous belly hanging nearly to the hem of the shorts.

"What do you want to know about something from that long ago?" Brazo asked, bracing himself in the doorway with both hands gripping the doorframe.

"We came across bones and while I was looking through missing person reports from back then, I came across the report about Evan Nestor. You were with him when he went missing."

"Yes, and I heard they found his body about a year later so I have nothing to tell you about anything you don't already know." The man took a step back and reached for the door.

"I want to know if you hit him with the butt of a rifle and tossed him in the river." Hawke peered into the man's face.

Brazo stopped, his eyes wide. "Who told you that?"

"I have a photo." Hawke watched the man for any tells.

The large man shook his head. "There isn't any picture of me taking a rifle to Evan. I didn't do it. We split up that day. Evan wanted to fish a spot that I didn't want to hike to. I told him to go and we'd meet back at the camp at five. He never showed. The next day I flagged down someone to get a hold of the authorities."

The man seemed genuine but until Hawke could get his hands on a picture of Brazo when he was younger, he wouldn't rule him out. "Did Evan talk about anyone he was having trouble with?"

Brazo thought about that. "He seemed preoccupied

73

but he didn't say anything about having trouble with anyone. His wife threw a fit when I picked him up. She wanted him to stay home. Evan told her she knew he was going on this trip for two months. She should have planned better."

Hawke made a mental note to find out where the woman was now and talk with her. "Thank you. If you think of anything else I'd appreciate a call." Hawke handed him a card with his cell phone number. "There is no statute of limitations on murder. And I believe the person who killed Evan Nestor also killed another man."

He left Brazo standing in his doorway and walked back out to his vehicle. A short man with a long gray ponytail and a pointed gray beard stood in front of the OSP truck.

"Who did you come to see? Do I need to keep an eye on one of the tenants?" the man's voice sounded as if he'd smoked a pack a day of cigarettes since he was old enough to walk.

"I'm only asking questions. No one here you need to keep an eye on." Hawke walked to the door of this vehicle. He stopped a moment and asked, "How long has Lucas Brazo been living here?"

"Twenty, maybe twenty-five years. Why? Is he who you were talking to? Someone turn him in for cruelty to animals?" The man acted as if it would delight him to have something happen to Brazo.

"No, I'm just curious. Do you happen to know if he lived in the county before he moved into this place?" Hawke would have to dig up some history on Brazo.

"I don't know. I moved here twenty years ago and took over this place. He was here when I did that." The man looked into the fenced-in area. "You sure I don't need to keep an eye on him?"

"I'm sure. He's no threat to anyone but his dogs." Which Hawke thought, he hadn't seen only heard. He slid into his vehicle and started it. As he drove away, he radioed he was on patrol and headed out to the Minam Grade to check on fishermen along the Wallowa River.

Chapter Nine

That night, after he'd given the horses and mule their grain, Hawke sat down on the couch with his work laptop and looked up Lucas Brazo. The man had moved here from Salem, where Nestor had been a lawyer. When Brazo lived there he'd been working for the city. It appeared the two had grown up together. He found a photo of the two in a newspaper story about a group of students who went to Washington D.C.

He also found the wedding announcement for Evan Nestor to Christa Croft. It was two years before Evan was killed. There was a story in the paper about Evan being missing. His wife was quoted as saying, "I don't know why he had to go to that place. It is truly Hell's Canyon."

Hawke typed Christa Nestor into the DMV records and she came up until a year after her husband's body was found. He tried her maiden name and it only came up until her marriage. She must have remarried. He went to records and looked up marriage licenses in the

Salem area the year she no longer showed up in DMV records.

There it was. Christa Nestor married Ford Pinson. Hawke stared at the name. Why was it familiar? He put it into the DMV records. Up popped the name and address. That's why it was familiar. The Pinson Ranch was in Imnaha. That was where Christa and Ford lived. Curious. He'd take a run out that way tomorrow.

《》《》《》

Saturday morning, Hawke woke early to check on the horses and mule. Just as he was headed out the door, the ham radio in the office started making noise. He hurried in and spoke into the handset. "Hawke."

"It's Dani. I'll be flying to the county today to bring out a family and bring in another one tomorrow. Want to meet for dinner in town?"

It was good to hear Dani's voice. It had been a while. "Copy. Time?"

"I should be at High Mountain Brew Pub by six."

"Copy. See you there." He smiled as he set the mic down. She'd only be home for a night. But this time of year, he looked forward to her one-night visits as she transported people from and to her lodge in the Eagle Cap Wilderness. Now he had something to hurry his day along.

"Dani will be home tonight," he told Dog as he walked out to feed the horses and mule. Dog bounced around and stopped by the feed room door.

"You need to make sure everyone behaves today so we don't have to hunt for you or put the horses in. I'll only have a few hours with her before she leaves again." He stood with his hand on his hips as he talked to Dog.

The dog's ears moved back and forth as if he were taking in everything Hawke said. And there had been many times when Hawke was sure Dog did understand every word. "Good boy." He patted Dog's head and opened the door to scoop grain for the three in the pasture.

After delivering the grain and some scratches, Hawke walked out to his work vehicle and slid in. Once he was out on the highway, he radioed he was on duty and headed to Alder, driving through the biggest town in the county in five minutes and heading toward Prairie Creek. In Prairie Creek, he turned left to take Little Sheep Creek Highway out to Imnaha.

The Pinson Ranch was north of the unincorporated town of Imnaha. As he drove into the small community the post office was on the left and fifty feet farther on the right was the store and tavern. It was too early in the day to enjoy one of the tavern's juicy burgers.

Hawke kept to the left and followed Lower Imnaha Rd. He drove close to fifteen miles up the road before he spotted the archway with the Rocking P brand and the sprawling two-story home at the end of the drive between two large outbuildings. One appeared to be an old barn and the other a new indoor horse arena.

The people milling around at the horse arena glanced at his State Police vehicle and returned to messing with their horses. The cowboys over by the barn, all stopped and stared as he parked in front of the walkway to the house.

One of the cowboys strolled toward him. When he was within speaking distance, he asked, "This have anything to do with Jimmy not showin' up for work today?"

Hawke shook his head. "I'm here to speak with Mrs. Christa Pinson."

The man studied him. "Whatcha need to speak to her about? She's been at the ranch for over a week. She can't be in trouble."

Hawke smiled at the man. "She's not in trouble. I have information about her first husband's death."

The man snorted and said, "That was a long time ago. She's been married to Ford for decades."

"I still believe she needs to know the truth." Hawke turned to walk up to the front door.

"You won't find her in there. She's giving lessons over in the arena." The cowboy pointed to the fancy horse trailers and women and girls fussing over their horses.

Hawke groaned inwardly. He'd hoped to talk to Mrs. Pinson alone. Gauge her reaction to the fact her husband died of murder rather than an accident. "When will she finish with the lessons?"

"This is an all-day workshop. She's providing lunch for the price they paid to come learn from her." The cowboy said it with admiration.

"What does she teach?" Hawke asked.

"How to deal with ornery horses. Well, she calls them troubled horses, but in my book they's ornery." He scratched behind his right ear and said, "But she does do miracles with them ornery horses."

Hawke was impressed to learn the woman, whom it had sounded like was from an influential family in Salem, was a miracle worker with horses. "Has the workshop started yet?" he asked.

"Yeah. She only works with two or three horses at a time. They're usually ones having the same issues."

A man by the barn hollered and the cowboy turned and waved. "I gotta go. It would be better if you came back tomorrow. Ford will be here then also. He's in town getting fencing supplies."

"Thanks." Hawke watched the cowboy join the others at the barn and then turned to the arena. He didn't want to come back here tomorrow. He'd rather get this done and get to checking fishing licenses and digging up more on the internet.

Settling his hat firmer on his head, he walked toward the arena. His stomach clenched as the females, ages from pre-teen to a woman who appeared too old and fragile to get up on a horse, stared at him as he drew closer.

A woman in her thirties, carrying a clipboard walked out of the arena with a girl of about eight. "May I help you?" the woman asked.

"I'm State Trooper Hawke. I'd like to have a word with Mrs. Christa Pinson."

The woman held out her hand, "I'm Fanny Pinson. My mom is busy at the moment. If you leave a card, she can give you a call on Monday."

Hawke shook her hand and said, "This is something I need to talk to her about in person."

The woman's eyes widened. "Did something happen to Dad?" The younger girl wrapped her arms around Fanny.

"No. Your dad is fine. I need to speak to her in private." Hawke insisted.

"I'll take you in to watch and when she finishes with this group, she'll have a fifteen-minute break. But I want to be present when you talk with her." Fanny's eyes narrowed.

"If your mom is okay with it," he said.

Fanny pivoted and shot over her shoulder, "Follow me and be quiet."

Hawke entered the fancy arena and took the seat on the end farthest away from where a woman with a long silver and blonde braid was astride a dun horse that couldn't seem to stand still. All he could see was the back of the woman and the rump of the horse as its feet moved up and down in a prancing cadence but it stood in one place.

The woman's voice was calm and steady, but not loud enough for Hawke to hear what she was telling the woman standing on the ground and the two sitting on animals who were similarly moving nervously.

Mrs. Pinson continued talking and settling herself even deeper into the saddle as her legs slowly moved away from the animal's side. Releasing the pressure of her legs on the horse's sides seemed to ease some of its agitation. As the horse moved less, she eased her hands closer to the animal's neck, releasing the pressure of the bit in its mouth. Eventually, the horse she was riding and the other two stood still. Their heads dipped a little in a relaxed stand.

Mrs. Pinson continued talking, leaving her legs slack along the horse's sides and the reins slack from where her hands rested on the saddle horn. In slow motion, she dismounted and held the reins out to the teenager who had been standing and watching.

The girl started toward the horse and its head came up, its ears twitching.

Mrs. Pinson said something and the girl moved slower, talking as she walked up to the horse. The animal stretched its neck and sniffed the girl's

81

outstretched hand. The girl then stroked the nose, the jaw, reaching up and scratching the animal behind the ear. And then she slowly moved her hand down the length of the neck and to the saddle horn. The horse began shifting its feet. Mrs. Pinson talked to the teenager and the horse as the girl did all the things that Mrs. Pinson had done before. After about ten minutes the horse was standing relaxed again, with a smiling teenager on its back.

Fanny walked out to the group, spoke to her mother, and pointed in his direction.

Hawke stood and started down the side of the arena as the three women and horses exited the far end of the arena and Fanny and her mother walked toward him.

"I'm Christa Pinson, what did you need to talk to me about?" the woman asked, her voice not near as soothing as it had sounded while she worked with the horse.

"Mrs. Pinson, we found the remains of a person near Sluice Creek on the Snake River."

"What would that have to do with me?" she cut in.

"We have reason to believe this person died around the same time as your husband went missing."

She placed her hand on her hips and said, "Again, I ask what that has to do with me?"

"There was unexposed film with the remains. I took it to the Oregon State Police Lab and it showed someone striking your first husband with the butt end of a rifle and putting him in the river." Hawke hadn't wanted to be so blunt but she had pushed his buttons by acting as if he were wasting her time.

Her mouth opened and then shut as her head shook slowly back and forth. "I-I don't understand."

"Your husband's death has now been ruled a homicide and I'll be working the case. I know this is sudden, but can you think of anyone thirty-six years ago who would have had a grudge against your husband? Maybe Lucas Brazo?"

"No, not Lucas. He and Evan were best friends from grade school. He was devastated over Evan's acci—" she sucked in air. "I can't believe it wasn't an accident."

Fanny put her arms around her mom. "Oh Mom, I'm sorry." Then she glared at Hawke. "Couldn't this have waited? If it's been over thirty years, why did you have to tell her now?"

"Because I need answers to my questions to find out who killed Evan Nestor." Hawke studied the younger Pinson. Her gaze didn't waver as she glared at him.

Shifting his gaze to the mother he asked, again, "Who had Evan had troubles with before his fishing trip?"

"No one. He got along with everyone. But I always thought it odd that he would fall in the river and not be able to get out. Then the autopsy said the body looked as it should for someone who had been carried that far down the river. Back then I wanted answers as to where he could have fallen in and how. But no one cared after it was stamped an accidental drowning." Mrs. Pinson released her daughter's arms from around her shoulders and took a deep breath. "Please let me know what you learn." She put her hand into the breast pocket of her Western shirt and pulled out a business card. "You can call and ask questions, too. I'd like to know what happened to Evan. It might have been half a lifetime ago, but I'd like whoever took him from me to pay."

"I'll do that. One more quick question. Had he and Lucas fished the Snake before?" Hawke pulled out his notebook and wrote what he already knew.

She sighed. "No. But it had been a dream of Evan and Lucas to either raft the river or fish the river. When I said rafting was too dangerous, given neither one of them had whitewater rafted before, they settled for fishing." She frowned. "But they picked the worst week to do it."

"Why do you say that?" Hawke asked, his pen poised over the notebook.

"My brother was getting married that weekend. Harry wanted Evan at his bachelor party but Evan used the excuse of promising Lucas a fishing trip. I found out later that Evan had known my brother planned to have one of Evan's former girlfriends, who was a stripper, at this bachelor party. Evan had chosen to go fishing to not get in a compromising photo with the ex. He went fishing to keep me from being jealous."

"How did you find out about his decision?" Hawke asked, scribbling in the book and looking up to see the woman's face soften.

"Lucas told me after he finished telling me that Evan was missing and presumed drowned. He was a mess. He said he thought he was helping Evan by agreeing to go so he wouldn't have to go to the bachelor party. Then after Evan's body was found and Lucas had time to grieve and could talk without choking up, he told me all about how they'd planned the fishing trip and how upset Evan was that I was so mad about them going. But he believed it would be better, in the long run, to have me unhappy over the timing than have my kid brother show me photos of Evan with Verena."

"Did your brother not like Evan?" Hawke asked.

Her brow wrinkled. "Harry and Evan never got along. Evan was all about getting ahead and working hard. Harry is a dreamer. He lives from day to day and most days he doesn't know where he's going to lay his head or get a meal. He was a bitter disappointment to my father. Where my father thought Evan was a younger version of himself." She thought a moment. "I think that's why I married Evan. I adored my father and marrying Evan would keep him around longer." She looked down at her hands. "Or was supposed to keep him around longer. Evan died before Father."

Hawke wondered at her wording. There wasn't anything in her words or tone that indicated she loved her first husband.

"Thank you. I won't take up any more of your day and I will let you know when I learn anything or have any questions." Hawke closed his notebook and slid it into his pocket.

"Thank you for letting me know. I always thought it strange that Evan, who took risks only in money, would succumb to an accident."

Hawke walked out of the arena and straight to his vehicle. As he drove away, he wondered how a man without any enemies could be smashed in the head with the butt of a rifle and pushed into a river.

Chapter Ten

After leaving the Pinson Ranch, Hawke drove the length of the Imnaha Lower and Upper Roads checking fishermen and then headed to Prairie Creek and up to Wallowa Lake to check boaters and those fishing. He spent the rest of the day thinking about what Mrs. Pinson had said in between talking to the fishermen.

At five-thirty he called dispatch to say he was finished for the day. He headed to Alder to meet Dani at High Mountain Brew Pub.

When he entered the pub, he found Dani visiting with Desiree Halver, a young woman whose family he'd helped out when he first started working in the county.

"Trooper Hawke, I was just asking Dani how she liked living with you." The young woman's eyes twinkled.

"I'm sure she said I'm set in my ways and hard to civilize."

Desiree and Dani both laughed.

"True," Dani said when she finished laughing.

"I have a table over here for you two. If you're lucky it won't get too rowdy tonight." Desiree led them to a table in the corner where Hawke could see everyone who entered and most of the open room.

There were already half a dozen men and women playing pool, most of the tables were occupied for dinner, and the bar area had a few high tables and bar stools left. He had to remember it was a Saturday night.

After they received their drinks and ordered their meal, Dani asked, "What have you been up to?"

He told her about his Snake River patrol, what Dog found, and he'd subsequently found, and that he was now working a double homicide cold case.

"Wow! I leave you alone for a month and you're digging up old murders to keep you occupied." She winked and laughed as their food was placed on the table in front of them.

"You left me in May. This is July. That's a lot longer than a month. A man has to find something to do when his woman is up in the mountains where he'd like to be." Hawke cut into the steak he'd ordered. The juices gushed out onto the plate. He glanced up. "I have missed you. Spending all winter together gave me a pretty good taste of what it's like having someone, other than Dog and the horses and mule, to come home to." He meant it. Before he met Dani and they bought the house together, he hadn't thought he was lonely. But after spending a whole winter with her, he found he liked the company more than the solitude.

"You know you can retire any time and come spend the summers with me at the lodge." She picked up her glass of beer and peered at him over the rim.

"That thought has been floating around in my head a whole lot more lately."

Dani put her hand on his. "If it helps, I've been missing you like crazy too."

He peered into her eyes and couldn't wait to get home and wrap his arms around her.

They ate their dinner with only superficial conversation. Dani asked how Herb and Darlene were and Hawke asked how Tuck, Sage, and Kitree were doing.

Desiree stopped at their table. "You might want to leave soon. I just heard there is a family reunion headed this way. It will get loud."

"Thanks for the warning," Hawke said, handing her what he figured would cover the meal and the tip.

"Anytime." Desiree walked back to the bar.

Hawke stood, waiting for Dani to gather her purse. His gaze roamed around inside the establishment and landed on a person at the end of the bar. Lucas Brazo. He walked Dani to her SUV and said, "Go on home. Dog will be happy to see you. I'm going to have a conversation with a guy I saw at the bar."

"Does it have to do with your cold cases?" she asked, opening her vehicle door and standing beside it.

"Yeah, he's a person of interest. If he's in there drinking because of my visit with him, I'd like to know more about his relationship with the victim. I also met the victim's wife today and she made out like she and this guy were good friends but he didn't seem like he cared for her much. Just want some clarification."

Dani put a hand on his arm. "Go talk to him but make sure you come home before I have to leave in the morning."

He leaned close and kissed her cheek. "I'll be home no more than an hour behind you. I promise."

"I'm holding you to that." She slid into her vehicle and he watched her drive out of the parking lot.

Hawke returned to the restaurant and slid onto the stool next to Brazo. The man didn't even look over at him.

Desiree walked down the bar to them. "Didn't expect to see you back in here."

"I'll have an iced tea while I talk with Lucas."

Brazo twisted his head and peered at Hawke through blurry eyes. "Do I know you?"

"We met yesterday. At your house. I'm surprised that you drove clear up to Alder to get drunk when Winslow or Eagle would have been an easier place to get a ride home." Hawke took the iced tea Desiree placed in front of him and nodded to her in thanks.

"We talked yesterday?" Brazo asked, staring into his drink.

"We did. I told you that your friend, Evan Nestor, is now a homicide, not an accidental death." Hawke studied the sallow face and jiggling jowls of the man beside him.

The man turned his head. Tears glistened in his eyes and snot trickled out his nose. "He was the best friend I ever had. No one else ever treated me like I had a brain in my head. They just called me the 'Fat kid.'"

"I want to know more about Evan and Christa's marriage," Hawke said.

Brazo swiped at his eyes with an overstuffed finger. "What about their marriage?"

"Was it good? Christa told me that you told her Evan went on the fishing trip to keep her from being jealous. Is she someone who gets jealous easily?"

"We did go on the fishing trip so Evan didn't have to go to Harry's bachelor party. Evan got wind that Harry had hired one of Evan's ex-girlfriends to be the stripper at the party. Evan always had a way of stopping trouble before it started. That's why he wanted an excuse. And it bothered him that Christa was angry with him over his choice. I told him to tell her why, she'd understand. But he said he didn't want her thinking he still had any feelings for Verena."

"You didn't answer my question. Does Christa get jealous easily?" Hawke restated.

"Y-yeah, well no. I mean I don't think she got jealous so much as once they were married, she believed Evan was hers. She was more possessive than jealous." Brazo scratched his head and waved his hand for another drink.

"How about I drive you home and we can talk some more on the way." Hawke shook his head when Desiree started their direction with another drink.

"I'm not ready to leave."

The reunion group arrived. Twenty people shoved and jostled their way into the air-conditioned building, blocking the exit.

Hawke didn't want Brazo to have anything more to drink so he could speak without slurring his words, though he was darn close to it right now. He knew to keep the man here he'd have to get him a drink. He waved to Desiree. "Bring him another drink but light on the booze. It doesn't look like we'll get out of here until that group is seated."

"That will be about fifteen minutes," she said. "They need to clear tables and put them together. The manager didn't want to save that much seating before the group arrived."

She returned with the lightly mixed drink and Hawke asked Brazo another question. "Do you know how Christa met Ford Pinson, her new husband?"

"She, Evan, and Ford went to college together. They were at OSU. Ford in agricultural studies, Evan in business, and Christa in animal science." He set his drink down. "I didn't go to a university. I went to a community college. Evan would still hang out with me even though some of his college friends would make cracks about me to each other. I hated it when he invited me to college things. The one time I pretended I had something else to do he begged me to come. He said he didn't like hanging out with them any more than I did but it was a time for him to build connections for when he got out in the business world."

"Was Ford Pinson one of those connections?"

Brazo started to nod his head and then changed it to a shake. "Ford wasn't at all the events."

"Did you know that Ford's family had a ranch not far from where you were fishing?" Hawke asked as the staff started seating the reunion group.

Brazo's head swung, his bloodshot eyes widening. "No. Really? I'd think if Evan had known that he would have asked him to join us." He raised a hand and made a circling motion with his index finger. "You know, to learn where the best fishing was and to make a bond with the man. Evan specialized in farm and ranch loans."

This was news to Hawke. Now he wondered if there was someone in the county thirty-six years ago who applied for a loan and was turned down by Evan.

The exit was no longer blocked. "Come on, I'll drive you home." Hawke helped Brazo off the stool which wasn't easy given the man's size and weight.

"What about my car?" Brazo asked as they walked over to Hawke's vehicle.

"You'll have to get someone to bring you up here to get it when you're sober." Hawke moved items from the backseat to the front passenger seat and pushed the man into the back seat.

Once the door was closed, Hawke walked around to the driver's seat and texted Dani that he would be a tiny bit longer. She sent him a thumbs-up emoji but he figured she wasn't going to be happy when he arrived. If she was awake.

Questioning Brazo any further was a bust. The man fell asleep before they'd cleared Alder city limits. Hawke used the silence to digest what Brazo had told him. Christa was possessive and Ford had gone to college with both Evan and Christa. He wondered if the Pinsons had been seeing each other secretly after the marriage between the college sweethearts.

Chapter Eleven

Sunday morning, Hawke drove behind Dani to the Alder airstrip and saw her off. She told him she had booked fewer people at the lodge for the weekend of the powwow so that she could stay home the whole weekend. Even though they both knew her crew could take care of a full lodge without her there.

Today and tomorrow were Hawke's days off, but he was feeling antsy. He returned home, hooked up to his horse trailer, saddled up Dot, filled his saddlebags with food for two days, and strapped on a bedroll. "Come on, Dog, we're going to look for the spots these photos were taken." He patted the pocket of the vest he wore. Maybe if he could determine the significance of the photos, he could narrow down who the body was. And if he had time, he'd stop by the dig site and see how they were coming along.

As he drove toward Alder to head to Imnaha and out to the Hat Point trailhead, he called Herb.

"Where are you going on your days off?" Herb

asked. "Up to the lodge with Dani?"

"No. She was just here picking up more guests. I'm headed to the Snake River over Hat Point. I'm taking Dot and Dog. We'll be back late Monday night. Thought I should let someone know."

"And you wanted me to keep an eye on the two you left behind."

Hawke chuckled. "Yeah. If you don't mind checking on them in the morning and giving them grain, that will make them feel less left out."

"Not a problem. Safe travels." Herb ended the call.

Hawke smiled at his good fortune to have had the Trembleys for landlords and now neighbors. They helped everyone and knew everything about everyone in the county. He made a mental note to stop by and see them when he returned to see if they knew anything about Ford Pinson.

He arrived at the Hat Point trailhead close to noon. Rather than take time to eat, he pulled a handful of jerky and an apple out of his saddle bag and put a bottle of water sticking out of the flap within easy reach.

Dog headed down the trail and Dot followed. Hawke ate his food and studied the terrain ahead of them. When he finished his food, he headed Dot off the trail to make the straightest line toward Sluice Creek. Sliding on shale and making their way down some rocky terrain for a little over an hour, they came to the edge of the cottonwood trees and hawthorn that lined Sluice Creek. Keeping just inside the tree line to stay out of the hot sun but avoid the worst of the thorny trees, bushes, and poison ivy, they continued another hour until he spotted people walking back and forth from the creek to the camp, which now consisted of half a dozen tents.

He rode into the camp, studying each person until he recognized Dave.

"Hawke, I figured you wouldn't stay away." Deputy Alden walked over to him and bent to scratch Dog's ears.

"The lab developed the film and thought I'd see if I could figure out where the photos were taken." Hawke dismounted and motioned for Dave to follow him as he led Dot down to the river to get a drink.

"The film also showed a man being murdered." Hawke studied Dave.

The deputy's gaze flew from where it had been watching the horse drink to Hawke's face. "Are you saying our remains witnessed a murder? And you think he was killed because of it?"

"The last photo is of a rifle being pointed at the photographer," Hawke said with the emotion he felt. The person had either been brave to take the photo, knowing the killer saw him or he had been foolish to stand there and let the killer see him.

"Man. That's something."

Hawke handed the envelope with the photos to Dave. "Take a look. It won't hurt to try and figure out where the person was standing." Hawke studied the photo Dave held of the two men arguing. He glanced at the rocks sticking up out of the water.

"Do you know who this victim is?" Dave asked, looking at the photo of the body in the river.

"Yes, Evan Nestor. A lawyer from Salem, he was here fishing with a friend. His death was cited as an accidental drowning." Hawke stared at the photo Dave held of the rifle pointed at the photographer. "I talked to his widow yesterday and his best friend who was with him here fishing."

Dave peered into Hawke's face. "Do you think the best friend did it?"

"My gut says 'no' but he's taking it pretty hard. Especially since it was thirty-six years ago." Hawke took the photo of the two men from Dave and held it up, glancing from it to the river. "Over there. That's where they were arguing."

Hawke walked upriver along the rocky shoreline. "There. That rock is behind them." He stood in front of the rock and then rotated to look up Sluice Creek. "The photographer had to have been up there somewhere." He took the photo of the rifle aimed at the photographer. "The killer has that rifle aimed high. That means the photographer was up there somewhere. Probably in the open. I wonder if after he was shot, he tried to hide in the bushes along the stream."

Hawke thought of the film in a canister in the back pocket of the vest. "He had enough time to roll the film back into the cartridge, put it in the canister, and shove it in the pocket of the vest. If the killer found him and finished him off, he must have taken the camera thinking the film was still in it. Or the photographer was a quick enough thinker that he put another roll in to make it look like he hadn't taken the film out." Hawke held out his hand to get the photos back from Dave. "Have you found more bones?"

"They are slowly adding more to the skeleton. We found the head, ribs, and pelvis. According to Dr. Galler, it's male."

"I wonder…" Hawke thought of the professor from OSU who had been missing since that same summer.

"Did you come across a missing male besides the man in the river?" Dave asked.

"I did. Professor Yu Chang from Corvallis. Did Dr. Galler say if there was a way to use DNA to figure out who the remains belong to?"

"He said there's a good chance that there will be enough DNA in the teeth to match if someone in his family is in the system."

Someone from the camp called to them. Dave and Hawke, leading Dot, walked back to the camp.

It was his Auntie Flo. She smiled. "I see you have come back."

"I wanted to check out the places along the river in the photos from the film I found." Hawke handed her the photos of the area along the Oregon side of the Snake River without the ones of the murder.

"These spots are downstream," she said flipping through them. She stopped and held up a photo. "This is at Salt Creek near Suicide Point." She looked up into Hawke's eyes. "You know about Suicide Point, don't you?"

Hawke studied her face. She was asking more than if he knew the history of the spot. He didn't. "I know that a Nimiipuu man, named Half Moon, and his horse fell at Suicide Point."

She nodded. "It is said that he wasn't alone and it wasn't suicide. Only the Whites called it suicide."

"That isn't the only unfortunate thing to happen in the area. On the Oregon side Salt Creek is where one of the groups of Chinese miners were digging for gold in 1887," Dave said.

Hawke's mind started rewinding like a movie. "If the body you found is Professor Yu Chang and these are photos he took, he could have been here documenting the Chinese miners." Hawke had the feeling he was onto the truth of who the bones belonged to. "I'll pass by tomorrow on my way out." He mounted Dot and whistled to Dog.

"Take care," Auntie Flo called after him.

He raised a hand in acknowledgment and kept Dot's head pointed north.

«»«»«»

Hawke and Dog came upon Sand Creek more than an hour from the encampment. There wasn't a sign of anyone using the cabin. He debated on spending the night but decided he'd rather have more time tomorrow to check out Salt Creek.

As the sun slid down below the west rim of the canyon, he rode by Suicide Point. Hawke studied the sheer rock cliff and wondered how a Nimiipuu horseman would have fallen to his death without aid from someone. Suicide was not something a warrior would think of doing. It would leave his family without someone to provide for them and disgrace everyone left behind.

He came to the south side of Salt Creek and rode about a quarter of a mile uphill from the river. They'd spend the night here and check around for a possible mine shaft in the morning. From his higher elevation, he could see lights coming on down at the campground closer to the river on the north side of the creek.

"Let's get some grub and sleep," he said to Dot and Dog as he unsaddled the gelding and put a feed bag with a ration of grain on the animal's head.

When Dot was munching away, Hawke dug in his bag for two MREs. He used the 'Meals Ready to Eat' often when he was up in the Eagle Cap Wilderness. It was too dry to start a fire and he didn't feel like waiting for water to boil on a sterno stove. Using his knife, he cut off the top of two heater bags, placed the MREs in next to the heater, and poured water in. After folding the tops down to keep the heat in, he rolled out his bedroll and positioned his saddlebags to use as a pillow or backrest so predators wouldn't be able to make off with their food during the night. Not that many would be interested in MRE packs, but they would like his jerky.

When that was finished, he opened one bag and pulled out the MRE. Cutting the top off, he dumped the spaghetti on a rock for Dog to eat. Then he opened the other bag, cut the top, and used a fork to eat his portion of spaghetti. He washed it down with water and a protein bar.

Dog burped and looked at him as if he wanted more.

"That's all you get tonight." Hawke stood and led Dot over to the water trickling about six inches wide in Salt Creek. The horse drank until he had his fill, and Hawke led him back to the camp, tying him to the closest large boulder.

He cleaned up the packaging from the meal and sealed it in a large plastic bag.

"Let's get some sleep. It could be a lot of scrambling through bushes and over rocks tomorrow." Hawke lay down, completely clothed, on top of his sleeping bag. It was too hot to crawl in and the full thickness gave a bit more cushion from the small rocks imbedded in the ground.

《》《》《》

The following morning, Hawke was up as soon as there was enough light to see. He used the sterno burner to make a pot of coffee. After a cup of coffee and a protein bar for himself and Dog, Hawke tethered Dot to a tree where he could forage for grass without getting into poison ivy. Then Hawke and Dog, using the photo, started down at the confluence of the creek to the Snake River and walked west, uphill to see if he could pinpoint the reason for the photo.

After an hour they stopped for some water and Hawke studied the photo closer. The photo specifically zoomed in on the shale rock slide. The area under the rock could have been flat enough for a camp. It would have been hidden from anyone on the river. But they would have had to carry their sluice boxes and equipment down to the river every day if their goal was not to be seen. He didn't understand the photo.

The other photos were farther downstream at Deep Creek. Where stories were told of 34 Chinese miners massacred by Wallowa County residents in 1887. Could this have been another site where the miners were working? Is that what Yu Chang was looking for?

Hawke took photos with his phone and then whistled for Dog. "Let's load up and head back to Hat Point. I want to search for the professor and see why he might have been out here thirty-six years ago."

He and Dog wandered back down to where Dot was standing with one hind leg cocked resting on the toe of his hoof, his eyes closed.

"Looks like you must have filled up on that grass," Hawke said, walking over and patting the horse on the neck before leading him to the saddle. Once the animal was all tacked out, Hawke swung up into the saddle and they headed upriver.

His mind swirled with what he knew and what he didn't know as his gaze took in the stark rocky Idaho side of the river. Jetboats roared by disturbing the solitude the deep canyon evoked. If it were up to Hawke only rafts and kayaks would be allowed on the river. Granted they would only be able to travel downriver and not up, but it would be better for the wildlife and the people like him who preferred to take in nature as it was not with a soundtrack of jetboats.

Dot walked toward the encampment at Sluice Creek as the sun beat rays straight down on them. Hawke dismounted by the river and let Dot drink and stand in the water. Today was hotter than any other he'd experienced while in this canyon. How had miners over a hundred years ago spent every day doing the hard labor of mining in this heat?

"You're back," a female voice behind him said.

Hawke turned to his auntie with a smile. "Saw what I could and headed back so I can be to work on time tomorrow."

She nodded. "Phil wants to send the lower jaw with you to see if DNA can be pulled from it."

This news made the cloud about the man's death lift a bit in Hawke's mind. "It would be good to know who he is. Though I think I know." He went on to tell her about the missing university professor and how the photos might have something to do with the 1887 Chinese massacre.

"That would make sense. But you would have thought if a professor went missing, they would have dug a bit harder to find him." Auntie Flo's brow wrinkled. "But then when have anyone other than a

101

White been a priority to law enforcement." She put a hand on his arm. "Excluding you. I'm sure you don't care about the color of a victim's skin. You always had an unbiased view of everyone."

Hawke dropped his chin to his chest. "I'm afraid being in law enforcement as long as I have, I don't judge a person by their skin color but I can be prejudiced against people who I see continually breaking the law."

"That is deserved. It isn't formed by the size of their nose or the color of their skin. It's formed by their previous actions. They are showing you exactly why you need to be biased because of their past." Flo looked back at the camp. "Come have lunch with me and you can get that jaw from Phil."

As they walked up the hill toward the encampment, Hawke asked, "How long do you plan to stay here?"

"Until they say there are no more pieces to find or until I'm called to check out bones that have been dug up from land where our ancestors have lived."

"If you can get away, Mom, Marion, and I, along with my friend Dani, will be at Tamkaliks in Eagle at the end of the month. I think Mom would like to see you if you have time to come." He thought he'd witnessed a hint of longing in his mom's face when he'd mentioned Flo.

She smiled. "I'll see if I can make it. No promises but I'll try."

"I'd like you to meet my friend, Dani, and my sister, Marion." Hawke's chest relaxed as Flo smiled and nodded.

At the tents, Hawke ground tied Dot and followed Flo over to the tent they were using as the kitchen. A table was laid out with bread, lunch meat, cheese, and condiments along with various bags of chips. Hawke made a sandwich and followed Flo over to another tent.

Inside Dr. Galler was moving between tables littered with bones. Hawke walked deeper into the tent and realized the man was putting together a human puzzle. The skeleton on one table was slowly being filled in with the cleaned bones from another table.

"Ahh, Trooper Hawke. Flo told me you'd be by today." Dr. Galler picked up a paper evidence bag slightly larger than a human jawbone. With gloved hands, he handed it to Hawke. "I'm sure you know where to take this to get a DNA sample."

"Yes. I'll get it to Clackamas tomorrow. I'm thinking about taking a trip over to Corvallis anyway." He glanced at his auntie. She nodded.

Why he needed her approval surprised him. He'd never wondered about getting anyone's approval his whole life, and now, this woman, had him seeking approval from her. Another thing to think about on his horse ride out of here.

He finished his sandwich with one hand while holding the bag in his other hand as he studied the skeleton taking shape on the table. "What are you still missing?"

"Mostly the small bones from the hands. We found a full leg and foot along with the pelvis, ribs, spine, and head. I sent a group up to the cave and they were able to find the rest of the arm but not the hand. They found the bones from his left leg down the creek about twenty yards from the rest of the skeleton. And the other arm bones under the tree where you found the piece of clothing with part of a zipper. I figure an eagle grabbed an arm and took off into the tree. There looked to be remains of a large nest."

Hawke nodded. He'd thought that might have been the case when he'd found the zipper. "Do you have enough to estimate his height and build?"

"Yes, he was five feet, seven inches. And I would say an average build. His bones don't appear to have had stress from carrying too much weight."

"Is there anything about the structure of the skull that might help with race?" Hawke asked, knowing that if it were a person of mixed race, it might be deceiving.

"I would say you are looking for someone of Asian race. It has pretty classic Asian measurements for the shape, eye sockets, and nasal opening." Dr. Galler looked up from where he was placing a bone in order on the skeleton. "Do you already have someone in mind?"

"Yes. I found a missing person at the time I believe this person was killed that fits. A professor from Oregon State University. Dr. Yu Chang. He taught history."

The anthropologist nodded. "You might just have the right person. But what was he doing here?"

"I hope to find out tomorrow. Thank you for all the work you are doing." Hawke exited the tent, wiping at the sweat trickling down his face. "How does he tolerate working in the tent without more ventilation?" Hawke asked Flo.

She smiled. "He is used to hot temperatures. And when he gets engrossed in what he's doing he forgets about any discomfort. If we didn't supply him with water, he'd dry up and the wind would take him away." She laughed and Hawke chuckled.

Hawke put the bag in his saddlebag and picked up

the reins from where they dangled from Dot's bridle.

"That's a good horse," Flo said.

"He was trained by a good friend. I keep asking her if she is Nimiipuu but she laughs and says she's a little bit of everything." Hawke swung up onto the saddle, looked around for Dog, and whistled.

He came bounding out of the bushes by the creek, his hair was full of small sticks. "What have you been doing?" Hawke asked as he urged Dot forward. He twisted in the saddle. "If we don't see you in a couple of weeks, I'll try to talk Mom into coming your way before winter."

"I'd like that, but she may not want to set foot in Idaho. I'll try to make it to the powwow."

Hawke nodded and returned his attention to the side of the canyon they had to navigate up.

Chapter Twelve

They made it back to the pickup and trailer by four. It had taken longer to go up as he'd stopped many times to let Dot catch his breath after climbing a steep section. Foaming on his neck and between his legs, Dot was happy to step up into the trailer and hang his head.

Hawke was glad he'd brought the younger horse and not Jack. Jack would have worked hard to get out of the canyon to please Hawke, but they would have had to stop even more often and the older horse would have been sore for several days after. Dot would most likely just be tired. His muscles were young and he had been packing Hawke around the Wallowas the last couple of years keeping him in shape. Jack had been staying out in the pasture more than being ridden.

On the way back, he decided to call Spruel today to get permission to take the skull to Clackamas and visit the college. He was even more certain the remains belonged to Yu Chang.

Once he was in cell service, Hawke called Spruel.

"Hawke, why are you calling in on your day off? Don't tell me you found another body," his superior joked.

"No. But I was down at Sluice Creek today and Dr. Galler gave me the lower jaw of the remains to take to Clackamas. I'd like permission to take it to the lab and drive down to OSU. From what Galler told me, I'm pretty sure the remains are that of Dr. Yu Chang, a professor from OSU who went missing at the same time as the death of Evan Nestor." Hawke needed Spruel's permission to make the trip across the state.

There was a prolonged silence on the other end of the call. He didn't know if Spruel was figuring out someone else to take the skull or if he was looking at the schedule to see if Hawke could be gone.

Finally, he spoke, "It looks like we have an overlap of troopers tomorrow. But you need to go straight over, do what you need to do, and get back. Ivy asked for two days off to check on her grandmother in Spokane. I'll need you the rest of the week."

"I'll get home, take a shower, and head toward Portland tonight. That will give me plenty of time tomorrow to do what I need to do and get back here." He started to end the call and said, "Thank you. I found the bones and feel like I need to give his family closure."

"Hawke, I know how you dig for justice. That's your saving grace when you take off like this." Spruel ended the call.

Hawke stared at the road and grinned. He had to retire before Spruel, someone young coming in wouldn't have the history with Hawke and wouldn't give him the leeway that Spruel did.

When he arrived home, Hawke washed down Dot, gave him extra grain, and let him out into the pasture to roll and rest. Then he went into the house, showered, changed into his uniform, made a quick sandwich, and drove Dog over to Herb and Darlene's.

He hoped to get as far as Boardman or The Dalles before he was too tired to continue driving. The closer he was to the Portland area the more time he'd have tomorrow.

《》《》《》

Hawke dropped the jawbone off at the OSP Lab in Clackamas after filling out all the proper paperwork. From there he grabbed some breakfast and headed down I-5 to Corvallis.

The college town was fairly easy to navigate, it was the campus that gave him trouble. He found the Administration Building and approached a row of windows with college personnel behind them. They, and the students at the computers in the room, all stopped and watched him. It appeared it wasn't often an OSP Trooper in uniform came to the college.

"I'm looking for the building where I can find the head of the history program," he said to the middle-aged woman behind the window.

"That would be The Autzen House. Go back out Jefferson and you can't miss it."

"Thank you." As he walked out to his vehicle, he kicked himself for not asking the name of the head of the department.

At the hall, Hawke went in search of the head of the history program. Following signs, he found the office of the head advisor and knocked on the door.

"Come in," called out a voice that while being

robust, was high enough pitched to be a woman.

Hawke opened the door and stepped into the office lined with bookshelves overflowing with books. A short, round woman sat behind the desk. She took off her glasses, allowing them to drop onto her ample breasts though they wouldn't have gone far since the frames were attached to a string of brightly colored beads around the woman's neck.

"How may I help you, Trooper?" the woman asked.

Hawke crossed the room, and said, "Ma'am, I'm Trooper Hawke and I'm working a missing person cold case. I believe the remains I found belong to a professor who was at this college in 1987."

The woman nodded. "Yu Chang. I always wondered what happened to him. I was a student of his at the time."

Hawke sat in the chair in front of her desk. "Did you happen to know what he was researching?"

"It had to do with Chinese history in Oregon. Specifically, the mining. All of his notes and things were given to his wife." The woman spun an old-fashioned Rolodex and pulled out a card. "This is the last phone number and address I have for his wife." She peered into Hawke's eyes. "Where did you find him?"

"Hells Canyon on the Oregon side. Does that mean anything to you?"

She nodded. "He was interested in the Chinese Miners who were massacred there. He believed that the group that was mining near Salt Creek left when they heard the gunshots from Deep Creek. He'd spent most of the year reading and making notes before he went to Hells Canyon." She shrugged. "I didn't realize that was when he went missing. All we were told was he didn't come back for Fall term and later I learned he was missing."

"Thank you for this information. I'll see if I can contact his wife."

"If she isn't alive, you can try to contact his daughter, Suzy Chang-Mills. She lives in Pendleton and has been trying to bring the underground tunnels there to life."

"Thank you again. Do you have a card in case something comes up and I need to contact you?"

The woman handed him a business card.

"Thank you." When Hawke was back out in his vehicle, he dialed the number from the Rolodex card. The number had been disconnected.

Pendleton was on his way home. He'd contact Carol when he arrived in Pendleton and get an address for Suzy Chang-Mills.

《》《》《》

Hawke pulled up to an older two-story house that appeared to have been built in the early 1900s but had been either re-modeled or kept up the last century. According to Carol, this was where Suzy Chang-Mills, her husband, and two children lived. It was just after dinner so the family should be home.

He stepped up the three wooden steps to the full-length porch with fancy woodwork and knocked on the thick wood door with a stained-glass window.

"I got it!" called a young voice before the door flew open. A boy of about twelve stood holding the door and staring at him. "I didn't do anything wrong, officer."

Hawke smiled. "That's good to hear. I'd like to speak with your mom if she's at home."

"She didn't do nuthin' either," the boy said, his face going from worried to angry.

"I know she hasn't done anything. I just want to ask her some questions to help me with an investigation I'm doing." Hawke remained on the porch, not wanting to appear pushy or that he would storm the house.

"Who's there?" a woman in her early forties asked, walking across the foyer toward them. "Oh!" she said, catching sight of Hawke in his uniform.

"Suzy Chang-Mills?" Hawke asked.

"Yes. Why are you looking for me?" She stepped back, motioning for him to enter the house.

Hawke stepped in, holding his hat in his hands, and waited for her to close the door. "Is there somewhere we can talk? And if your husband is home, it might be a good idea for him to join us."

The woman stared at him a moment as if she hadn't heard what he said, then touched her son on the shoulder. "Go ask Daddy to come into the house, please."

"I can holler out the door," the boy offered.

"No, just walk out and tell him." She smiled at the boy and when he ran down the hall, she motioned for Hawke to walk into what must have been the parlor when the house was built. It had comfortable furniture arranged so everyone would have a good view of the television sitting on the mantle above an obsolete fireplace.

It wasn't five minutes and a tall man with brown hair, receding from a wide forehead, appeared in the doorway. He glanced at Suzy and then they both sat on the couch, staring at Hawke.

"Does this have something to do with Cara?" Mr.

Mills asked.

"I don't know who Cara is," Hawke said with a smile, "but no."

Suzy slumped against her husband. "She's our daughter. She left on a trip with a couple of her friends yesterday. They were just driving up to Spokane to hang out with someone's cousin. When I saw you, I thought…"

"I'm sorry to have given you such a fright. No. I found the remains of who we are pretty sure was your father." He studied her face. First, it was shock, that rolled into relief.

"Finally, I'll know what happened to him. Where did you find him?" she asked.

"Along Sluice Creek in Hells Canyon on the Oregon side," Hawke's gaze drifted to her husband. The curious expression on his face said the location meant nothing to him.

Suzy's face became red and her eyes narrowed. "Mother knew that was where something happened to him. But when she reported him missing and that was where he was last seen, no one did anything. I know. I looked up the records for that summer and they didn't even call out a search party because they had no tangible evidence that he was in that area." She stood and paced the floor. "My mother told them what he was looking for and that he would be near the area where the Chinese miners were massacred."

The husband perked up. "You mean he was near where we went for the monument ceremony?"

"You were thirty-two miles away. And I'm not sure why he was at Sluice Creek when it was nine miles upriver from Salt Creek. If anything, he should have been between Deep Creek and Salt Creek, not past them both." Hawke studied the woman who had stopped pacing and now stood staring at a photo of a young Asian couple at what looked like their wedding.

"My mother died twenty years ago from a broken heart. She didn't believe the people who told her that her husband had become tired of his life and took off to start a new one."

Hawke shook his head. "That isn't what happened." He waited for the woman to look at him. "Your father was killed."

She strode over to the couch and folded onto the cushion beside her husband. "How do you know that he didn't just fall and hurt himself and died waiting for help?"

"He may have waited for help that never came but he was shot at."

"You found the bullet?" she asked.

"Not yet, but the forensic and anthropology team are sifting through the ground where I found his remains and if there was a bullet in him, it should be found in the ground under where he lay."

"Then how do you know he was shot without proof?" Mr. Mills asked.

The young boy returned to the room and sat next to his mother.

Hawke inhaled and studied the family. "I found a canister of film that had photos of Deep Creek and Salt Creek. It also had photos of two men arguing down by the river, one man swung a rifle at the other, then the second man floating down the river, and a photo of a rifle pointed at the photographer." He paused.

Suzy sucked in air and said, "He took photos of a

killing and then was shot because of it?"

"That is what I've pieced together. I'm working on who would have wanted to kill the man in your father's photos. They were taken from such a distance and so long ago that trying to enlarge the photo and see the face of the killer, it's indistinguishable. But I'm working the cold case and I will have a name for you." Hawke held out the photos of the area that her father had taken. "From what I hear, you have continued reviving the history of the Chinese in Oregon."

She took the photos, leafed through them, and peered up into his eyes. "Mother and I never for one moment thought he left us. We always knew something had kept him from coming home." She set the photos on the coffee table. "I went on to study the history of the Chinese in Oregon and have moved around curating different establishments of historical significance."

"I was hoping you might have some of his papers from before he disappeared. Something about what he was looking for?" Hawke pulled out his notebook. "All I know is he was there doing research. While I'm sure what he was doing had nothing to do with why he was killed, I don't like unsolved things. I'm curious as to why he was at Sluice Creek. Can you put his papers together for a State Trooper to pick up in the next few days?"

Suzy shook her head. "That won't be necessary. I did my master's thesis on his research of the 1887 massacre. You'll find all of his work and mine in that." She turned to her husband. "Steve, could you make a copy of my thesis and bring it out here for Trooper Hawke?"

He nodded, squeezed her knee, and stood, walking

out of the room.

"Do you have any leads on who killed my father?" she asked.

"It's been thirty-six years, but I'm working through the possibilities. Since it has nothing to do with your father's life, because it was a case of him being at the wrong place at the wrong time, I have to dig into the man he witnessed being killed."

She nodded. "But you will let me know who it ends up being?"

"Yes."

"Good."

"Mom, why are you talking about killing and your father?" the boy asked, his face a mask of confusion.

"I'll explain it all to you when the trooper leaves," she said, smoothing his hair.

Mr. Mills returned with a folder of papers. He handed it to Hawke. "I hope this helps. Her father's disappearance has bothered Suzy her whole life."

"I understand. That's why I wanted to contact his family as soon as I was pretty sure it was him. We'll know for sure when they get a DNA sample. Have you had one done?" Hawke asked.

Suzy's face glistened pink. "Yes. I wanted to see if Father was still out there and asked to have information about anyone who matched mine sent to me. I have met some distant cousins but a close match never came up."

"That's good to know you're in the system. That means if it is your father, the match should come up." Hawke stood. "I'm sorry to have taken up so much of your time. I will let you know as soon as I know anything."

Suzy and her husband stood. "Thank you for

coming by. This has lifted a shadow that has been following me everywhere."

"You're welcome." Hawke walked out to his pickup feeling good. He'd given a woman closure on an event that had definitely scarred her. But she had followed in her father's footsteps and was doing good work for the history of Chinese in Oregon.

Chapter Thirteen

Tuesday morning, Hawke went through his usual chores and got ready for work. Dog had been happy to see him when he'd picked the animal up from the Trembleys the night before. This morning, he was on Hawke's heels as if he were afraid to be left behind. That was unusual for the dog. He didn't mind staying at home with the horses and chasing deer and ground squirrels.

Hawke opened his work vehicle door and Dog jumped in. "Hey! You know you can't go with me when I'm on regular duty." He grabbed Dog around the chest with his arm and lifted him out.

Once on the ground, Dog behaved as if he'd been beaten. The animal had never acted like this before. Hawke pulled out his phone and called his friend Justine. She raised and trained bird dogs and had found Dog for him years ago.

"Hawke, do you need a bird dog?" she asked in a joking tone.

"No, but I need some help with Dog." He went on to describe how the animal was acting.

"It sounds like something traumatic happened to him while you were away yesterday. Did you ask Herb about it?"

"No. I just picked him up last night and we didn't say anything more than 'Hi and bye.'"

"Take Dog with you and find out what happened. Then see if you can reenact it with him and show him it wasn't that scary." Justine always had good ideas. But Hawke didn't see the point in scaring him again.

"Okay. I wanted to talk to them today anyway." He ended the call and opened the vehicle door. "Come on. You can ride as far as Herb and Darlene's.

Dog jumped in and took up his regular passenger position of sitting and peering out the windshield.

Hawke shook his head, started the vehicle, and drove the dirt road between his property and Herb and Darlene's house. The road hadn't been there before Hawke and Dani purchased the property. Herb had worn the track as good as a road, going back and forth helping with the care of the horses and Dog when Hawke was busy and Dani was in the mountains.

Hawke parked in front of the house and held the door open for Dog to jump out. He didn't. He didn't even look at Hawke.

Leaving the vehicle door open, Hawke walked around to the back porch door and knocked. The smell of something baking made his stomach growl even though he'd eaten a bowl of cereal.

Darlene opened the door. "Hawke, I didn't expect to see you this morning. Did you smell the blueberry muffins clear over at your house?" She smiled and returned to the stove where she stirred something in a pot that smelled fruity.

Hawke entered the cheerful kitchen he knew well from many breakfasts and late night snacks when he'd lived over their arena. "I had some questions to ask you and Herb about the Pinson family out Imnaha and Dog is acting weird this morning. I wondered if something happened when he was here yesterday."

"Herb would know more about the Pinsons than I do. He's been on a couple of committees with Harvey and now Ford. As for yesterday, Herb said something about Dog sniffing around in the barn and the tom turkey attacking him." She lifted the pot off the stove, turned off the burner, and set the steaming pot on a pad on the counter.

"He's never been scared of turkeys before, but then he's never had one attack him either." Hawke wondered how he could get Dog over the trauma of the turkey.

Herb stomped into the house through the back door. "What's with Dog in your work vehicle? I tried to get him to come out and he wouldn't."

"I think his encounter with your turkey yesterday scared him." Hawke picked up the cup of coffee Darlene set in front of him and sipped.

"Dog isn't scared of anything," Herb said, settling on the chair across from Hawke and picking up his cup of coffee.

"I can't think of anything else that would make him stick to me like Velcro and not want to get out of the vehicle at your place." Hawke studied the couple. They both nodded their heads.

"I also need some information on the Pinson family down at Imnaha." Hawke pulled out his notebook and pen.

"Ford and Christa? Or Harvey and Marvella?" Herb asked.

"Ford and Christa. I found photos that show Christa's first husband was murdered. He didn't die by accidental drowning as stated in the coroner's report."

"No kidding… Huh." Herb sat, sipping his coffee.

Hawke could tell the man was spooling through his memories. "Any chance the two of them had been together before the first husband was killed?"

"Not that I know of. It was known they had met in college but there wasn't any gossip about them being cozy before the first husband's death," Darlene said, sliding into the chair next to Herb and pushing a plate of still-steaming muffins toward Hawke.

"Did Ford date anyone before?" Hawke asked.

"Do you think he had something to do with the first husband's death?" Herb asked.

"I don't have any suspects, just digging into everyone who might have benefitted from the man's death. Or anyone who held a grudge against him. It just feels strange that someone would follow him down along the Snake in Hells Canyon to kill him unless it was something pretty tangible."

"What about the man who was with him?" Herb asked.

"I've talked to him twice. He's still broken up about the death. Whether it's because he didn't get away with murder or because they were best friends and he was shocked to lose him. I don't know. But I am digging more into his past as well."

"You are going on the assumption that Ford killed this man to get his wife?" Darlene asked.

"It makes sense that someone who didn't live that far from the area would make his way down Hat Point and kill the man in his way of getting the woman he wanted. Then make it look like an accident and bide his time until things had all blown over and get himself reacquainted with the woman he wanted." Hawke thought it made for a plausible scenario. Only Professor Chang had witnessed the killing and therefore had to be silenced as well.

"Christa seems to be quite the horsewoman. Do you know if she was training horses while she was married to her first husband?" Hawke asked.

Darlene and Herb shared a gaze before Darlene said, "She's built her reputation off what she learned from Ford's mom."

Hawke leaned back in his seat. He needed to dig more into Christa's life before becoming a Pinson. "Thank you for the information."

"We didn't give you much," Herb said, picking up a muffin.

"I guess I'll take Dog with me today. He's not going to get out here and I don't want him hiding away in the barn all day. Tonight, I'll bring him over and see if we can get him to see the turkey attack was a one-time thing."

Herb shook his head. "It probably wasn't. This old tom is pretty ornery."

"I see. Then I guess Dog will be staying home until you eat that tom." Hawke picked up two muffins. "One for me and one for Dog."

Darlene grinned and said, "I expected as much. Have a good day."

"Thanks, you too." Hawke left the house and

walked back to his vehicle.

Dog sat in the passenger seat still staring straight ahead.

"How about one of Darlene's muffins?" Hawke said, sliding behind the steering wheel and placing a muffin on the seat beside Dog.

His mouth opened and he gobbled up the treat without losing a crumb.

Hawke chuckled and started the vehicle. He had the muffin eaten by the time he hit the highway. The radio crackled as he reached for it to call in and say he was on duty.

"Possible suicide attempt at Six Pines trailer park on Fourth Street in Eagle."

"Copy. I'm headed that way," Hawke said into the mic.

"Is this Hawke?"

"Affirmative."

His phone buzzed. Hawke read the name and slid his finger across the screen where it sat in a holder on the dash. "What's up, Calvin?" Hawke asked the county deputy.

"I'm just about to Eagle, do you have thoughts on what this is?"

"Could be a guy I talked to yesterday about my cold case. His name is Lucas Brazo." Hawke eased up on the accelerator as he took the curve through Winslow faster than he should have been driving in town. But his lights were on and cars were getting out of his way.

"I just parked at the park office. Want me to wait or scope it out?" Calvin asked.

"Scope it out and if he becomes agitated, tell him

I'm on my way. I think it has to do with his friend being murdered thirty-six years ago."

"Okay, I'll see what I can find out." The call ended.

Hawke exited the city limits and pressed down on the accelerator. He glanced over at Dog who had curled up in a ball on the seat. He hoped this wasn't going to be another traumatic day for him.

Easing off the accelerator as he came to the curves along the Wallowa River, Hawke mentally pictured Eagle and the fastest route to the trailer court. As soon as he hit Eagle city limits, he slowed down but kept the lights flashing as he continued on Main Street and turned onto Fourth Street.

Slowing down at the mobile park, he spotted Calvin standing at the office with the manager who had spoken to Hawke the day he was here. Scanning the area he didn't see Lucas. Had the man already killed himself?

Parking next to the county vehicle, Hawke opened the door and sprang out. He strode over to the deputy. "What's going on?"

"According to Bales, here, Lucas doesn't own a gun." Calvin nodded toward the manager.

"But since he is a fisherman, I'm sure he owns a knife or something else he can harm himself with." Hawke spun and strode through the gates and down the road toward the mobile home in the back.

Calvin caught up to him. "Dispatch said he threatened to shoot himself."

"That doesn't mean he won't use some other method. Is he on the phone with someone?" Hawke asked.

"Yeah, it was a person from the suicide line that

called it in."

They stopped at the door of the mobile home. "Get a subpoena to procure the transcript of the conversation. I'm going in and talk to him."

Hawke knocked on the door. The dogs started yapping and the mobile home shook. "Lucas, I know you're in there. This is Trooper Hawke. I brought you home the other night. Remember?"

"Go away. I don't want to talk to anyone but the lady on the phone." His words were slurred. Had he been on a drunk since Hawke brought him home from High Mountain Pub?

"The lady you're talking to called us. She's worried. Can I come in so I can tell her you aren't going to hurt yourself?" Hawke had talked to several people over the years who felt their best way out was to kill themselves. Only one did eventually do it.

"I don't want you in here. I don't want to see or talk to anyone." The words came out in a sob.

Hawke grabbed the door knob and wasn't surprised when it turned. Most people who threaten suicide just want help, not to truly end their lives. He opened the door and stepped in. Three Chihuahua mix dogs attacked his ankles. His duty boots kept them from doing more than slobbering all over his boots and hooking their teeth in the hem of his pants.

Lucas spun toward him and wobbled. Hawke reached out, holding the man's weight the best he could to lower him onto the sofa that had been raised with railroad ties. The man didn't fall as far as he would if the couch had been at the regular height off the floor.

"Go away, I don't want to be here. I don't want you here." Lucas swung at Hawke, causing the cell phone in

Lucas's hand to fly out the open door. The dogs took off yapping after it.

"Hey. I'm here to listen and to help." Hawke grabbed a sturdy chair that sat at the kitchen table and placed it in front of Lucas. "Nothing is going so wrong that the only way to fix it is to end your life."

"What do you know?" Lucas slurred and swung an arm like a dramatic silent movie actress.

"I know life doesn't always go as we plan. But you seem like the type who can reinvent yourself. From what I read you were pretty good at your job with the City of Salem. What made you move here?" Out of the corner of his eye, Hawke saw Calvin peek in.

"I came back to ask around about Evan. It didn't make sense that he would lose his footing and fall in the river. Because that would be the only way he'd end up in the water. We didn't have a boat. We paid someone to bring us to where we camped and to pick us up the day we were leaving." Lucas ran his thick fingers through his long straggly hair. His pudgy face was wrinkled in frustration. "None of it made sense. Nothing makes sense."

"None of what? The trip? His arguing with Christa?" Hawke eased his notebook out of his pocket, keeping eye contact with Lucas.

"How he went missing and then learning he'd drowned. He was scared of the water. That's what didn't make sense about his drowning. He wouldn't have taken any chance to fall in. He commented about how the river terrified him when we were going through one of the rapids."

Hawke studied the man. "Then why did he suggest fishing on the Snake River? He had to have heard about the rapids and unexpected rise and fall of the water."

"That's what didn't make sense. I kept telling him we could fish anywhere, but he insisted we fish Hells Canyon."

Hawke wondered if the trip had been a ruse to meet someone. But who? "When did he start talking about the fishing trip on the Snake?"

Lucas rubbed his face with a puffy hand and shook his head. "I don't know. Maybe a month before we went."

"Do you want to find out what really happened to Evan and get your life back on track?" Hawke asked.

The man stared at him with bloodshot eyes and saggy jowls. "What are you talking about?"

"I think this downward spiral you're in started when you couldn't make sense of Evan's death." Hawke waited as the words sunk into the man's alcohol-saturated brain.

Lucas nodded slowly. "Yeah, I didn't understand and no one could give me answers. I moved here to try to find out more, but I was an outsider and no one would answer my questions."

"Then you became frustrated and started drinking." Hawke nodded to the table full of empty booze bottles.

The man ran a hand through his greasy hair again. "Yeah. If I get drunk enough, I forget Evan and the worry when he didn't come back to the tent. Then the days of trying to locate him before I had to go back to work."

"I'd like you to sober up and help me figure out what happened to him. I could use someone who knew Evan back then to walk me through his life and who could have wanted him dead." Hawke closed his notebook. "Can you help me do that?"

Lucas nodded.

"Do you have someone who can come help you clean all these bottles out and give your house a good cleaning?" Hawke stood, replacing the chair by the kitchen table.

"There's a woman in the park who cleans houses to make extra money." Lucas tried to push to his feet but his legs wobbled.

"Why don't you sleep it off for now and I'll talk to her. What's her name?"

"Wendy Fielding. Her trailer is the second one on the left when you come into the park." Lucas leaned back on the couch and closed his eyes.

"I'll talk to her and have her come check on you in a few hours." Hawke could tell Lucas had already dropped off to sleep. Having taken some of the man's anxiety away had helped him to rest.

Hawke stepped out of the trailer and found Calvin holding the three chihuahuas. "Put them in the trailer and we're done here."

Calvin placed the dogs inside the trailer and closed the door. "Why was he wanting to off himself?"

"He's torn up over discovering his friend was murdered. It seems he moved here to prove his death couldn't have been an accident. I asked him to sober up and help me with information about Nestor's life. I figure his best friend can tell me more than his wife. A best friend from grade school would know a lot about the victim."

"I sure wouldn't want anyone talking to my best friend I've had since second grade." Calvin grinned. "I'd never have made it in law enforcement if anyone had talked to him."

Hawke chuckled. "I think most of us have something in our childhood that was on the wrong side of the law. At least we figured out which side we wanted to be on." They had walked toward the entrance to the park. Hawke stopped at the second trailer on the right. "I'm going to ask the woman who lives here to check on Lucas and clean his house. He said she cleans houses to make extra money."

"I'll let you write up the report on this since you did all the talking." Calvin waved and headed to his county vehicle.

Hawke walked up to the ten-by-ten deck on a 70s model single-wide mobile home. The area up to the deck was dirt and gravel. Several pots of flowers bloomed adding color alongside a self-standing porch swing. He walked up to the door, heard the sound of a television show, and knocked.

A dog barked and the television went quiet. The knob jiggled and the door opened. A woman Hawke guessed to be in her 60s, stood in the doorway peering up at him. She had to be five feet if not a few inches shorter. Her limbs looked as if they held little flesh or muscle. Her short curly brown hair had streaks of gray. Her brown eyes peered up at him as she tipped her head back slightly.

"What can I do for you?" she asked, straightening her wire-rimmed glasses on her long, slender nose.

"Are you Wendy Fielding?" Hawke asked.

"I am. Why do you want to know?" She crossed her arms, holding his gaze.

"I just came from Lucas Brazo's place."

She snorted. "That man was useful when he first

moved here. Not anymore. What did he do? Drunk and disorderly?"

"He called the suicide helpline. I responded." Hawke motioned for her to come out and sit on the porch swing.

She made kissing sounds and a small white fluffy dog stepped out of the house. They both sat on the swing.

Hawke glanced around and found a bucket. He set it upside down in front of her and sat, so she didn't have to look up at him.

"I'm sorry he felt the need to reach out like that," the woman said, sounding as if she meant it.

"He's drunk."

"Well, he's been in that state ever since he found out his friend was killed and hadn't died by accident."

Hawke studied her. "What do you know about that?"

She shrugged, her thin shoulders poking up through her t-shirt. "Just what he's told me over the years. He didn't believe it was an accident, but since he found out he was right, he seems to have lost it."

Hawke nodded. "I told him to sober up and help me with the investigation. He's known the victim since childhood. I'm hoping he can help me piece together his friend's life up until his death." He glanced toward Lucas's place. "He said you clean houses for extra money."

"I do. My social security just barely pays for this place and groceries. I like to have extra for emergencies and sending gifts to my nieces and nephews."

"I'd like you to go check on Lucas in a few hours. I left him sleeping it off. But he needs all those empty bottles and the full ones thrown out. Then if you could go in tomorrow and clean his house. I'll be back tomorrow to see if he's sobered up enough to help me piece things together." Hawke stood and held out forty dollars. "You can let me know tomorrow if I owe you more."

He walked to the steps leading off the deck and she said, "Why are you doing this?"

Hawke faced her. "I need his help in solving this cold case, and I believe everyone has a reason they are on this earth. Lucas's is to help me find his friend's killer."

Chapter Fourteen

Hawke and Dog spent the rest of the day checking fishing licenses and listening to radio chatter about a kid who tried to evade the county and state police. The chase had happened in the north area. Hawke had been patrolling Highway 82 along the Wallowa River before it entered the Minam River.

It was drawing close to time for him to call it a day when Spruel called him. "Hawke, there's a woman at the office looking for you. Her name is Suzy Mills."

"I can be there in twenty minutes," Hawke said. "Tell her to meet me at the Blue Elk."

"Okay, I'll pass that along. Does this have anything to do with your double cold case?"

"It does." Hawke ended the call, closed the door he'd had open as he'd sat watching the last group of anglers he'd checked, and patted Dog on the head. "We'll have a good dinner tonight."

He started his vehicle and wondered what had brought Suzy Chang-Mills to Wallowa County.

《》《》《》

Walking into the Blue Elk tavern in Winslow, Hawke easily found Suzy. She sat at a tall table directly underneath the establishment's mascot. An elk head that had been dyed blue and the horns painted neon blue. She sipped what looked like a soda. A folder sat on the table beside her drink.

"Hawke, you want your usual?" Ben Preston, owner of the establishment, called to him from the bar.

"Yes, thank you," Hawke replied and sat in the chair across from the woman.

She raised an eyebrow. "You come here often?"

"I've been in the county nearly twenty years and been single most of that, I believe every place that serves food has had me at their place on almost a monthly basis." He hung his cap on the back of the chair.

Ben arrived with his iced tea. "You ordering?"

"I'd like to have two cheeseburgers, one without pickles, and two fries to go for when I leave," Hawke said, picking up his tea and drinking.

"You must have Dog with you to order one with pickles." Ben slapped him on the back and left.

"Your dog likes pickles or is that a nickname for someone?" Suzy asked.

"My dog, named Dog, likes pickles. He is a rare one." Hawke smiled and asked, "What brings you to Wallowa County?"

"I went through my father's things and found this information on what he called the Snake River Project." She pushed the folder across to him.

There didn't seem to be very much inside. Hawke opened the cover and found a neatly typed page with

132

dates and reference numbers. He put it to the side and found what looked like a photocopy of letters written in Chinese. Setting that to the side, he found photos of Deep Creek.

"Is this what you used to write your thesis?" he asked.

"Have you read my work?" she leaned forward.

"No. I arrived home too late last night and had to get to work this morning. I was going to read it tonight." He pointed to the photocopied letters. "Can you read these?"

"Yes. They are letters that were sent from some of the miners to their families back home."

Hawke studied her. "I thought they didn't know the names of the miners."

"My father was able to find documents from the Sam Yup Company and through a process of elimination find four of the massacred men's families. When he reached out to them, they sent the letters their ancestors had received from the men mining in the Snake River."

"Your father must have been working on this project for a long time."

"Close to ten years before his death. It started with an exchange student from China who mentioned to my father he had an ancestor who had died in Oregon while mining. After my father talked to him, he realized it was someone mining along the Snake River in Hells Canyon." Her face scrunched up and a frown wrinkled her brow. "My father was working on something that no one talked about until after his death when a person working in the Wallowa County courthouse in nineteen-ninety-five found the hidden documents from the trial of the local men who massacred the Chinese miners." She shook her head. "If my father could have had access to that information, he wouldn't have needed to go looking for proof of their existence in Hells Canyon and he would still be alive today."

Hawke understood the woman's anger and resentment. He'd come across atrocities done to his people, the Nimiipuu, Cayuse, and Umatilla tribes, and felt the anger, resentment, and frustration. But it was people like her father who dug for the truth who brought the horrendous acts to light and to hopefully bring about change in humanity.

The man's commitment to finding the truth made Hawke admire and respect him.

Something nagged at the back of his mind. "Did the letters mention Salt or Sluice Creek? Because from what I know, the miners were at Deep Creek, where the memorial was placed."

"Yes, one of the letters mentions a small group was at Salt Creek mining. Why he went to Sluice Creek, I don't know." She studied Hawke. "If he had stayed at Salt Creek, he would not have come across the murderer that killed him."

Hawke shrugged. "We will never know why he went there. But he was brave to take photos of a crime being committed. I'll make sure he is mentioned as one of the reasons we bring the killer to justice."

"If the person is still alive," Suzy said. "It was thirty-six years ago. If the man was in his forties then, he could be eighty now. He would most likely not even last a year in prison. And yet two men lost all those years because of him." She picked up her drink and downed the rest of it. "I'll head back to Pendleton. I just wanted to speak with you again. Last night I was in shock. All these years my mother and I thought he had come to harm, but no one would listen. I want to know who killed my father and the other man. And why. I would like answers even if there is no one to pay for the crimes." She slid off the tall chair and walked to the door.

Hawke stared after her. He watched her get into a sporty-looking car, back out, and head toward Eagle.

"Here you go," Ben said, walking up to the table with a bag.

"What do I owe you?" Hawke asked, pulling out his wallet.

"Twenty-two." Ben touched the photo. "That looks like Deep Creek."

"It is." Hawke handed him twenty-five. "Do you know the area well?"

"I spent some time down there during summers with my cousins. We'd ride horses down to the river and explore. I couldn't believe it when the whole Chinese massacre was uncovered. That's a sad piece of this county's history."

"It is never a good thing to suppress the bad things that happen. It can only lead to more bad things happening." Hawke put the photos and papers in the folder, slid off his chair, and picked up the bag. "Thanks."

Out in his vehicle, he handed Dog his burger and unwrapped his own. On the way home they ate in silence. Hawke was more determined than ever to catch the killer or if the person was dead, bring his actions to light.

《》《》《》

Wednesday morning, Hawke left Dog at home, watching over the horses, and planned to head to Eagle to check on Lucas. The man could hold the answers that Hawke was seeking. If he could stay sober long enough to remember anything.

He stopped at the Rusty Nail Café in Winslow for breakfast. He'd made stopping here at least once a week a priority ever since he met the owner, Merrilee Grady. She was a feisty woman who'd run the restaurant with a small crew ever since her husband left her with two small children. She'd lost both children in the last twenty years and used the restaurant as an excuse to get up every morning.

"Hawke, did you find out what scared Dog?" Justine asked, as she poured a cup of coffee at his usual spot at the counter.

"Yeah." He scanned the establishment. Half a dozen locals and several tourists took up three of the tables. Raising the cup of coffee to his lips, he spotted Wendy Fielding sitting at a table by herself.

"Well, what happened to make him scared?" Justine asked.

Hawke turned his attention to the waitress. "I guess a tom turkey attacked him. Herb said Dog was snooping around in the barn and the turkey surprised him. He wouldn't even get out of the pickup at Herb's yesterday morning." Hawke twisted his neck to see if Wendy was still at the table. "When did she arrive," he asked, nodding in the woman's direction.

"Wendy? Why on earth are you interested in her?" Justine asked, leaning on the counter next to him and whispering.

"I paid her yesterday to clean up someone's house

and just wondered if I shouldn't have trusted her."
Hawke was having his doubts the woman had followed
through with what he'd asked.

"She'll head over to old man McGruder's place
when she finishes breakfast to clean his house. Go ask
her."

"Bring my usual breakfast over there, please."
Hawke stood and caught a glimpse of Merrilee through
the window between the room and the kitchen.

"Morning, Hawke. Working on your usual."

"Thanks, Merrilee," he said and waved. Walking
up to the table where Wendy sat alone, he watched the
woman's head come up from where she'd been reading
a book. Her eyes didn't look wary but she looked
uncomfortable with him walking in her direction.

He put a hand on a chair. "Mind if I sit with you?"

The woman glanced around the café and then
shrugged. "I guess you don't like eating alone."

"I don't mind it. I've done it for a lot of years. I
just want to ask about Lucas. Did you go back over and
check on him yesterday?" Hawke set his cup of coffee
on the table in front of him.

"I gave him about three hours and went over. He
was waking up but still half drunk and groggy. He
asked me if he'd really tried to kill himself and if there
had been cops there." She sipped her coffee and added,
"You might want to go by today and refresh his
memory."

"That's where I'm headed after here. Were you able
to get rid of the booze?"

She nodded. "I had to wait until he dropped off
again, but I took all the full and partial bottles out. I'll
clean up the rest and the house when I finish at Alfred

McGruder's."

Hawke nodded.

She pushed her empty plate to the center of the table. "Sorry to leave after you made a point to sit with me, but I need to get over to Alfred's." She stood. "And after seeing the mess at Lucas's, I can tell you, you'll owe me about as much as you already paid me by the time I'm finished." She studied him.

"As long as his house is cleaned up that's fine." He nodded as she walked away from the table.

A few minutes later, Justine set his breakfast and utensils on the table in front of him. "Did you find out what you wanted to know?"

Hawke grinned at his inquisitive friend. She'd helped him on a couple of the murder cases, unfortunately, one of them had been putting her father and sister in jail for murder. "Yes, I did."

"Seen Dani lately?" Justine asked, picking up the dishes Wendy had left behind.

"She was out picking up more guests over the weekend. Why?" Hawke was glad that Dani and Justine were friends, but they also liked to gang up on him.

"Will she be out the weekend of the powwow?" Justine held all the dishes in one hand.

"We're planning on going. Why are you interested?"

"She told me about your sister being a dancer. Thought I'd check it out and meet your family." The sadness in her voice told him she missed having family, even if they hadn't been nice to her.

"We'd love to have you join us. I'll have Dani give you a call when she gets home and let you know when we'll swing by and pick you up."

"No, you don't have to pick me up. I can drive myself. I just want to be there at the same time." Her cheeks grew pinker.

"Okay. Then I'll have Dani let you know when we'll be there." He smiled and said, "I'm nervous. It's been a long time since I participated in a powwow."

She put a hand on his arm. "You'll be fine."

"Justine! Order!" Merrilee's gravelly voice called.

"Enjoy your breakfast," Justine said, hurrying to the window to pick up the order.

Hawke finished his meal, thinking about the powwow and wondering if any of his relatives from Lapwai would be there.

Chapter Fifteen

Knocking on Lucas Brazo's door, Hawke peered around the mobile court. Most of the homes were from the 70s and 80s. The owner Bales stood at the gates watching him. The dogs barked on the other side of the door. Their high-pitched yips were enough to wake the dead. The thought sent a shiver up his spine.

Hawke pounded harder. "Lucas, it's Hawke, answer the door."

The dogs started howling. Hawke tried the knob and it turned. He stepped in and put his hand over his mouth. The stench of feces—human and dog—met him. He stared at the body of Lucas Brazo as his dogs ran past Hawke's feet and out the door.

The man's eyes were open, staring up at the ceiling, his hands clutched the neck of his shirt.

Hawke stepped out onto the small porch and radioed dispatch. "Hawke here. I have a twelve-forty-nine." He went on to give the address and requested Dr. Vance, the county medical examiner. Once the

140

information was given, Hawke walked back into the trailer and studied everything.

All the full and partial booze bottles had been removed as Wendy had said. But there was a bottle on its side beside the couch. An amber liquid of about a quarter inch covered the downward side.

Hawke pulled out his phone and took photos of the body and the bottle. Then he tugged a latex glove out of his pocket, shimmied his hand into it, and picked up the bottle. He placed the bottle on the kitchen table so it wouldn't get knocked over when more people arrived.

He walked down the narrow hall, tiptoeing around the piles of dog poop, and peered into the bathroom and the bedroom in the back. It appeared the dogs had slept in the bed while their owner slept and eventually died on the couch. Hawke made a mental note to ask Wendy what time she'd been here to check on Lucas.

The sound of a vehicle stopping took him back out to the living room. One of the dogs had returned and curled up on the victim's stomach.

Calvin walked into the house. "Yeesh!" he said, covering his nose and stopping just inside the door. "Did he finally do himself in?"

"I don't think so." Hawke nodded to the table with the bottle. "I'd asked the neighbor to remove all bottles of alcohol from here and I found this lying on the floor next to the couch."

"You think someone poisoned him?" Calvin asked, his curiosity overriding his aversion to the smell.

"If so, we know that Evan Nestor and Professor Chang's killer is still alive." Hawke's phone buzzed. He answered. "Hawke."

"I heard there was a death at Six Pines where there

was a suicide attempt yesterday," Sergeant Spruel said.

Hawke explained how he'd come back to check on the man who was of interest in his cold cases and found him dead.

"By his own making?" Spruel asked.

"I don't think so." He went on to tell him about the neighbor and the bottle found by the couch.

"Stay there and get all the information you can. I'll send Lange and have Ivy cover for you." Spruel ended the call.

Hawke felt a bit of relief that he could now put more time into the cold cases since this one might just be connected. But he wouldn't know that until the liquid in the bottle was examined at a lab. However, to get an autopsy done on the victim, he had to find enough evidence that this was foul play to convince D.A. Lange.

He could, now that he was the lead on the homicide, bag the bottle. Hawke caught Calvin's gaze. "See if you can find a lid for the bottle on the table. I'm going out to grab evidence bags out of my rig. We need to find enough evidence to convince Lange this is a homicide."

Calvin nodded and started looking around.

Hawke walked out of the trailer and spotted Dr. Vance and another county vehicle driving into the mobile court.

He walked over to Dr. Vance's car and opened the door for her. She stepped out in running shoes, dark blue slacks, and a sleeveless flowered shirt, showing off long brown arms with brightly colored bangles at her wrists.

"What do we have?" she asked, leaning back in the

car and pulling out a light blue doctor's coat. She slid her arms in and buttoned it before picking up a bag and a pair of paper booties to put over her shoes before she entered the house.

"Male, in his sixties. Overweight, possibly drank himself to death." Hawke didn't move when she started to walk.

Dr. Vance glanced back at him. "Is this a suspicious death?"

He shrugged.

"That means you think it is and are waiting to see what I find." She flashed him a bright smile. "I like it when you give me challenges."

Hawke chuckled and followed the doctor back into the mobile home with his evidence bags.

"I found the lid," Calvin said when Hawke stepped through the door. He glanced at where the deputy pointed and saw the bottle had been capped.

"Good." Hawke walked over to the table, wrote on the evidence bag, and placed the bottle inside. He left the bag on the table.

The new deputy stood at the door of the mobile. "What do you want me to do, Hawke?"

"Talk to all the people who live in this court and the manager. See if you can learn if anyone came to see the victim last night or this morning and get a time." Hawke waited for the deputy to walk away and then he asked Calvin to help Dr. Vance.

"What are you going to do?" Calvin asked.

"I'm going to look through his bedroom to see if I can find anything that connects him to my cold cases."

"You already know he was a friend of one of the victims and with him at the time of his death." Calvin waved a hand toward the body Dr. Vance was examining. "He could have killed himself because his murders came to light."

Hawke shook his head. "He didn't kill anyone. He lost his best friend that day. He started drinking feeling he'd let his friend down. Lucas told me he moved here to try and figure out what had happened but no one would talk to him."

"You're hoping he came up with some information you can use," Dr. Vance said, turning from her examination.

"Something like that. What do you think?" Hawke stepped closer to the doctor and the body.

"If his skin was blue or gray, I would think he died of alcohol poisoning. He reeks of alcohol." She walked over to the table with the bottle in the evidence bag. "Could I get a whiff of this?"

Hawke opened the evidence bag and took the lid off the bottle. He held it out and Dr. Vance sniffed.

"That smell is around his neck and face. I believe the drink was poured into his mouth. I think it would be safe to rule out suicide. But I'm not sure what kind of poison. The body isn't showing any of the usual signs." She walked back over to the body and pointed to the hands clutching his shirt collar. "He was trying to get more air. While this could be caused by heart failure or lung failure, which could happen to someone in his shape and age, I can't swear it wasn't a natural death until there are tests run."

"Do you have an idea of the time of death?" Hawke asked.

"From his body temperature, it could have been anywhere from ten to twelve hours ago. But this mobile home is hot and stuffy. The body wouldn't have cooled at the same rate as it would if the home were cooler. So it's just an estimate."

There was a commotion outside the mobile home moments before District Attorney Lange stepped through the open door. The small living room wasn't large enough to hold many more people. "Spruel told me to get over here, you have a homicide that might connect with two cold cases." Lange was a small man who got to the point. At first, Hawke didn't like the man but after discovering that the D.A. had been framed by a revenge-seeking lunatic, Hawke and Lange were on better terms.

Hawke stepped forward. "Mr. Lange, this man was best friends with the first cold case victim." Hawke went on to explain how he believed this man had information that would have helped Hawke with the cold cases.

"That's all interesting, but is this suicide or homicide?" Lange faced Dr. Vance. "Gwendolyn, have you had a chance to inspect the body?"

"I have." She went on to explain to Lange what she had told Hawke.

Lange walked over to the evidence bag on the table. "You believe there is something in this bottle that killed him?"

"That is what we both think," Hawke said, motioning to Dr. Vance.

"You think it is worth the taxpayer's money to have an autopsy done on this man?" Lange ran a hand over the hair combed back from his forehead.

"I am sure that this is homicide and the person who killed him committed the crimes thirty-six years ago."

Hawke was positive his finding Professor Chang's body and asking questions had made the killer nervous.

Lange studied him and then faced Dr. Vance. "Do you agree?"

She nodded.

"Then contact Seth at the funeral home and have him pick up the body and transport it to Clackamas. And get that bottle off to forensics in Pendleton." Lange took a long look at the inside of the mobile home, then the body, and walked to the door. He turned back to face them. "If this goes to trial, I want every piece of evidence you can find to connect this killing to the other two." He spun back to the door and left.

Hawke held back the grin. He'd thought it was going to be harder to convince Lange that this wasn't a suicide. He smiled at Dr. Vance. "Thank you for the initial examination."

"You're welcome. I'll be interested in learning what was his cause of death." She left the mobile home and Hawke handed Calvin a small digital camera. "Start taking photos of the body and the whole room, please. I'll be in the bedroom digging around, shout if you find something interesting."

"Sure thing." Calvin took the camera and started clicking.

Hawke walked down the hall and into the bedroom. On his first look in the room, he'd noticed three boxes stacked in the far corner. He made his way over to the boxes and opened the top one. It had a photo album on top. It was filled with photos of Lucas and Evan as kids and up through high school and some taken as adults. From the grayed lower right-hand corners, the book was looked at a lot. Hawke figured every time Lucas was drunk or started thinking about Evan, he would look through this album.

He set the book to the side and began methodically going through each photo and scrap of paper in the box. It did appear as if Lucas had been trying to discover what had happened to his friend. He had a couple of notebooks with names of people in the county he'd talked with. None of them gave him more than they didn't know the man he was talking about and didn't know of anyone who might.

He would have had a hard time finding someone who knew Evan since he hadn't lived in the county and his wife hadn't moved to the county until she married Ford Pinson. Evan had no relatives here. Hawke found photos of the wedding between Evan and Christa. They appeared to be happy, staring into one another's eyes for most of the photos. Ignoring the happy couple, Hawke studied the people in the background.

He put one in an evidence bag. One of the men standing in the background looked a bit like Ford Pinson. As he continued to study the photos, he stopped and studied another photo. It looked like Ford and a woman much younger and fuller than Wendy Fielding. It was a pretty strong resemblance. He'd have to ask her about the photo. He placed it in with the other photo.

Hawke recognized photos taken on the Snake River. Lucas must have taken them during their trip. He put all of them into an evidence bag to go through later. Lifting the top box off and placing it on the floor, he started going through the next one. This one appeared to be a box of things that had belonged to Evan. His diplomas, sports awards, prom photos, and a wedding album.

Sitting back on the bed, Hawke stared into the box. He would have thought this would be stuff that Christa would have kept or given to Evan's family if she hadn't wanted it. How had Lucas ended up with it? And why?

"I finished up with the photos." Calvin's voice made Hawke flinch. "Sorry didn't mean to sneak up on you." The deputy said in a joking tone.

"I was deep in thought." Hawke stood and stretched his back. "Did you find anything interesting?"

"Nothing out of the ordinary for the way he lived and ended his life." Calvin shrugged.

"Take a few photos in here. Especially these boxes." Hawke sidestepped out of the corner to make room for Calvin to get close enough to take photos of the articles in the box.

"Man, I didn't save this much of my memorabilia." Calvin raised the camera to his eye and clicked.

"It's all stuff from the first victim, Evan Nestor." Hawke decided he needed to visit with Christa tomorrow.

"Really? What kind of weird fascination did this guy have with him?" Calvin studied Hawke.

"They grew up together. From what I got out of both Christa Pinson and Lucas, they were like brothers."

"Still. I wouldn't keep all this stuff if my brother died. I'd give it to his kids or our parents."

"That's what I thought. It seemed odd he had it. I'll talk to Christa about it." Hawke motioned for Calvin to move. "I'm going to put it out in my vehicle."

"You want me to carry a box?"

"Yeah."

Hawke stepped into the living room as Seth Kahn

from the funeral home came through the front door with one end of a gurney. "Is there enough room in here to use this thing?"

"There will have to be. He's too large for you to try and get him out of here without wheels," Hawke responded. "You made it here fast. Did Lange call you?"

Seth continued in with another tech at the back end of the gurney. "Dr. Vance called and said to do a pick up here and take it directly to Clackamas. I guess she didn't have time to do the autopsy."

"D.A. Lange wanted it sent directly to Clackamas." Hawke knew it might take a little longer to get information on the body than if Dr. Vance had done the autopsy, but the results would be undisputable if the body went straight from here to Clackamas.

A second man on the back end of the gurney walked in. His name tag said 'Ted.' "Whoa, he's a big ole boy."

Hawke set his box down on the kitchen table next to the bottle and helped move the body onto the gurney. Once the body and gurney were out of the mobile home, Hawke picked up the box and carried it out to his vehicle. He placed it on the back seat when Bales hurried up to him.

"How long will it be before I can rent that home out?"

Hawke studied the man. "I'm thinking at least a week. Maybe longer."

"A week! I need to keep a steady income coming in." Bales grabbed his ball cap, picked it up, and slammed it back down on his head.

"This is a crime scene. We'll be putting up tape and

expect you to help keep people out of there until we take the tape down." Hawke moved so Calvin could place the other box in the back seat.

"While you're here." Hawke pulled out his notebook. "Did you see anyone visit Lucas last night or this morning?"

Chapter Sixteen

Wendy Fielding walked up as Hawke was helping Calvin string crime scene tape around the porch of Lucas's mobile home. "What's going on? What happened to Lucas?" she asked.

Hawke met her before she could get any closer. The heat of the day made the house smell even worse. They'd left the windows open and the smell was seeping out. "I came to check on him this morning and found him dead." Hawke studied the woman. Her eyebrows rose and her mouth shaped an 'O.'

"No! He was just sleeping last night. What happened?" She glanced at the home. "Where are the dogs?"

Hawke nodded to a neighbor on the other side of the street. "Mrs. Dover took them. She's going to find them homes."

Wendy nodded. "She does that kind of thing, usually with cats."

"Are you certain you took every bottle of booze out

of his house last night?" Hawke asked.

"Yes. I even checked the cupboards. Why?" It was her turn to study him. "Did he die of alcohol poisoning?"

"The medical examiner didn't think so but there was a bottle found on the floor beside him."

Wendy folded her arms. "I took all the booze bottles out of his house. Every one of them, even the empties."

"Do you think he went out somewhere last night and bought a bottle?" Hawke could tell she was thinking as she took her time to reply.

"No. He wasn't in any condition to drive or walk."

"Would he call someone to get him some?" Hawke had been briefed by the deputy he'd sent to talk to all the residents of the mobile home park. The deputy said nearly everyone said they barely knew the man, and no, they didn't hear anyone come or go during the night.

"As far as I know the only friends he had were me and Otis Powell. They'd meet up for coffee once a week at Al's Café. And Otis goes to bed at nine. I know because Lucas complained about it."

Hawke jotted down in his notebook, *talk to Otis Powell*. "Were you at Evan and Christa Nestor's wedding?"

Wendy's body jerked and she peered at Hawke. "I don't know who you're talking about."

Hawke pulled the evidence envelope out of his back pocket and pulled out the photo of Ford and the young woman who looked like Wendy. He held it out to her. "This photo taken at their wedding has Ford Pinson and a young woman who looks a lot like you in the background."

She gripped a corner of the photo with her thumb and finger and stared at it.

Calvin walked by. "That's done. I'm going to upload the photos, write my report, and call it a day."

"Thanks for your help," Hawke replied not taking his gaze off the woman staring at the photo. She was taking so long, he figured she was coming up with a lie. He tapped the top of the photo. "Any idea if that's you or not?"

She nodded her head. "That's me. It's amazing how one photo can bring back a torrent of memories." Wendy handed the photo back to him. "I didn't know the names of the bride and groom. Ford told me he had a wedding to go to and he didn't want to go alone. I offered to go and we had a wonderful weekend in the Salem area. I barely remember the wedding. Other than I sat a lot by myself. Because he'd left me sitting alone, he'd been more than attentive the rest of the weekend."

He could tell she was remembering something good by the distant look in her eyes. "Were the two of you a couple?"

She shook her head. "No. Not for my lack of trying. He wasn't interested in me for a wife. When he married Christa, it never dawned on me that she was the woman whose wedding we'd attended. It wasn't until Lucas moved here and pulled out photos asking questions about Evan, that I put two and two together. Christa had married Evan instead of Ford. That must have ate at him. He was used to getting everything he wanted."

Hawke was reminded that he had yet to meet Ford in person. He hoped the man would be at the ranch when he went there the next day. "Do you think Ford had something to do with Evan's death?"

"I don't see how, but I can't really say."

"Did you ever bring that up to Lucas?" Hawke wondered if Lucas had caught on to it.

"Nope. I didn't say a thing. He didn't realize I was the girl who had been at the wedding with Ford so I just pretended to not know anything about anything."

"Did you hear anyone come in or out of Six Pines after you were in Lucas's house?" Hawke had a feeling that whoever came to the house had parked out on a street and walked in. But what about the dogs? Every time he'd been here, they had barked like crazy. "Did you hear his dogs barking last night?"

Wendy thought a moment. "No. But they were making a fuss when I left for work. I figured they wanted out and were having trouble waking Lucas up since he'd drank so much yesterday."

"You didn't go let them out and check on him?" Hawke asked.

"No. I was running late and wanted to have breakfast at the Rusty Nail before I cleaned Alfred's house."

Hawke couldn't think of anything else to ask. "Thank you. If you hear or think of anything, give me a call." He handed her one of his business cards.

"Okay. I hope you find out who killed him if it wasn't a natural death." Wendy pivoted and walked slowly toward her home.

Hawke made sure the door was locked and slid into his vehicle. It was late afternoon. He didn't feel like driving out to Imnaha tonight so he headed toward Al's Café in Eagle on the off-chance Otis would be there. And he could get a late lunch, early dinner.

Stepping through the jangling door of Al's Café, Hawke was greeted by Lacie Ramsey. She and her husband had owned the restaurant for the last five years.

"Hawke, it's been a while since you had one of our burgers," Lacie said, walking toward him with a glass of iced tea.

Taking off his hat, Hawke wiped at the sweat tickling his brow. "Thanks, this is what I needed." He took the glass and guzzled down half of it before scanning the restaurant. He didn't see Otis. "What day and time does Otis Powell come in here?"

"Today is Wednesday. He should be here tomorrow morning about nine. That's when he and Lucas get together for coffee." She indicated the table he stood beside. "Are you planning to sit down and eat?"

"Yeah." He pulled out a chair and sat. "I'll have a burger and a salad, please."

"Coming right up." She spun around and headed to the window between the dining area and the kitchen. She pinned up his order and returned with the pitcher of iced tea, refilling his glass.

Hawke did a slower scan of the other people in the establishment. Only a handful were locals. It was the height of tourist season for the county.

The door jangled and heads turned. Hawke craned his neck and spotted OSP Trooper Steve Shoberg walking toward him.

"Need something cool to drink?" Hawke asked, pushing a seat out for the other trooper to sit.

"I'll get something to go. Spruel said you had something that needed to go to Pendleton. I'm headed out to LaGrande with some paperwork and said I'd pop on over to Pendleton for you." Shoberg had his hands on his duty belt, scanning the people as he talked.

"It's in my vehicle." Hawke stood, shoved his cap on his head, and called to Lacie. "I'll be right back."

She waved a hand and he walked out to his vehicle with Shoberg.

"Spruel said you might have a homicide that goes with your cold cases," Shoberg said as Hawke unlocked his vehicle.

"I'm positive it does, but making it all fit together may take some time." Hawke handed the other trooper a small box he'd filled with evidence. Once Shoberg had a hold of the box, Hawke touched the bag with the bottle. "This is the most important. I believe it contains more than booze." He grabbed his laptop. "I'll get the forms filled out and sent to the lab so all you have to do is drop them off."

"Good, because I don't have a clue what they are. Talk to you tomorrow." Shoberg walked over to his vehicle, unlocked the trunk, and put the box inside.

Hawke walked back inside with his computer. He picked up his drink and went to a table in the corner where no one could see what was on his computer from over his shoulder. He opened the computer and pulled out his notebook. He began logging in the items for forensics to check for fingerprints and in the case of the bottle also the contents to be analyzed.

"Here's your early dinner," Lacie said, holding his plate of food.

"Set it there." He pointed to a spot up and to the side of the laptop. "I'll get to it as soon as I finish filling out these forms."

He finished, closed the computer, and shoved it to

the side. As he pulled the plate of food toward him, his radio crackled. Hawke lowered his ear to the back of the mic to listen.

A disturbance at the High Mountain Brew Pub was called in. He listened to see if there was enough law enforcement handling it. Two Alder City police and a deputy were headed there. He didn't see a need for him to miss this meal.

He ate his salad and then the burger, keeping an ear out for the radio to see if he might still be needed. By the time he finished eating and headed back to Winslow to type his report about Lucas Brazo, he was officially off duty. As he pulled into the Winslow State Police office, he called in that he was done for the day.

He entered the building through the back and went straight to his desk. The light was on under the door of the sergeant's office. While Hawke should give him an update, he knew the man probably wanted to get home to his family.

That was one thing Hawke was lucky about. He'd not had anyone at home worrying about him. Well, Dog probably worried, but that was because he liked his biscuits and going out on trail rides. As for a person worrying about him, he had only himself. Of course, now that he and Dani lived together, she worried a little when she was off the mountain. When she was working at the lodge, she didn't know when he came and went and didn't have time to worry about him.

He placed his hat on the back of his chair, and took off his duty belt, placing it on the counter beside his computer. As the computer booted up, he walked into the conference room/lunch room and grabbed a cup of coffee. He'd need to keep awake to get all of this information written up properly. If he didn't make sure to include all the information that showed this to be a homicide and not a suicide Lange would be on his ass.

The clock on his computer showed 8:30 when he put the last document in the file he'd started for the Lucas Brazo homicide. Hawke stretched, yawned, and turned off his computer.

It looked like he'd be having breakfast at Al's Café in the morning to catch Otis as early as he could and then head out to Imnaha to have a chat with the Pinsons.

Hawke put his hat on, grabbed his duty belt, and flipped the lights off as he left the building. The door locked automatically behind him and he slid into his vehicle, thinking about a hot shower and a handful of oatmeal cookies with milk.

The drive to his house took less than ten minutes. He pulled up to the house and found Dog sitting on the porch, wagging his tail.

"Good to see you, too," Hawke said, bending down and patting the dog's head. He carried his laptop and duty belt into the house and then walked back out to the barn to check on the horses and mule. The three geldings stood at the gate. They must have seen the lights of his vehicle when he drove up the lane.

"You can't be hungry. You've been eating in that lush pasture all day," he said, patting their foreheads and walking to the barn to grab three alfalfa cubes. Back at the gate, he fed them the cubes, patted their necks, and walked to the house, with Dog trotting beside him.

In the house, he stopped at the office to see if anyone had left a voice message. The light blinked twice. He hit the replay button.

"Gabriel, I have a ribbon shirt made for you. Do you think Dani would like a ribbon skirt to wear to Tamkaliks? Call me back." The phone beeped that the message had ended. Hawke smiled at how excited his mom sounded about the whole family attending the powwow. He glanced at the clock. She would still be awake.

Hawke called his mom.

"Hello?" she answered.

"I just heard your message on my home phone. You know you can call my cell phone."

"I don't want to disturb your work for something that isn't important."

He knew the ribbon shirt and skirt were very important to her. "Thank you for the shirt and I'm sure that Dani would appreciate a skirt."

"You think so?"

"Yes. I'm sure she will love it."

"Okay. I have the fabric and Marion said she's the same size so I can use her to know how big to make it." There was a pause. "You're sure you'll make the powwow?"

"Yes. I've marked the days off on the calendar at work. I will be there for you and Marion."

"*Qeʔciyéwyew*," she said softly.

Her saying 'thank you' in her language told Hawke just how much the upcoming weekend meant to her.

"We will have a wonderful time as a family. Oh, and my friend Justine wants to hang out with us," he added to make her see how committed he was to being in attendance.

"That's wonderful! I'll let you go. You had a long

day. *Ta'c cik'éetin'*."

"Good night." Hawke ended the call and punched the button for the other call.

"Trooper Hawke, this is Fanny Pinson. Please call me back at…" she rattled off a cell phone number.

Hawke found a pen and paper and played the recording again to write down the number. Why had the daughter of Ford Pinson called him?

Hawke dialed the number on the paper and listened to the phone ring.

"Hello?" a female voice answered.

"This is Trooper Hawke. You left a message for me to call."

The voice whispered, "I can't talk now."

"I'm coming to the ranch tomorrow. We can talk then."

"No!" came a harsh whisper. "I can't talk to you here."

"Can you meet me at eleven at the Imnaha store?" he asked.

"No. But I can be out riding my horse. Do you think you'll be at the ranch around eleven?"

"Yes."

"I'll meet you on the road between Imnaha and the ranch." The call ended.

Hawke wondered what was so important and yet secret that Fanny couldn't just meet him at the store and tell him.

Chapter Seventeen

Hawke was up early, graining the horses and getting ready to leave for Eagle to get breakfast and visit with Otis.

Just as he started out the door, the ham radio crackled to life.

"Hawke, this is Dani. Over."

"Dani, what's up? Over."

"I wanted to let you know that I'll be coming out on Sunday to drop off a family if you want to have lunch together. Over."

"Sounds good. I'm headed out to have breakfast and talk with a person. Catch you up on Sunday. Over."

"Have a good day. Over."

"You too. Over." He hated making the contact so short but he disliked talking on the radio. Especially when it was a conversation that others could overhear if they were on the same frequency.

Plucking his hat off the coat rack by the door, he stuffed it on his head and stepped out of the house, nearly tripping over Dog and losing his grip on the laptop. "What are you doing laying in front of the door?" he asked, bending and petting the dog's head.

"You take care of the boys today. I'll try to get home earlier tonight." As he moved to step around Dog, the animal squeezed closer to his legs. "What's wrong, boy?"

"Gobble Gobble!" sounded close by.

Hawke spun toward the sound and found the biggest tom turkey he'd ever seen prancing around from the side of the house. Dog tucked his tail and backed behind him.

"Is this the bird that scared you?" Hawke asked, setting the laptop on a bench by the door and stepping off the porch, waving his hat. "Hah! Hah! Get home!" Hawke hollered, swinging his arms.

The turkey cocked his head to one side, eyeballing him.

Hawke took a couple of lunging steps, shouting, "Hah! Hah! Get out of here!"

The turkey puffed up his feathers, flapped his wings, stretched his neck toward Hawke, and charged.

Hawke could only think of one thing to do that wouldn't hurt the bird. He ran toward the barn and into a horse stall. He stood in the corner near the door and waited for the turkey to come in after him. The second the tom passed through the door, Hawke slipped out and closed the door on the bird.

Breathing hard, he pulled out his phone and called Herb.

"Morning, Hawke," he answered. "What was all the shouting I heard over there?"

"Your tom is in a stall in my barn. That damn thing

was going to attack me, so I lured it into the barn and locked it up. I think it's time you butchered him." Hawke was still gasping for air as he walked out of the barn. Dog sat at the corner of the house staring at him.

"As soon as we get enough eggs from the hens, he'll be butchered. I'll come get him and keep him locked up better."

"Dog and I would both appreciate that." Hawke was at the side of the house. He didn't blame Dog one bit for being scared of that menacing tom. "I'm taking Dog with me today. He's not going to want to stay at your place and now he doesn't feel safe here either."

"I am sorry. I didn't think that old tom would stray that far."

"No harm, just try to keep him locked up. I can't take Dog to work with me every day." Hawke ended the call. "Come on. You can go."

Dog's ears went up, and Hawke swore he saw a smile.

Hawke walked to the porch, picked up his laptop, and headed to his work vehicle. Dog sat by the door waiting.

"Did you invite that tom over so you could go to work with me today?" Hawke asked, opening the door.

Dog jumped in and sat in the passenger seat, staring forward.

"You wouldn't tell me if you did," Hawke said, roughing up the hair on Dog's head and starting the vehicle.

On the drive to Eagle, Hawke called dispatch to let them know he was on duty. At Al's, Hawke had to circle the block to find a place to park. It seemed Thursday was a popular day for the locals to have

163

breakfast out.

Walking through the door, it jangled and heads turned in his direction. He nodded and smiled at the locals he knew as he made his way over to the table where Otis sat by himself. "Mind if I join you this morning?"

The old farmer shook his head. "You might as well keep me company. I didn't find out about Lucas until I got here this morning." The man raised a cup of coffee to his whiskered face and drank.

Lacie arrived at the table with a cup of coffee and a menu for Hawke.

"Thanks," he said.

"Two days in a row," she said and hurried away to refill coffee cups.

"Who told you about Lucas?" Hawke asked.

"Joe Morton. He said his nephew works for the funeral home and they had to take him all the way to Clackamas for an autopsy." The man stared at him. "Does that mean it wasn't natural causes?"

"I believe someone put something in a bottle of booze," Hawke said, taking a glance at the menu.

Lacie appeared at his side as he set the menu down. "What'll you have?"

"Sausage, eggs, over easy, and the English muffin, for here. And a breakfast sandwich to go. Dog's with me today."

"I'll get that up." She walked away.

"I told him all the time, he needed to quit drinking. It was going to kill him. But I hadn't thought it would be from someone else's hand." Otis took a drink of coffee. "Who would want to kill him?"

"Had Lucas ever mentioned his friend Evan?"

Hawke asked, picking up his coffee.

"Yeah, he's the reason Lucas moved here. Trying to find out what happened to him. He didn't believe his friend drowned."

"He drowned but it wasn't by accident. We've discovered evidence that shows Evan being struck unconscious and then shoved in the river. He drowned but it was due to his being unconscious while floating in the water." Hawke sipped his coffee, watching Otis.

"So, he was right? It wasn't an accident?" Otis asked.

"Did Lucas ever mention anyone he was talking to about Evan?"

Lacie placed a plate of pancakes in front of Otis. "Here's your sugar-free syrup. Enjoy."

"Thanks, Lacie," Otis said, his eyes shining with happiness. He glanced up at Hawke. "This is my favorite day because I don't have to eat oatmeal for breakfast." Cutting the pancake into bite-sized pieces he said, "Don't get married. Your wife will starve you trying to keep you alive."

Hawke laughed. "She just wants you around for a long time."

"Well, maybe I'm ready to go. Maybe I'd rather die happy than feel like I'm missing out on good food." Otis smothered the pancake with the syrup and forked a bite in his mouth.

Hawke let the man enjoy a few bites before he asked again, "Did Lucas ever mention anyone he talked to about Evan?"

"Lots of people when he first moved here. But in the last few years, I think he gave up trying to find out anything. It was as if he'd lost hope. That's when he

165

started drinking heavier." Otis shoveled in a few more bites.

Lacie returned to their table with Hawke's breakfast and refilled their coffee cups. "How's it tasting, Otis?"

The man smiled. "Like heaven, Lacie. Like Heaven."

"That's good to hear. Burt has been perfecting his pancake mix. I think this is his best yet." She walked away and Otis watched her.

"She is the prettiest and nicest lady in this whole county," he said.

Hawke smiled. "I think it's because she lets you eat whatever you want when you come in here."

Otis picked up his coffee. "That could be but she is a nice lady."

"Yeah, she and Burt are a great addition to the county." Hawke dug into his breakfast, wondering how the locals felt about Christa when she first arrived.

"Have you ever met Ford Pinson's wife, Christa?"

Otis stopped eating and studied him. "Don't think I have. But Lucas brought up the names a time or two. They have something to do with his death?"

"Not that I know of." He wasn't going to have Otis start rumors that could get slander charges brought up against Hawke and the OSP. The Pinsons were a prominent family in the county.

"Do you know Wendy Fielding?" Hawke decided to figure out where she might fit into all of this.

"She's the lady at the mobile park who cleaned Lucas's house once in a while. I think she did take him food now and then too."

"Was there anything more between them?" Hawke

asked.

Otis glanced up from where he'd been scooping up the last of the syrup from his plate. "You mean like romantic?"

"Or strong friendship?"

"I don't know if you'd call it strong, but I think they were friends. Lucas didn't seem to be interested in women. He was focused on proving his friend didn't accidentally fall into the river." Otis put down his spoon and picked up his coffee. "I think he felt guilty for leaving his friend alone. For being lazy and overweight and not being able to hike where his friend wanted to hike."

Hawke had the same feeling. But in his gut, Lucas had been right. Evan hadn't died by accident. And Hawke's gut said neither had Lucas.

《》《》《》

On the drive out to Imnaha, Hawke stopped one out-of-state driver for driving 30 miles an hour over the speed limit. The man was cocky and Hawke didn't feel bad giving him a ticket. Then the guy made a crack about whether he was a trooper or dog control since he had a dog in his vehicle. Hawke wished the man had been going even faster so he could have given him a higher ticket.

He stopped at the Imnaha store to get something to drink. A young woman with red curly hair was behind the counter, helping a customer.

Hawke stood beside the door, scanning the establishment looking for the owner or his wife. The mounted elk, deer, and moose heads that lined the upper walls of the establishment were starting to show a little bit of age. Memorabilia filled in the gaps on all the flat surfaces. A large black barrel stove, with a stovepipe like a pillar, stood in the middle of the room. A glance at the ceiling revealed the folded bills that were stuck like large spit wads.

It was a long open building. The bar, with stools to sit and eat or drink, were along the left side. Behind the wood stove sat a pool table. The right side had groceries on stocked shelves behind five tables for people to sit and eat or have a drink. The back of the building had a storeroom and restrooms. Hawke preceded that direction to see if Tyler was around.

"Trooper, I can help you," said the young woman.

Hawke pivoted and walked over to the counter. "I wanted to talk with Tyler or Mandy."

"They headed to a family reunion this weekend. Is it something I can help you with?" She nodded as the bell over the door clanged and a customer walked in.

"No. I just wanted to visit with them about some of the people who live down here." He walked over to the cold drink case and found an iced tea. "I'll take this." He handed her the money and exited behind two women dressed in hiking shorts, boots, and hats.

Settling behind the steering wheel of his vehicle, he opened the bottle of tea and drank half of it. He was about half an hour early. He wasn't sure if Fanny would be near the road yet for their talk. He scratched Dog behind the ears and finished off his drink.

After sitting in the parking lot of the store for ten minutes, he started up his vehicle and slowly drove north along the Imnaha River. He wondered how Fanny planned to meet up with him when the Pinson ranch was across the river from this road.

Five miles before the bridge to cross over to the

ranch, Hawke spotted a person riding alongside the opposite side of the road. He slowed even more and watched as the horse and rider crossed the road.

He stopped beside her lowering the passenger side window. "This is a strange place to meet," he said.

She pointed back across the road. "When you continue, you'll see a barely discernable road toward the river. Take it and follow it along the river until you come to that old grove of fruit trees. I'll be there."

He continued on watching in the review mirror as she crossed back across the road and disappeared. Watching her in the mirror, he almost missed the road she was talking about. It was barely a quarter of a mile from where she'd stopped him. Following the road, it took him down closer to the river and into the grove of old fruit trees.

Fanny stood beside her horse waiting for him.

Hawke wondered at all the secrecy. What could she have to tell him?

He stopped the vehicle, opened the door, and stepped out, letting Dog out to pee on trees and get a drink from the river.

"What do you have to tell me that needs to be a secret?" He knew she wasn't alive when Evan was killed and even if she had been she would have been a toddler. But that would have made her Evan's daughter and not Ford's.

"Ever since you showed up at the ranch Mom has been acting weird. She and Dad were in the office a long time that evening when he returned home. I want to know if you think they killed the man you were talking about."

"I don't know who killed Evan Nestor. But I do

169

know your mom was married to him at the time and the three of them, Evan, your mom, and Ford were friends in college. When she gave me vague answers it made me wonder if she had something to hide. I'm back because Evan's best friend and a man who has been trying to figure out what happened thirty-six years ago was killed last night. Some of the things I found in his house, I'd like clarification about and your mom can tell me about them."

"I see." She bit her bottom lip and blew out a breath before saying, "Is there a way for me to get a sample of this Evan's DNA?"

Hawke studied her. "Why?"

"I think he might be my father. When I did a DNA test, I was contacted by someone who said we were cousins, but Ford had never heard of the person. So, I managed to get a sample from him when my daughter did a school science project. It came back I'm not even close to his DNA."

"What did your mom say when you asked her?" Hawke now wondered who contacted who before Christa and Ford married.

The woman's face grew red. "I haven't asked. If she's been lying to me all these years there has to be a reason. I wanted to have proof before I brought it up. Then she wouldn't be able to talk her way out of it."

Hawke wondered if this mother-daughter relationship had gone downhill since Fanny did the DNA test or before. "You could write to the person who contacted you and ask for the names of her relatives. I would think that would give you a start at figuring out who your biological father is."

"I'm waiting for her reply but thought maybe I

could get something more substantial from you and the case."

"Sorry, if the person who contacted you doesn't reply, then you should look up living relatives of Evan Nestor." Hawke whistled for Dog. He came running up from the river with wet legs, belly, and face. "Were you trying to catch fish?" Hawke asked the dog.

He faced Fanny. "Did either of your parents go anywhere last night?"

"Dad had a meeting with the cattlemen's association in Alder. Mom was helping someone with a horse north of Alder. Why?" Fanny watched him.

"Just wondering. Guess I'll see you at the ranch."

"Yes, but don't let them know we talked." The woman took a step toward him with her hand stretched toward him in a pleading pose.

"I won't." He slid into the vehicle, backed up, and slowly drove out to the road and up onto it.

As he drove the rest of the way to the ranch, he tossed around the information he'd just gathered from Fanny. Why would Christa keep Fanny's father secret from her if it wasn't Ford? In this day and age, he didn't understand it. People who never married had children together.

Turning to cross the bridge and go under the archway at the ranch, Hawke studied the main house and wondered what the two running the ranch now had done in their past that they were hiding it from their child.

Chapter Eighteen

Christa walked out of the arena as Hawke pulled up to the main house. Two cowboys were mending tack by the barn. A man, Hawke didn't see the last time he was here, stepped out of the barn and walked toward the vehicle.

Parking, Hawke rolled the windows down and stepped out.

"What can I do for you trooper?" the man asked, his hands on his hips. He had dark curly hair with gray interspersed.

"This is the trooper I told you about the other night," Christa said from behind Hawke.

"Senior Trooper Hawke," he said, holding out his hand to shake.

The man reluctantly shook and said, "Ford Pinson. This is my ranch. What can I do for you?"

"I have some questions for you and your wife." Hawke glanced at Christa and touched the bill of his cap as he dipped his head, in a cowboy-style greeting.

"Let's go inside, it's getting hotter today than it was all week." Christa walked to the front of the house.

The girl he'd seen on his last visit ran down the hall toward them. "Grandma, can I have two cookies?"

"Yes, but take them and a glass of milk out to the patio. I don't want crumbs all over inside," Christa said, waving for Hawke to take a seat on a leather chair in what appeared to be the great room. The furniture was all leather and large paintings of cattle, cowboys, and horses covered the walls that weren't floor-to-ceiling windows. Heavy tables that looked like it took a whole tree to build stood solid next to the chairs and couch.

Hawke sat, placing his hat on his knee and pulling out his notebook and pen.

"Why did you need to talk to us?" Ford asked, sitting on the couch with his arm around Christa.

"Did your wife tell you we found photos of the way her first husband died?" Hawke decided to start by seeing how much Christa had told her husband.

"She told me about the photos and that Evan's death wasn't an accident. But what does that have to do with us? That was over thirty years ago." The man frowned at Hawke.

"There is no statute of limitations on murder. I'd think you would want to find out who killed him and the professor who took the photos of the murder." Hawke kept his gaze trained on the couple. They stared forward, but Christa's hand slipped into Ford's.

"Of course, we'd like to know who did it. But we don't have anything to tell you. If we did, we would have brought up concerns back then." Ford said.

"You two were seeing each other when the murder happened?" Hawke asked.

"No!" Christa spat. "What gave you that idea?"

"Your husband made it sound like you two were conversing at the time your first husband was killed." Hawke scribbled in his notebook as if he were writing down something significant.

"We were only friends back then. It was Evan's sudden death that brought us back together," Christa hastily said.

"As something other than friends?" Hawke asked, peering up at the woman expectantly.

The woman's face flushed and she said, "You're messing with my words."

Ford stood up. "You can just get out if you are going to sit here and suggest that we had anything to do with his death. We didn't."

"What about Lucas Brazo? He was Evan's best friend. He came to the county to find out what really happened to Evan. Did you take him seriously when he said he couldn't believe that Evan had an accident?" Hawke watched Ford walk over to a window and stare out. Christa stared at her husband's back.

"When was the last time you saw Lucas?" Hawke asked Christa.

She jerked her head around to look at him. "What?"

"When was the last time you saw Lucas Brazo?"

"I-I'm not sure. Six months ago, maybe. He would call once a month and ask how I was doing. At first, I thought it was kind. But as it kept happening month after month, year after year, I started to hate the calls. Why couldn't he let things go? Why couldn't he leave me alone?"

"You won't get a call this month. He's dead."

Hawke saw relief in her eyes before she feigned sorrow.

Ford slowly turned from the window his eyes narrowed. "You came out here to ask us if we had anything to do with his death. For crying out loud, he was an alcoholic."

"How do you know that?" Hawke asked.

"The whole county knows that. He didn't try to hide it." Ford walked back to the couch and sat beside his wife.

"Did he come to you with any suspicions he had about who might have killed Evan?" Hawke asked.

Christa shook her head. "Nothing concrete, just that there was no way Evan fell into the river."

"Because your husband was scared of water?" Hawke asked.

Christa's eyes met his. "He wasn't. Anyway, not that I knew of. Who told you that?"

"Lucas. He told me that Evan was scared of the boat and feared the water. That there was no way he'd get close enough to the water to fall in accidentally." Hawke studied both of them.

"How well did you know your husband?" he asked, studying Christa. Her eyes pinged back and forth in their sockets as if she were looking for an answer.

"What are you trying to say?" Ford asked in an accusing tone.

"Did you really know if he had enemies?" Hawke asked. He turned his attention to Ford. "In college, did Evan get along with people or did he make enemies?"

Ford scoffed. "The only enemies he had were the jocks who pushed him around and called him a geek. Otherwise, he got along with everyone. That's what makes your accusations he was killed hard to believe."

"Who were some of the jocks?" Hawke asked.

"You can't seriously think one of them followed him on his fishing trip and killed him." Ford was starting to look worried.

"Sometimes animosity can carry on out of school. Did any of them cross his path in his career?" Hawke thought it was a long shot but one never knew.

"Declan Smith, and Harry, Christa's brother," Ford said, nodding toward his wife.

"That was just joking around," Christa came to her brother's defense. "He liked to see how far he could push Evan to make sure he wouldn't get violent with me. That's all."

Hawke raised an eyebrow. "Your brother bullied Evan to make sure he'd be a good husband?"

She shrugged. "It was just his way."

Since they were talking about family, Hawke asked Christa, "Why did Lucas have boxes of Evan's memorabilia? School photos, awards. If you didn't want them, I would have thought they'd have gone to Evan's parents."

"Evan's parents died when he was in high school. He lived with Lucas and his family during his junior and senior years. When I didn't want them after Evan died, I gave them to Lucas since he was the closest family I knew about."

And that was why Lucas felt as if he had to find out the truth about his friend. They were nearly as close as brothers. "I found some photos of your wedding in the boxes." Hawke slipped his hand into his pocket and pulled out the photo of Ford and Wendy. "Do either of you remember this woman?"

Christa studied the photo and looked at her

husband. "That girl came with you. Evan and I had never met her before."

Ford's face grew taunt as he said, "Wendy Fielding. I asked her to be my plus one at the wedding and reception." He stared at the wall over Hawke's head. "She's a local. We were at a bar and I mentioned I had a wedding to go to and no date, she offered to come along."

"Any reason why she offered? Were you two dating?" Hawke asked.

The clomp of boots coming down the hallway had them all peering at the hall.

Fanny stepped into the room. "Oh! Sorry." She began backing down the hall.

"It's okay, pumpkin, the trooper is just leaving," Ford said.

Hawke shook his head. "I'm not leaving until I have all of my questions answered."

"Then I'll leave you to your questions." Fanny spun around and hurried down the hall.

"Were you and Wendy dating at the time you took her to Evan and Christa's wedding?" Hawke asked.

"No. What gave you that idea?" Ford said loudly.

"The way Wendy explained the weekend it sounded like you two knew each other well." He let the implication hang in the air between them.

"I barely saw her after that weekend. I only had one person I wanted to marry. And it wasn't Wendy. I told her that on our way to the wedding." Ford's gaze drifted to his wife.

She gave him a weak smile, possibly realizing his words were damning, given her husband was killed only two years after the wedding, practically in Ford's backyard.

"And who was that woman?" Hawke asked, his pen poised over his notebook.

Sweat beaded Ford's forehead below his graying hair. The room was a perfect temperature not too cold and not too hot. The only reason for the sweat had to do with him finally realizing what he'd said.

Ford grabbed Christa's hand and said, "This woman. I fell in love with her in college but she only had eyes for Evan. Then after his acci-death, I pursued her, and she finally gave in."

"When was Fanny born? Before you married Ford or after?" Hawke asked, hoping to get some clarification.

Christa's face paled. "After, why are you asking me this? Her birth should have no bearing on my first husband's death."

Switching up the questions to keep them on their toes, he asked, "Where were you the weekend Evan and Lucas went fishing on the Snake?"

She sputtered, "I-I was at my brother's wedding in Spokane. Why? I couldn't have killed him if that's what you're thinking. Was I mad he left me to go to the wedding alone? Yes! But not enough to kill him."

"But you could see why he didn't want to go given the way your brother treated him." Hawke studied her.

She stared down at her hands where her fingers were twined together. "True, I don't blame him but I didn't like being there without Evan. All my family kept asking where he was. Why hadn't he come to the wedding? It was embarrassing. I had to tell them he picked his best friend and a fishing trip over my family celebration." She glanced up. Tears glistened in her eyes but they also held anger. "I was ready for a good fight with him when he returned. But…he didn't return. Then I felt awful for having been so angry about being there alone."

Hawke leveled his gaze on Ford. "Where were you that weekend?"

"You expect me to remember where I was that long ago?" He glared at Hawke.

"I would think it would stick in your memory if it was the weekend that Evan went missing. You had to have heard about the search for a missing man on the Snake and they would have mentioned his name." Hawke continued to hold the man's gaze.

Ford broke the contact, his gaze landing on Christa. "I was wrangling cattle and joined the search for him. I knew Christa must have been worried and I wanted to help."

"Maybe be her hero by finding the man who had abandoned her family wedding to go fishing?"

They both flinched. As he'd suspected, she had called Ford when she was upset with her husband. He had known where Evan would be. And quite possibly, his wrangling had been in Hells Canyon.

"Could I have the phone number of your brother and your parents?" Hawke asked, turning the page he'd been writing on and presenting a fresh page and his pen to Christa.

"Why do you want to talk to them?" she asked, writing their numbers on the pad.

"I'm following all leads." Hawke motioned for Ford to take the pad. "Give me the names and phone numbers of the people who were here that weekend."

"I can't remember everyone from back then. And

some of them have died or left." Ford didn't take the pad from his wife.

"Then any of the ones you do remember. Or else I'll go out and start questioning all of them. That should get them wondering what kind of a person they are working for." Hawke held Ford's gaze.

Ford pulled out his phone and started writing down names and scrolling through his phone for numbers. When he handed it back, Hawke noticed he hadn't put down anyone with his last name. "Were there any of your family here that weekend?"

"My mom and dad. Dad's been gone four years and Mom doesn't remember much of anything past her childhood. She's in a care facility for dementia in Lewiston." Ford stared at a photo on the wall of two people who must have been his parents.

"Do you have any siblings?" Hawke asked.

"My brother, Jordan, and a sister, Erica. They are both older and weren't at home that weekend. They were married and living with their families."

"I see. And neither one of them wanted the ranch?" Hawke found it interesting the youngest of the children ended up with the family ranch.

"No. They both couldn't wait to get out of the county. They rarely come back. If I want to see them or their families we have to visit them." Ford's tone told how he resented the fact they didn't visit.

"Thank you. That's all for now. If I think of something else, I'll be back." Hawke rose.

"You could just call," Christa said.

Hawke smiled. "Then I wouldn't get to drive out here."

Ford walked him to the door. "I don't know why

you are so insistent on finding a killer. The verdict of an accidental death appeased Christa. Now that you say it's murder, she's been on edge and worried what everyone will think."

"Everyone deserves to have justice. Knowing that he was killed and the killer most likely killed Lucas, I believe that person needs to be found and charged." Hawke put his hat on his head and walked out to his vehicle.

It was after noon and he was hungry. Hawke continued along the Imnaha River on Upper Imnaha Road until he found a good spot to pull over. He dug into the cooler in his back seat and pulled out a package of jerky, a package of cookies, and water.

They walked over to a boulder and Hawk sat, eating, tossing bites to Dog, and spinning everything he learned at the ranch around in his mind.

Chapter Nineteen

Following the Upper Imnaha Road to Grizzly Ridge, Hawke turned left and then right onto Camp Creek Road. As he wove his way back to a main road, he stopped and checked licenses and asked if the fish were biting. He was on Zumwalt Road nearing Alder when his phone buzzed. It was Spruel.

"Hawke," he answered.

"Where are you? I've been trying to call you for a couple of hours."

"I was down on the Imnaha and came through Trail Creek and now on Zumwalt. What's up?" Hawke asked.

"The result came in on the liquid still in the bottle. It had xylazine, an animal tranquilizer, mixed with the alcohol. You were right, it was a homicide."

"I'm sure it's whoever killed Evan Nestor. Now I want to know who Lucas called and who he talked to before he died. I don't remember seeing a phone." Hawke thought back to all the items they had bagged and a phone wasn't one of them.

"You can go see if you missed it in the morning. You aren't going to get home for another two hours. Did you learn anything new?"

"I did." Hawke went on to tell Spruel about the brother, the previous relationship of Ford and Christa, and his conversation with Fanny.

"You had a productive day and tagged some fishermen. I'll catch up with you tomorrow." The call ended and Hawke grinned. He'd had a productive day and knowing that Lucas's death wasn't from natural causes gave him satisfaction he would find Evan, Professor Chang, and Lucas's killer.

By the time he pulled into the High Mountain Brew Pub, Hawke's stomach was growling and Dog was fast asleep. He left the windows halfway down and parked in the shade of a large cottonwood on the far corner of the parking lot. He didn't need a do-gooder saying he left his dog in an oven of a vehicle. Which he would never do, but some of the people who believed they needed to police parking lots to find animals left in cars, were overzealous in proving their point and would break windows and vandalize the vehicles to shame the pet owners.

The parking lot was full and he was glad he'd been able to nab a spot in the shade. He crossed through the parking lot and cars, noting most of the licenses were from out of state or other parts of the state. Many locals who moved away came back in the later part of July for class and family reunions and Chief Joseph Days. A weekend of rodeo, drinking, a parade, and amusement park rides.

Next weekend was the powwow. That brought the tribal people whose ancestors had once lived on this land from reservations to celebrate. They stayed on the powwow grounds during the weekend, visiting with family and seeing friends.

Hawke pushed open the establishment's doors and felt the whoosh of cold air. That could be another reason the place was packed. Not all eating establishments in the county had air conditioning. It was a draw this time of year when the temperature was in the 90s.

Heads turned and people watched him walk up to the bar.

Desiree was on duty. She smiled. "Hawke, are you looking for dinner or a person?"

"Dinner. All I had was jerky and cookies for lunch. And Dog ate most of it."

Desiree laughed. "You have to quit spoiling that dog or he's going to walk all over you."

"He already does."

"Do you want a table or sit here at the bar."

"I'd prefer a table since I'm in my uniform."

"You got it. Let me go clean that table over in the corner." Desiree came out from behind the bar as a man walked up waving a hundred-dollar bill.

"We need more drinks, Doll," the man said.

"I'll be right with you," Desiree said, walking past him, carrying a wet towel.

The man reached out and grabbed her by the arm. "I said we need drinks."

"And I said, I'll get them after I've cleaned this table." She tried to shake loose. When fear sparked in her eyes, Hawke stepped in.

"Take your hand off the lady," he said in his most threatening tone.

The man turned angry eyes on him. "Says who?"

Hawke stomped on the man's foot. He released Desiree to throw a punch at Hawke. He countered and twisted the man's arm behind his back. "Now, you can wait patiently for her to come back and take your order or you can leave now. Your choice."

The man started slinging cuss words and calling him every name he'd heard before. Hawke kept pressure on the man's arm, moving him toward the door. "Call City Police and have them come pick him up," he called to Desiree who stood where the man had accosted her. She nodded and dived around the end of the bar.

Hawke took the man out to the sidewalk in front of the pub.

"Let me go!" the man shouted and tried kicking backward at Hawke. "You have no right to hold me."

"You assaulted the bartender and took a swing at me. Before the City Police take you away, they'll go in and get her statement." Hawke tweaked the man's arm higher up his back.

"Ouch, this is harassment!" he shouted as two men walked out of the pub.

"Damn, Harry, why can't you just ask for drinks nicely," the tallest of the men said.

"Trooper, we can take him from here." The shorter man said.

"I'm waiting for the city police to come get him. He assaulted the bartender and has been attacking me. You'll have to pick him up from the city jail." Hawke held each man's gaze briefly before Harry started struggling.

"Ow! Let go of my arm!" Harry shouted.

"When you stop trying to harm me or get away, I'll loosen my hold." Hawke decided it was worth putting his cuffs on the man and getting them back later then making his muscles sore. He pulled out the cuffs and hooked one to the man's wrist that was up behind his back and then swiftly captured his other hand and snapped the other cuff on. The man tried slamming his head backward into Hawke's face but he felt the man's body whipping and stepped to the side. Harry nearly went over backward. Hawke reached out and stopped his fall as the city car pulled up at the sidewalk.

Officer Craig Herold stepped out of the car. "What do you have, Hawke?"

"He assaulted Desiree and swung at me, not to mention the dancing we've been doing out here waiting for you." Hawke pulled Harry over to the patrol car.

Craig held the door open, and Hawke lowered his suspect into the back seat of the vehicle.
Craig closed the door and pulled out his notebook. "Are these men witnesses?"

"No, we're his friends. What's this crap about grabbing our buddy when all he did was ask for drinks," the shorter man said, standing on his toes and pushing his face out toward Hawke.

"He did ask for drinks and then he grabbed the bartender by the arm and squeezed so hard I'm sure we'll find bruises. I stepped in and he took a swing at me." Hawke walked by the two men and indicated for Craig to follow.

Inside, Hawke led Craig over to Desiree who was pouring drinks. "You need to tell Craig what happened. And make sure you show him your arm. I'll be over at the table figuring out what I want for dinner."

Hawke walked over to the cleaned-off table, took off his hat, and set it next to the utensils rolled up in a napkin. He watched Craig take down Desiree's statement, then walk over to where he sat.

"You want to officially give me your statement?" Craig asked, taking the seat across from Hawke.

After telling what happened, Hawke pointed out several of the people who were close by the altercation. "You might want to get their statements as well. I have a feeling Harry isn't going to let this go away."

Craig nodded and as soon as he walked over to talk to the people Hawke mentioned, Desiree appeared.

"What can I get you for dinner?" she asked, placing a glass of iced tea on the table in front of him.

"I'll have the chicken fried steak, mashed potatoes, and a salad, please." He handed the menu to her.

"Thank you for stepping in." She raised the short sleeve of her blouse and showed him the red and purple marks from the man's fingers squeezing her arm. "I've never had someone get that violent so quickly. He must have been drunk when he came in."

"Or high. He'll be locked up for a while and hopefully will cool down."

"He dropped this on the floor." She pulled a hundred-dollar bill out of her pocket.

Hawke called Craig over and slid the bill over toward him. "You might want to bag this and give it to the guy that's in your car. He was flashing this when he assaulted Desiree. He must have dropped it in the ruckus. She found it on the floor."

Craig glanced at the bill and pulled a small evidence bag out of his back pocket. He put the bill inside, sealed and wrote on the bag. "I'll make sure it's given to him if he calls in a lawyer." He winked at Desiree. "Good faith and all that. I think I've got all I need. Have a good dinner."

After Craig left, Desiree still hung by Hawke's table.

"Something else you want to talk about?" Hawke asked, picking up his iced tea.

"Hey! Who's working the bar!" someone called out.

"I'll ask when I bring your dinner." She hurried back to the bar and Hawke watched her for a few minutes. What could be on her mind?

He found out when she brought his meal to the table and slid onto the chair across from him.

"Bud's taking over while I take a break," she said, placing a glass of soda on the table in front of her.

"That's good. What did he have to say about the guy who grabbed you?" Hawke glanced over at the owner of the pub. He was busy filling orders.

"He said, he'd stay behind the bar with me the rest of the night. It is busy and I could use the help."

Hawke nodded. "It's a bit crowded in here tonight."

"Bud wants to put outdoor seating off that end of the bar. Then things will really be busy with more seating." She sipped on her drink, finally released the straw, and said, "The man you took home the other night, Lucas. I heard he died. Was it from excessive drinking?" She wrung her hands and stared at him.

"No, he was drugged by someone. Why were you worried he'd died from drinking?" Hawke saw the relief that had flashed in her worried eyes.

"I didn't cut him off like I did other people because of his size and he was never a nasty drunk. I thought maybe I'd given him one too many and that I-I'd killed him." She placed her entwined hands on the table and peered into his eyes. "I was ready to turn myself in if that were the case."

Hawke smiled and patted her hands. "You didn't kill him. You wouldn't kill anyone, of that I'm sure. But from now on, don't allow an alcoholic to have as much as they want, no matter how nice they are. It's not good for them."

She nodded and asked, "You said he was drugged. Who would want to kill him?"

This was a good opener. "When he came in here did you ever see him with anyone or did he always come in and sit alone?"

"Mostly alone, but there was a woman who would meet him once in a while...no make that two women. The first time I thought, 'Wow, he's picking up a nice-looking lady.' Then they met again and I guess about once a month, they'd meet here."

"Nice looking? Describe her." Hawke pulled out his notebook to write down the description.

"Probably around his age, only she looked a lot better. Slender, athletic, suntanned face, cowboy boots, long silver and blonde braid down her back."

Hawke glanced up. That meant Christa Pinson had been meeting Lucas here once a month. Why hadn't she mentioned that? "And the other woman?"

"It's just been the last couple of months. I'd say the woman was in her thirties, curly auburn hair about shoulder length. Athletic body, dressed in the usual ranch clothing. Are they responsible for Lucas's death?"

"No. I don't think so. Did you see a resemblance in the two?" He was sure it was Christa and Fanny. And he was sure that Fanny had met with Lucas to ask about Evan, a man she now believed to be her father.

"Now that you mention it, yes, they could have been related. I believe the older woman is married to Ford Pinson."

Hawke nodded. "She is. Her first husband was best friends with Lucas." He decided not to tell her any more. He saw an arm waving in his peripheral vision. He glanced at the bar. "I think Bud needs you back at the bar."

She turned in her seat, and Bud waved his arm again.

"Thank you again. And your dinner is on me." She slid off the chair before he could protest.

When he left, he slipped twenty dollars under his plate for a tip.

As soon as he opened the vehicle door, Dog was on his feet drooling.

"Back up or you won't get these fries and bites of steak I brought for you." Hawke pushed the dog over into the passenger side and then handed him the food. "Let's go home. Tomorrow, I need to find Lucas's phone and see if I can find out if any of the bones at Sluice Creek show signs of foul play."

Chapter Twenty

Friday morning, Hawke spent thirty minutes proving to Dog that the turkey wasn't anywhere around the house or barn. When the dog finally understood he wasn't going with Hawke, he tucked his tail between his legs and walked out into the pasture with the horses.

Hawke laughed at the comical sight and slid into his vehicle. First on his agenda was to go to Eagle and find Lucas's cell phone. If it wasn't there, then the killer took it. Most likely to hide the fact that he or she had called Lucas.

But first, he stopped at the Rusty Nail for breakfast.

"Good morning, Hawke," Justine said when he walked up to the counter.

"Morning, Justine." He peered through the window into the kitchen. "Morning, Merrilee."

"Hey there, Hawke. Your usual?" Merrilee asked.

"Why don't you spice it up today and give me sausage."

She waved a spatula. "I can do that."

Hawke settled at the counter but spun the seat to study the other patrons. Today there were more locals than tourists. "Good crowd today."

"You can tell it's getting close to the end of the month when all the excitement happens around here." Justine poured a cup of coffee for him.

"Will Wendy Fielding be in this morning?" he asked.

"No, she only comes in one day a week. Is she in trouble?" Justine put a hand on her hip.

"No, I just had a couple of questions for her regarding one of her neighbors." He still hadn't ruled her out as a suspect. She had known Evan and Lucas from before and she could have cleared out all the booze bottles and left the one behind with the drug in it. That reminded him.

Hawke pulled out his phone and searched for xylazine. When the results came up, he sat up straighter, staring at the screen.

"What's on there that makes you look as if you are holding a snake?" Justine asked.

"Nothing. I was looking up something and the results surprise and don't surprise me." He cleared the screen and wondered which veterinarian the Pinsons used.

Once his plate was clean, Hawke thanked Merrilee for the good food, paid and tipped Justine, and headed to his vehicle. Before he left Winslow, he swung by the OSP office.

Sitting in Sergeant Spruel's office, he filled the sergeant in on what had transpired at the pub the night before and said he would be going to sign his statement after he tossed Lucas Brazo's home searching for his

192

cell phone.

"If you can't find the phone, find out from someone what his number was and we can get a subpoena and do a search to find out who he called and who called him," Spruel said.

"I think I already know who called him. Did you look up what xylazine is used for?" Hawke asked.

"Yeah, it's an animal tranquilizer."

"Mostly used on horses." Hawke stood. "I requested information about Christa Pinson from when she was Christa Nestor. I know she is into horses now, but I want to know how long she has been and who the Pinsons use for a vet. We need to find out where the drug came from."

"I'll read through the report and give you the highlights. Then I'll call the vets and see who works on the Pinson horses."

"Thanks. I'm headed to search the mobile home and have a talk with Wendy Fielding, if she's around. I'll stop back by on my way to Alder." Hawke stood.

"I'll try to have all the information for you and a subpoena ready if you don't find the phone." Spruel tapped on his keyboard. "If you can close the two cold cases and the current case, you'll have outdone yourself."

Hawke didn't care about the number of cases closed. He cared about justice for the dead and the ones they left behind.

《》《》《》

At Six Pines, Hawke parked outside the fence, in front of the office. Mr. Bale came out with his arms crossed as if he planned to bar Hawke from entering the court.

"When are you going to take that tape down and let me get someone in to clean up that trailer? I need to get rent from all of them to make a living," Bale said.

"It's not the end of the month and I'm sure Lucas paid for this month. We'll let you know when we're through investigating." Hawke passed the man and continued down the narrow, paved road that ran between the trailers. He noticed the crime scene tape flapping in the breeze as if someone had crossed the line and didn't care if anyone knew. Hawke spun around and studied Bale. He could tell by the expression on the man's face, he'd gone in the mobile home. Hawke strode back toward the office. The man started to walk away, his long gray ponytail catching the morning sun.

"Hold up!" Hawke shouted. "Unless you want to be brought in on charges of tampering with a crime scene."

Bale stopped and slowly faced him.

Hawke stopped close enough to the short man that Bale had to tip his head up to look him in the eye. "Did you enter the crime scene?"

"Why would I do that?" Bale asked belligerently.

"Exactly. No one should have crossed that tape. But it appears to be ripped in the middle, not like it came loose on an end. "I knew you weren't too bright but this…"

"Hey! You can't call me stupid!" Bales stood up on his tiptoes, trying to appear larger.

"I didn't. I called you not bright. Why did you go in there?" Hawke crossed his arms and waited.

Bales stared at him, slowly lowered onto his heels, and dropped his gaze. "I wanted to see if there was anything worth money that I could hock to help with the fact I wouldn't have rent money until you finished up."

Hawke couldn't believe the gall of the man to steal from a place that was still under investigation. "You stole from a crime scene? What did you take?"

"Nothing much. Just some furniture and the electric appliances." Bales's eyes narrowed and his face reddened. "He's not going to need them!"

"They are all part of the investigation until we find out who killed Lucas." Hawke decided to scare the man. "One of those things you took could have evidence that will lead us to his killer. I could let word get out you took items from the crime scene and see who shows up at your door to keep you quiet."

"I never—No one would—" he stopped stammering and said, "You can't do that."

Hawke grinned. "Oh, yes, I can. You are no better than the killer since you crossed crime scene tape and took evidence." He narrowed his eyes and peered hard at the man. "Did you take the items because one of them has your fingerprints on it from killing Lucas?"

The man backed up as if he'd been blasted with a gust of wind. "N-no! I didn't kill him."

"I'm going to go look for what I came for. When I finish, there better be every single item you took from Lucas's house in the back of my vehicle." Hawke pivoted and strode toward Lucas's mobile home. He noticed several of the neighbors standing on their porches or in their yards watching. He wondered how many of them had heard what he'd said to Bales.

At the house, the smell wasn't as bad as the first day. The open windows and the feces drying kept the smell tolerable. He hoped whoever cleaned the house before the next renters were good at their job. The obvious place for the phone would be on or around the couch. Hawke pulled off all the cushions and shoved his gloved hands down into all the nooks and crannies of the furniture's frame.

No phone but lots of food. He nearly gagged when he pulled his hand out and it was covered in melted chocolate. He washed the gloved hand in the sink and returned to tip the couch over and inspect underneath. Given the piece of furniture sat on railroad ties there was plenty of room for numerous things to get kicked underneath.

He didn't find the phone but there was a flash drive. He put that in an evidence bag and wondered why he hadn't found a computer. Lucas would have needed a way to either put information on the flash drive or to see what was on it.

He also found a well-used stockman pocket knife. It didn't look like anything the man he'd known for a short time would use. It was worn smooth, but when he opened the three blades, they were sharp and ready for use. As he inspected the knife, he discovered a barely discernable brand etched on the metal at the end of the handle. In the dim light, he couldn't make it out.

Hawke bagged the knife and moved on to looking through all the cupboards and drawers again, only this time he took things out and shook them. He didn't come up with a phone or a computer. After two hours, he decided the killer must have taken the phone and the computer.

Out in the fresh air, Hawke held the evidence bags in his hand and stood still, facing the mobile home. He closed his eyes and thought back to the night he'd brought Lucas home from the High Mountain Pub.

Lucas had been wobbly from the drink and having slept all the way to Eagle. He'd been disoriented. Hawke had opened the door, which hadn't been locked. He'd helped Lucas to the couch. It was easier than navigating the large man down the narrow hallway.

After Lucas had plopped on the couch, Hawke had surveyed the room. In his mind, he scanned it as he'd seen it that night. There wasn't a computer in the living room. Or on the kitchen table. He remembered seeing bottles and dirty dishes. But he hadn't gone into the bedroom.

Hawke walked over to Wendy's home and knocked on the door. A dog barked but that was all. His mind abruptly flew to the night he brought Lucas home. The dogs hadn't been in the house. They hadn't barked or tried to chew on his boots. Where had the dogs been that night? They'd been there gnawing on his boots the morning of the suicide attempt.

As he headed down the steps off the deck, a woman next door called out, "She's working this morning. She'll be back around one."

"Thanks." Hawke wandered over to the woman. "Did you happen to know Lucas Brazo?"

"Not really. I knew who he was, but he kept to himself. Drank a lot from the bottles in his garbage and then those yapping dogs. You'd have thought he'd have been deaf. Some nights I could hear them clear over here." She nodded accentuating her statement.

"Did you hear them the night he died?" Hawke asked.

"Not until early in the morning. Then you came

and they went scattering all over the place. I'm sure Shirley has found them all homes by now. She's good at that." The woman smiled.

"Do you remember seeing anyone visit Lucas the night before he died?"

"I only saw Wendy go in with a couple of garbage sacks and come out an hour later with them full and clanking."

"What about the dogs? Did they bark when she went in?" Hawke asked.

The woman thought. "No, I don't remember them barking, but then she didn't knock on the door, she just walked in. I figured she'd called and told Lucas she was coming."

"Thank you," Hawke said and strolled back to his vehicle. Once the evidence bags were stored in his glove box, he pulled out his notebook and wrote down everything the woman had told him. He circled the dogs hadn't barked when Wendy entered the house. Had Wendy visited so often that the dogs didn't bark at her? That would make sense that the neighbors hadn't heard any barking. And when she went in to take away all of the bottles, she could have easily left the one with the drug in it. But what would be her motive?

He needed to have another chat with her. She'd be back in two hours. He could run to Alder, sign his statement, and grab lunch then come back down here and try to catch her at home. Or he could grab a burger to go at Al's, check fishing licenses in the canyon, and come back by here on his way to sign his statement. That made more sense.

Pulling his phone out of his pocket, he called Al's Café.

"Al's Café, Lacie speaking, how may I help you?"

"Hi Lacie, it's Hawke. I need a burger to go and I'll be there in fifteen minutes."

"We'll have it ready. You want fries and an iced tea?"

"Yes."

"See you in fifteen." She ended the call and Hawke smiled.

Chapter Twenty-one

At 1:15 Hawke drove back toward Eagle to have a chat with Wendy. He'd given out two citations for fishing without a license and broke up a fight between a drunk fisherman and another man because the drunk had butt into the other man's fishing hole.

He still had a lot of things to do today that pertained to the cold cases and the homicide. In Eagle, he turned down Fourth Street and parked in front of the Six Pines office. He still had the items Bales had put in the back of his vehicle from this morning to take to the evidence room. He doubted any of it would have anything to do with the crime, but he wasn't going to let Bales use stolen property to pad his wallet.

Stepping out of the vehicle, Hawke's gaze landed on a car parked next to Wendy's place. That must mean she was home. He'd left his vehicle at the office due to the lack of space for more than one vehicle per home, and the one-lane road in and out of the place.

As he walked by her car, he found Wendy and the

neighbor he'd talked to that morning, sitting on the deck, sipping a cold drink. Wendy's small white dog lay on the porch swing between the ladies.

"See, I told you he'd be here," the neighbor said in a gleeful voice.

"Trooper, I'm surprised you wanted to see me again. I've told you everything."

Hawke smiled at the neighbor and said to Wendy, "There has been some new evidence come up and I wanted to ask you more questions."

"I see," Wendy took the glass out of her neighbor's hand and said, "Irene, you need to leave. I'm sure this police matter doesn't need you blabbing it all over Eagle."

Irene huffed and stood. "If that doesn't take all. Here I come and let you know this trooper wanted to talk to you and you don't even let me listen in."

"It would be best if we talked alone," Hawke said, hoping the woman wouldn't try to eavesdrop.

"I'm leaving. And don't ask me to help you with anything again." The woman stomped over to her home and slammed the door.

Wendy chuckled. "She'll be back as soon as you leave wanting to know everything."

Hawke nodded to the inside of the house. "We could go in there for privacy."

She shook her head. "No, I've opened the windows but it's too hot to sit in there. I'll get you a glass of tea and we'll sit out here and talk quietly." Wendy rose and walked into the house with the glass she'd taken from her neighbor.

The dog watched as Hawke settled himself on a small folding chair he found tucked in the corner of the deck.

Wendy returned with his drink, handed it to him, and sat on the porch swing, petting the dog. "What has come up?"

"A couple of things. The night I brought Lucas home from High Mountain Pub, his dogs weren't in the house. But the day when the suicide attempt call came in, the dogs were in the house. And your neighbor, Irene, said the dogs didn't bark when you cleaned the bottles out of the house. Where would they have been? And when would they have been returned home?"

Wendy nodded her head as he talked. "Sometimes when he put them out, they'd run all over the place and people here would gather them up and put them back in. Could have been the dogs got out at some point before I went over to clean up the bottles and he didn't want to bother gathering them up, knowing people would put them in the house if they were a bother."

Hawke studied her. She wasn't telling the truth. She wasn't keeping eye contact and her hands gripped her knees. "Is that really what you know to have happened?"

"It's just speculation. I don't know what happened." Her gaze drifted over his left shoulder.

He'd leave that for now. "I found a flash drive under the couch. Did Lucas have a computer?"

Her eyes widened at the question. "No. I think he used the computers at the library."

"Did he go there often?" Hawke hadn't thought about the man using a computer let alone going to the library to use one.

"I don't know. Before he started drinking so much, he had a job and would leave every morning and come home in the evening. But about the time he retired, he started drinking more and leaving his home less." She thought a moment. "But he talked about his friend more."

"Do you think he was digging harder into how Evan died?" Hawke asked, studying Wendy to see if the question annoyed her.

"Maybe, but he wasn't thinking as clearly as when he first started asking questions. I think it was more all in his head and nothing really of substance." She nodded.

"Then his digging up information that might implicate Ford Pinson wouldn't have bothered you?"

She'd been staring at a potted plant. Her head swung toward him and her gaze met his. "What would give you that impression?"

"Your intimate weekend with him during Evan and Christa's wedding. You obviously liked him back then and you haven't married. I wonder if you still like him and would do things for him?"

She snorted and said, "The reason I haven't married is Ford showed me how shallow and callous men can be. I'd rather be alone than live with someone who treated me like I didn't matter." Her face reddened as she said, "I did everything he asked that weekend and when he dropped me back off at my house, he told me that he never wanted to see me again and that I'd just been a way to ruffle feathers." Her eyes sparked with anger. "Ruffle feathers! Of all the asinine things to say when I thought he'd cared for me."

"Do you clean for any veterinarian clinics?" he asked.

The abrupt change of topic had her staring at him.

"What?"

"I asked if you clean any veterinarian clinics."

"No, why?" Her eyes narrowed.

"Just a question. Okay, I think that's it for now." Hawke finished off his drink and stood. "I might have more questions later."

He walked to the three steps off the deck and faced her. "Ask around about the dogs. I'd like to know where they were and when they were put back in with Lucas." He continued off the deck and down the drive to his vehicle. He didn't look back to see if she acknowledged his request. It would give her something to think about and maybe she could come up with an actual person who had taken the dogs, other than herself.

Hawke stopped at the Eagle Library. It was a small building with a built-in table across the back wall where four computers sat for public use. Hawke smiled at the young man standing behind the check-out counter.

"Do you work here often?" Hawke asked.

"I'm the head librarian for this branch of the Wallowa County Library System."

"Do you know Lucas Brazo?" Hawke noticed there was a mother with two small children in the Children's section.

"Yes. And I heard the news. The way he took care of himself it's no wonder he died."

Hawke thought it best to leave the young man believing he'd died of natural causes. "Did he come in here and use the computer?"

The man grinned. "Yes, about three years ago, when I first started working here, he came in with a binder and asked how he could put the information from the binder on something smaller that he could take back and forth. Work on it here and take it home with him. I told him I could buy him a flash drive. I did, and then I showed him how to make a document and save it to the drive. After he put all the stuff from his binder onto the drive, he just brought the flash drive and a notepad with him when he came in."

Hawke was impressed that Lucas had the foresight to put all the information he'd collected into an easier way for people to read it.

"Thank you. And when was the last time he was in here?"

"A day or two before he died. I can't remember exactly. I can look at the log-in book. Everyone who uses the public computers has to fill out the date and time when they use one." He walked to the table with computers and over to a book that sat at the end. He flipped backward through the pages and stopped. "This past Monday at ten. When we opened."

Hawke wrote the day and time in his notebook. "Thank you. You've been very helpful."

"Does your asking all of these questions mean his death wasn't natural?" the man asked.

"It does look like a suspicious death." Hawke started for the door.

"He talked to a lady when he left here that day. She was sitting in a car across the street. I happened to look out the window when he walked straight across the road to the car. They didn't look happy to see one another."

Hawke turned and walked back to the man. He pulled out his notebook. "Can you tell me what kind of car and what the woman looked like?"

"It was a fancy SUV. She had long silver-blonde hair in a braid."

"Thank you. This had been most helpful. Could I get your name, please?" Hawke wrote down the man's name and as he walked out of the library, started figuring out how to get back out to Imnaha for another chat with Christa Pinson.

《》《》《》

At the Alder City Police Station, Hawke walked in and asked to see Chief Browning. The receptionist picked up a phone, recited Hawke's name, and then told Hawke to go to the Chief's office.

He liked Browning. The man had been instrumental in helping Hawke discover a serial rapist in the county and bringing in his killer. The tall, thin, red head, rose from his chair and held out a hand in greeting when Hawke walked through the door.

They shook hands and Browning motioned for Hawke to have a seat. "I imagine you're here to sign your statement about the altercation at High Mountain last night?"

"Yes. I had a few things to clear up down in Eagle before I could get this way. Is the man still in custody?"

Browning shook his head. "He seems to be someone with money. His lawyer persuaded Judge Vicker that Harry Croft was an upstanding citizen and had just had one too many drinks with his buddies."

Hawke snorted. "He's an arrogant ass who should still be in jail for assaulting Desiree and me." Then the last name struck him. "Did you say Croft?"

Browning tossed a folder toward Hawke. "Yes, his sister is part of your cold case. He claimed he and his friends came to the county to visit his sister and take in the rodeo."

Hawke studied the chief before pulling the folder

closer and opening the file. The man's sister was Christa Pinson. This was the Harry who'd bullied Evan. And whose wedding Christa had been at while her husband was being killed.

"He's staying with his sister until the rodeo? That's two weeks away. Why would he come and stay that long?" Hawke's mind was spinning with why the man was here. "Did he say when he arrived?"

"Not really. He was vague on did we mean to the pub or actually in the county?"

Hawke glanced up and could see that Browning hadn't liked the man either.

"Interesting. He could be connected to my cold cases and the current homicide." Hawke needed to get out to the Pinson ranch. But first, he had to look at the information on the flash drive he'd collected from the crime scene.

"If you hand me my statement, I'll get it signed and take off. I have information to look into."

Browning picked up his phone and asked someone to bring in a file. Once it arrived, Hawke signed and thanked Browning for his information.

"Let us know if you need help with anything."

"I will." Hawke was glad that in the county, because there were so few law enforcement officers, the city, county, and state police worked well together.

Out in his vehicle, Hawke drove through the Shake Shack, ordered a chocolate shake, and then parked on a side street with the windows down. He opened his laptop, turned it on, and inserted the flash drive.

Hawke spent the next hour reading the information that Lucas had compiled. Most of it was conjecture, but he had honed in on the people who had Hawke's attention. Ford and Christa Pinson, and Harry Croft. Wendy wasn't in any of Lucas's findings.

«»«»«»

It was late afternoon. Hawke decided to wait until the morning to head out to Imnaha and the Pinson Ranch. If he was lucky there might be some more forensic reports in that would help him come up with reasons to go out there and not just look like he was harassing the family, especially now that he knew Harry Croft was staying at the ranch.

He went on up to Wallowa Lake and checked boaters and fishermen for licenses and asked how the fishing was. Standing on the dock, after talking with a family in a boat, he stared up at the mountains. He would have much rather been up there checking anglers than down here. But until he figured out who had killed Lucas Brazo, he would stay down here digging up information.

It was time to call it a day. He slid into his vehicle, radioed he was off duty, and headed toward Prairie Creek and home.

His phone buzzed. He didn't know the number and pulled over in a wide spot to answer.

"Hawke."

"It's Wendy. I found out where the dogs were."

"Where?"

"Dougie Jones. His mom said he was going around to the neighbors looking for jobs. You know, like mowing lawns, pulling weeds, that kind of thing. Lucas asked him to watch the dogs because he wasn't feeling well. When Dougie asked his mom, she said, he had to bring them to their house and take them back in the morning, not whenever Lucas decided to want them in the middle of the night."

Hawke thought about this. Had it really happened or had Wendy concocted the story and the woman would go along? The best way to find out would be to talk to the boy.

"Okay, thank you. Where does Dougie live?" Hawke asked.

"They are two doors down on the opposite side of Lucas's trailer," Wendy said.

"Thanks, I'll swing by in the morning and talk to him." Hawke ended the call, pulled back on the road, and headed toward Eagle. He wasn't going to wait until morning. He wanted to make sure he received the exact information.

Hawke parked in his usual spot at the mobile home park and walked to the house two houses down on the right from Lucas's house.

He knocked on the door and stepped back when a boy of about ten answered. "Wow, are you a real cop?"

Hawke smiled and nodded. "Oregon State Trooper Hawke. Are you Dougie?"

The boy's brow furrowed and he took a step back. "Yeah? Why?"

"I heard you took care of Lucas Brazo's dogs the other night."

"I did and I didn't get paid cause he died." The boy's suspicious gaze turned angry.

"What did he say he'd pay you?" Hawke asked.

"Twenty bucks. But when I put the dogs in his house, he was asleep so I figured I'd get the money later."

"What time did you take the dogs to his house?" Hawke asked.

"Before mom went to work. I have to be here to watch Joey while she's at work in the summer."

"What time does your mom go to work?"

"She leaves at eight to be there before the store opens at eight-thirty." Dougie glanced over his shoulder. "She's taking a bath right now."

"How much before eight did you take the dogs over?" Hawke asked, wondering if the boy was worried his mother would disapprove of him answering the questions.

"Seven-forty-five. His house stunk! Mom said it was because he was a big man and didn't clean the house or himself well."

Hawke held back the smile that twitched his lips. "How did you get the dogs?"

"I knocked on his door to see if he had any chores, he wanted me to do. It's how I make money to help mom. He said I could take care of his dogs cuz he didn't feel very well. I asked when he wanted them back and he said in the morning. Mom said I could keep them overnight." The boy grinned. "It was fun having the dogs to play with and they slept on my bed. Joey liked Squirt, so I let him sleep with her."

"Did you take the dogs outside after you brought them home?" Hawke wondered if someone had been lurking about the house.

"Yeah, Mom had me take them out on leashes before we went to bed. She was afraid they'd take off or try to get in Mr. Brazo's house."

"Did you see anything when you were out walking the dogs?" Hawke asked.

"I saw someone come through the gate and then duck into the shadow along the fence." He shrugged.

"Do you see that a lot?" Hawke asked, wondering if there was someone in the court dealing drugs.

"Now and then. Usually, it's a man going to Mrs. Popular's house." The boy grinned.

Hawke raised an eyebrow. "Is that really the person's name?"

"No, it's what my mom calls her. I don't know what her name is but she gets lots of men callers and sometimes there is a lot of noise that goes on when they are there." The boy raised his face, howling and then panting. "I think she has a dog in there that gets riled up when she gets visitors. But I've never seen her with it."

A chuckle tickled Hawke's throat. It was evident to him that Mrs. Popular was either a sex-driven woman or she was making money by selling herself. Not his problem at the moment. "Did you go near Lucas's house when you had the dogs out?"

"We made a circle of the park and I went back in the house." Dougie waved his arm to show he had walked around in front of all the homes inside the park.

"Did you see anything at Lucas's house when you walked by?" Hawke had his notepad out writing down about seeing someone walk in the gate.

"No. His lights were off and the dogs didn't try to go in."

"Dougie, who are you talking to?" A short woman with wet dark hair walked up to the door. "What do you want officer?"

Hawke touched the brim of his hat. "Ma'am, I'm State Trooper Hawke. Dougie has been explaining that he had Lucas's dogs the night of the man's death."

"Why do you need to know that?" She narrowed her eyes and put a protective arm around her son.

"I was just wondering where they had been when Wendy cleaned all the bottles out of his house and then they were with him when I discovered his body. Dougie has done a fine job of explaining things to me." He smiled at the boy and then returned his attention to the mother. "Did you hear or see anything that night?"

"When I went to bed, I saw a light bobbing between the trailers opposite of us."

Hawke shifted to look across the way. "How were they bobbing between?"

"Like someone with a flashlight was walking along the fence behind them. You know, like they were headed to the gate." She pointed to the gate.

"How long after Dougie took the dogs out was that?" Hawke asked.

"Ten, maybe fifteen minutes." She shrugged.

"Thank you both for your information." Hawke pulled out his wallet and handed the boy a twenty. "You did a service and should be paid."

Dougie's face lit up as he grasped the bill. "Thank you! Mom said I'd just have to chalk it up to a good deed." He turned to his mom. "Look!"

"Thank you, Trooper, that wasn't necessary."

"When someone does a good job, they deserve to be paid." He touched his hat and walked back to his vehicle. Someone had been in Lucas's trailer and most likely left the bottle of booze that killed him.

Chapter Twenty-two

Saturday, Hawke dressed for work, fed his animals, and settled into his vehicle. Once he was on the highway headed toward Alder, he called dispatch to let them know he was on duty. When he'd returned home last night, there had been an email from Sergeant Spruel with the name of the veterinarian Christa used and a report from forensics that they weren't able to get a decent image of the man in the photo holding a gun. They were however positive it was a man. Hawke had responded asking if they could determine his size.

At the moment he had two men in his sights. One was tall and lanky, the other average height and stocky. A thought struck him. He hadn't asked Dougie about the size of the person he'd seen lurking in the shadows the night of Lucas's death.

He didn't have a phone number for the boy so he'd called Wendy and asked her to talk to Dougie about the person he saw enter the park that night. "Get a description if you can."

Hawke pulled off the highway onto Fish Hatchery Road. He was headed to Dr. Ashley's Vet clinic. Spruel had determined she was the vet who worked on the Pinson animals.

The clinic had just opened when he walked through the door.

"Hawke, what brings you here so early in the morning? Nothing wrong with your animals I hope." Dr. Ashley walked out of the back carrying a box of bandages.

"Nothing wrong with my guys, thanks. I need to know about one of your customers." He held his hat in his hand and drew his notebook out of his pocket.

"Who?" Dr. Ashley set the box down and leaned her back against the counter. Her arms crossed, which didn't bode well for what he wanted to ask.

"I understand you doctor the Pinson animals."
She nodded.

"Have they ever had a need for xylazine?" Hawke asked.

She uncrossed her arms and studied him. "What are you getting at?"

"I need to know if anyone in that household could get their hands on the drug." He held up a hand. "This has to do with an investigation I'm on."

"Christa brought in one of her older mares for an injection last week. She has tried to get me to give her some so she doesn't always have to bring in her horse. But it's a controlled substance and I have to keep track of every vial I have." Dr. Ashley recrossed her arms and stared at him.

"Was she ever left alone with the drug?" He poised the pen over his book.

The woman's nostrils flared. "Christa went to college to be a vet but never took the final exams to become one. She knows all the rules and would never take something that could get me in trouble."

"Okay. Who came with her?"

Dr. Ashley stared at him for several seconds and said, "Ford."

"Was he ever left alone where he could get hold of the drug?" Hawke studied her as she thought.

"Christa asked me a question about the medicine and then one of her other horses. We walked to the office and I asked my technician to clean up the area. Ford was standing at the mare's head petting her when we walked out."

"Who was the technician?" Hawke asked.

"Brittney. She works well with the animals and keeps the areas clean." Dr. Ashley narrowed her eyes. "I hope you don't suspect her of anything."

He held up his hands, one holding his hat and pen, the other his notebook. "I just want to talk to her and see what Ford did after you left."

"She doesn't work on Saturdays. You'll have to catch up to her at home." She walked around to the back side of the counter and started tapping on the keyboard. She wrote on a sticky note and handed it to Hawke. "Here's her address."

"Thanks." He motioned to the computer. "Any chance you could look and see if you're missing any xylazine?"

Muttering under her breath, the veterinarian tapped on the keyboard. Her fingers stopped moving and she stared at the screen.

"Something wrong?" he asked.

"We're missing a fifty-milliliter vial."

Hawke walked out of the clinic with a smile on his face. If Brittney could put Ford anywhere near the drugs, he would have Lucas's and most likely Chang and Evan's killer.

《》《》《》

Brittney lived in Alder in a small older house on the edge of the city park. Hawke parked in front of the house. A compact car sat on the grassy drive beside the house. That was a good sign she would be home.

Hawke stepped out of his vehicle and the front door opened. The young woman he'd talked to while looking for who killed Reverend Betz, stood on the small porch her eyes wide and her face pale.

"Hi, Brittney. Do you remember me?" he asked.

She nodded. "I haven't done anything wrong. Why are you here?"

"I need to ask you some questions about the last time the Pinsons were at the vet clinic."

Brittney glanced around at her neighboring houses and ushered him inside. "I can't tell you much."

Hawke stepped into the small living room of the 1950s home. The original wood floors thumped under his boots.

Brittney remained by the door.

Hawke faced her. "I visited with Dr. Ashley and she said that she and Mrs. Pinson went into the office and Mr. Pinson was with the horse while you were cleaning up." He pulled out his notebook.

She nodded. "I was putting Dr. Ashley's instruments away and checking the horse's breathing."

"What did Mr. Pinson do while you were cleaning up?" Hawke asked.

"He stood by Coco's head, petting her and talking to her." She took a couple of steps away from the door. "He helped me carry the instruments and things into the back where I clean them."

"Did Dr. Ashley use all of the medicine in the vial on the horse?"

Her eyes widened. "No! If she'd used a whole vial, it could have killed Coco. It was just enough to help alleviate her pain."

"What did you do with the leftover medicine?"

Brittney stared at him. Hawke could see her mentally going through her movements that day. "I don't remember putting it back in the cupboard. Did you ask Dr. Ashley if she did?"

"Did you carry it in from where you worked on the horse?" Hawke asked.

Again, she stared and slowly shook her head. "I don't remember picking it up. Dr. Ashley must have. Sometimes she picks up the leftover controlled drugs and puts them in her pocket to keep anyone from taking it."

"What about Mr. Pinson? Was he near where the drug was sitting?" Hawke's fingers itched to write down that Ford had access to the drug and most likely took it.

"The cart with all the instruments, medicine, and stuff we used was not far from the horse's shoulder. He could have reached over and taken the vial when I was turned or bent over picking something up. But why would he want the drug?" She studied Hawke.

"That's a good question. One I plan on asking him. Thank you for your help." Hawke closed his notebook and shoved it in his shirt pocket.

Brittney stepped back to the door and opened it. She smiled timidly. "I'm sorry I wasn't friendly when you arrived."

He smiled and touched his hat. "That's okay, lots of people get nervous when a police officer wants to talk to them. Dr. Ashley said you are doing good work. I'm happy for you." He walked out of the house grinning. The young woman's mouth dropped open at his last words. He hadn't wanted to badger victims of Reverend Betz but he'd had to find his killer for the sake of justice.

«»«»«»

Hawke drove to Imnaha and the Pinson Ranch. Everything he'd learned was bouncing around in his head. Ford had to be the killer. He'd had access to the xylazine, lived within a horse ride from where the first murder took place, wanted the wife of the man he'd killed, and could have been recognized by Professor Chang since he was a professor at the college at the same time as Ford was going to school there.

It was Dog finding the bone, and subsequently, the parts and film from the professor that stirred things up. But all justice should be served.

Hawke pulled up to the Pinson Ranch house and turned off the engine. The place was quiet except for the occasional horse snort or whinny. He stepped out and walked up to the house. He knocked on the door with the brass horse head knocker and waited.

A woman he'd not met before came to the door. "How can I help you?" she asked.

"I'd like to talk with Mr. Pinson." Hawke held his hat in his hands.

"He and Christa's brother went on a fishing trip."

"Then may I speak to Christa?" Hawke wondered if the fishing trip had been planned or was a way for the two men to be hard to track down.

"She, Fanny, and Alicia are at a horse show in Reno."

"When will any of them be back?" Hawke asked, angry that he couldn't confront them but at the same time realizing it would give him more time to dig up evidence against Ford.

"The women on Tuesday. The men, I'm not sure. They had enough food for a week." She started to close the door.

Hawke put a hand out stopping the door. "Where were they going fishing?"

"On the Snake River."

He removed his hand and strode back to his vehicle. He had a hunch he knew where they were fishing. Some place where they could keep an eye on the excavation of the professor's body if Dr. Galler and the rest hadn't found all the bones already.

The two could be in on it together. Tomorrow, he had to meet Dani for lunch, but Monday was his day off, too. He, Dot, and Dog would make another trip off Hat Point and down into Hells Canyon. He wanted to see if Harry and Ford were just fishing.

Chapter Twenty-three

Sunday morning, when Hawke hadn't heard back from Wendy about Dougie's description of the man he saw, Hawke decided to go ask the boy himself. He and Dog set off for Eagle.

At Six Pines park, they walked up to Dougie's house and Hawke knocked on the door. It was only eight and he hadn't thought about other people might be sleeping in, until Dougie's mom opened the door yawning, wearing her pajamas.

"Sorry Ma'am. I have a question to ask Dougie," Hawke said.

"It's eight o'clock on a Sunday morning. And you're not in uniform."

He smiled. "It's my day off, but I have a question that's been nagging at me." He shrugged.

"Come in, I'll start some coffee and wake Dougie up."

"Can Dog come in or do you want him to stay outside?" Hawke asked.

The woman stared at Dog sitting beside Hawke. "Is he friendly?"

"Yes, and house-trained," he added.

"He can come in." She headed toward the kitchen area.

Hawke followed with Dog on his heels. Sitting in a chair at the small kitchen table, Hawke motioned for Dog to sit. The animal's nose twitched as he sniffed the air.

The woman left the kitchen calling to Dougie. A few minutes later, the boy entered the kitchen, wearing pajamas and rubbing his eyes.

"Mom said you want to ask me something?" He sat down in a chair, his shoulders drooped and his arms crossed on the table. He appeared barely awake.

Hawke rose, poured himself a cup of coffee, and opened and closed cupboards until he found glasses. He grabbed a glass out of a cupboard and poured the boy a glass of milk. Sitting back at the table, he took a sip of his coffee and smiled.

"You said you saw someone come through the gate and go behind the trailers the night you watched Lucas's dogs. Can you describe the person to me?" Hawke pulled his notebook out of his pocket.

Dog lay down. The clicking of his nails on the floor caught Dougie's attention.

"You have a dog?" He dropped to the floor and petted Dog.

"Yeah. He likes coming with me when I'm not working." Hawke watched the boy stroke Dog's head and scratch his chest. "How tall do you think the person was?"

"In feet? I don't know."

"Did they seem tall?"

Dougie laid his head against Dog's shoulder and closed his eyes. "The fence was above his head when he walked by. But he ducked under Irene's clothesline."

Hawke was pleased with the boy's references. They could experiment with heights to discern how tall the person was. "Was the person skinny or larger?"

"You mean fat?" Dougie opened his eyes and stared at him.

"You tell me? How would you describe the build of the person?" Hawke had written what the boy had said so far in his notebook.

Dougie scrunched up his face and said, "Not skinny, but not fat. Not like Lucas. I don't know for sure. He wore a long coat that covered most of his body. I don't know if he was the size of my mom or you."

Hawke latched onto the clothing. "I know it was dark. Did the coat appear dark or light colored?"

"Dark and it was kind of stiff."

Oilcloth duster. Typically worn by a cowboy.

Hawke thought about the weather and how hot and dry it had been lately. Why would someone wear an oilcloth coat that was heavy and hot? To hide their body.

"How long did you watch the person walking?" Hawke asked, jotting down the last things Dougie had said and his own thoughts.

"From the gate until I couldn't see him when he went behind Mrs. Popular's trailer." Dougie sat back up in the chair one hand on his glass of milk and the other on Dog's head.

"Can you show me how the person walked?"

The boy stared at him for a moment and stood. He walked to the counter and back to the table. It looked like how the boy normally walked.

His mom entered the kitchen. "What are you doing?"

"He had me walk across the room," Dougie said, petting Dog.

"Dougie, watch me walk across the room." Hawke stood and walked to the kitchen door, then the counter, and back to the table. "Did it look like that?"

The boy shook his head. "No, not really."

"Would you walk to the counter and then back to the door, please," Hawke asked Dougie's mother.

She looked at him with a perplexed expression but did as she was asked.

"That's what the person walked like!" Dougie said loudly.

Hawke had a feeling he needed to do more digging. "Thank you. Can you get dressed? I want to do some experiments outside to determine the height of the person."

Dougie shot to his feet and headed to the door, he stopped and swung around. "Can Dog help us?"

"Yes, he'll help us," Hawke said.

"Good!"

When the boy left the room, his mother studied Hawke. "What is he going to do?"

"Help me determine the height of the person he saw walking in the shadows the night Lucas was killed."

Her hands clutched together in front of her sternum. "Will this put my boy in danger?"

"No one needs to know he is helping me."

She shook her head. "Everyone will know if he is seen talking to you and then you accuse someone."

"All he has to do is stand where he was standing that night and tell me what he sees. He won't be identifying any person, only their size, and that could be half of the population of Wallowa County." Hawke stood when Dougie burst into the room towing a younger boy behind him.

"Can Joey help?" Dougie asked.

"Sure." Hawke led the way out of the trailer and stopped in the area in front of the trailer. "You, Joey, and Dog stand where you were the night you saw the person. I'm going to grab a walkie-talkie from my pickup. You run get it from me at the gate then go back to your brother and Dog."

"Come, Dog," Dougie said as Hawke walked away.

He turned and made the motion for stay. Dog walked back to the boys and stayed. Hawke continued to his vehicle and found the set of walkie-talkies he and Kitree had played with the last time they had gone on a trail ride.

Back at the gate, Dougie ran toward him. Hawke showed the boy how to make the radio work. "I'm going to walk along the fence. You tell me if I need to be closer to the fence or farther away. That will help me determine the height of the person."

Dougie nodded and ran back to Joey and Dog. The younger boy knelt on the ground by dog, hugging him around the neck.

Hawke began walking and his radio crackled. "Closer to the fence," came Dougie's voice.

He moved closer.

"There!" the boy shouted. Hawke didn't need the

224

radio to hear him.

Hawke continued along the fence, going behind the trailers. He saw why the boy said the person had to duck under the clothesline. It ran from the fence to the back of the Irene's mobile home. He ducked and asked Dougie, "Am I bending more or less than the person did?"

"More."

That meant the person was shorter than his six feet. But tall enough to have to duck under the clothesline. He estimated the height of the line at five foot eight inches.

He continued on behind the trailers until he came to the back of Lucas's trailer. Both doors were on the front side of the trailer. The person would have to walk into the open to go through a door. But he noticed that a bucket was turned upside down under the bedroom window. He walked over and found the screen lying on the ground. The window was shut.

Reaching up, pressing his palms against the window, he pushed up. The window opened an inch. Hawke slid his fingers under the window and shoved it all the way up. It was large enough for a person with smaller shoulders than his to get into the house.

He walked around and was met at the door to the trailer by the boys and Dog.

"Do you need more help?" Dougie asked.

Hawke handed the other radio to Joey. "No, Dog and I are good. Thank you for the help. You can keep the walkie-talkies."

Joey's bottom lip stuck out. "I'd rather have the dog."

Hawke smiled. "Sorry. Dog's been with me too

long. He wouldn't make you a good friend."

Dougie took Joey's hand. "Come on. You know what Mom said. We can't have a dog until we can figure out how to buy the food for him."

"Thanks for your help," Hawke said, and he and Dog entered the trailer. Dog stopped just inside the door and scanned the area.

"I know you smell the ankle biters but they aren't here. You can wait or follow, it's up to you." Hawke continued through the living room and down the hall to the bedroom. Forensics had gone through the room but they hadn't realized someone might have come through the window. He doubted there would be prints because someone coming to leave a bottle of booze laced with xylazine would be wearing gloves.

He hoped to find something else. And he did. There was hair stuck in the aluminum casing of the window sash. Short, dark curly hair with some gray.

Chapter Twenty-four

After dropping the evidence bag with hair off at the Winslow OSP office to be transported to the lab in Pendleton, Hawke and Dog headed to the airport between Alder and Prairie Creek to take Dani to lunch.

Hawke stood in front of the office with Hector Ramirez the manager or the FBO of the airstrip.

"Dani radioed in for fuel and a spot to tie down for a few hours," Hector said, chewing on the end of an unlit cigar. "Tell her to use her usual spot."

"I'll let her know." Hawke watched as Dani taxied her plane to a stop in front of the office. The small airport only handled private aircraft and had a mechanic along with Hector as the only people other than plane owners who hung out there.

The plane stopped and Dani climbed out. Hawke hurried out to the plane to assist with opening the back door. A man, a woman, and two kids about eight and ten climbed out. Hawke climbed in the back and handed out suitcases and backpacks. As he climbed back out, he watched Dani shake hands with the family before they walked toward the parking lot.

He walked over to Dani, hugged her, and said, "Hector said to tie up at your usual spot after you fuel."

"Thanks. Meet you at the fuel tank." She climbed back into the plane and taxied over to the fuel tanks.

Hawke jogged over and placed the chocks behind and in front of the wheels as Dani turned off the engine and climbed out.

"Thanks for coming," she said, grasping the fueling hose and dragging it out to the plane.

"It's Sunday and I'm not working. No way would I miss getting to see you." He stood beside the fuel tank.

Dani walked over, flipped the switch, and gave him a hug. "Have you and Dog been staying out of trouble?"

"I have a lot to tell you when we eat lunch," he said.

They finished fueling the plane, and Dani taxied it over to a spot with tie-downs. Hawke put the chocks at the tires again and tied it down as Dani went in to pay for the fuel.

They met at the pickup and loaded up.

"Where do you want to eat?" Hawke asked.

"How about Olive's? I don't feel like all the noise that will be at High Mountain and I don't want to sit in the pickup and eat if we order from the Shake Shack."

"Olive's it is," Hawke said, leaving the airport and heading toward Alder.

At Olive's, Hawke and Dani took a seat in the corner. Olive, the owner and a Nez Perce descendent, handed them menus. "What are you drinking today?"

"Iced tea for me, with lemon," Dani said.

"Same, no lemon," Hawke said.

"I'll go grab those while you decide what you'd like." The woman strode over to the counter and the drinks.

When she returned with their drinks, Hawke ordered a cheeseburger with pickle to go and a plain burger for himself. Dani ordered a Rueben and fancy fries. Once Olive left with the order, Dani asked, "What's going on with your cold cases?"

Hawke filled her in on what he'd learned so far and that he had his suspicions of who the killer might be.

"Who?" she asked in a low voice, leaning over the table toward him.

He shook his head. "Too many people in here to say. Someone might hear and say something."

"Is it someone you suspected from the beginning?" she asked.

"Yeah. If the results on the hair I found come back, how I think they will, I've been on the right track all along." Hawke sipped his tea and asked. "How's things up at the lodge?"

"Good! Kitree has started taking families out on trail rides. I won't let her go with all adults, especially if they are all males."

Hawke's face heated thinking what could happen to the girl if a group of men who had no morals went on a ride with her. "I'm glad you are thinking that way. And the family trips don't usually stay out too long."

"Yeah. But it makes her feel important to take a family now and then. I had a hard time talking Sage into letting Kitree do it. She's so protective." Dani's tone held concern for both the child and the woman.

Hawke understood both the women's concerns.

Sage had lost her biological daughter to illness and had become overprotective of her adopted daughter. But Kitree was now thirteen and more intelligent than most people three times her age.

"It will be hard for Sage to allow Kitree the freedom to learn and become an adult."

Dani smiled and put a hand on his arm. "Yes."

Olive walked up with their food, placing it on the table. She smiled at them. "Enjoy."

"Thank you," Hawke said, pulling out several napkins and wrapping Dog's cheeseburger up before he picked up his hamburger and bit into it.

They were quiet for several minutes as they ate half of their sandwiches.

"Are you still able to get off next weekend to attend the powwow?" Hawke asked.

Dani took a drink and nodded. "Yes. We will only have two families for the weekend and this coming week it is a horse riding group who will be staying and taking day trips on their own horses."

Hawke smiled. "Good, then you can relax and enjoy the dances." He cleared his throat. "Mom made you a ribbon skirt to go with the ribbon shirt she made me." He knew Dani was interested in their heritage but was hesitant to jump in too quickly having been kept from it by her parents.

Her face lit up. "Really? She made me a skirt?"

Hawke nodded. "She wanted to know if you would like one. I said I thought so."

Tears glittered in Dani's eyes. "I've never owned clothing that is a part of my culture."

"Mom was excited to make it for you. She has waited a long time for her children to embrace our culture."

"I'm not your mom's child," Dani said, a bit of sorrow in her voice.

"Everyone is family to my mom. Look at all the children she's cared for over the years while their parents worked hard to make a better life for them. She considers anyone she's ever talked to as part of her family."

"I can see that." Dani smiled. "I'm glad I know her." She picked up her iced tea. "And you."

Hawke's chest swelled with love and admiration for the strong women in his life.

They finished their meal and took Dog's cheeseburger out to him. Three bites and the burger disappeared.

"That was quick," Hawke said. "Do you have time for a drive or do you want to go home for a couple of hours?"

Dani glanced at her watch. "I have one hour until the family I'm flying in arrives." She sighed. "And I should go over my aircraft before they arrive."

"Dog and I can hang out with you while you do that." Hawke wished she were staying all week until the powwow but he knew her sense of work and responsibility were as strong in her as they were in him.

"That's nice, but you don't need to. I'll be busy checking things and won't really be able to visit."

He parked where he'd parked to pick her up by the fuel tank. "Okay. If you're good, then I'll pack some food and head to Hat Point to ride down into the Snake and see if I can find some people of interest who are supposed to be fishing."

Dani grinned. "I could tell you were itching to be

somewhere."

He wasn't sure if that pleased him or irritated him. He was pleased she realized he wanted to be after Ford and Harry, but it irritated him that she so easily sent him on his way. *You can't have it both ways*.

"It wasn't that obvious, was it?" he asked, as they both exited the pickup and met at the front of the vehicle.

"Hey, we are both work-driven individuals. And the best part is we understand that. I'd love to stay with you longer, but I need to make sure everyone, workers and clients, are doing okay at the lodge. You have a double cold case and an open murder you want to solve. You won't be able to relax until you do."

He wrapped his arms around her and kissed her. She was his equal in all ways. "Thank you for understanding. Let me know when you're flying out on Friday. I'll be here."

"I plan to be here by four on Friday. I know things are going on at the powwow on Friday but I can't get away any earlier." She peered into his eyes and he saw she meant she wished she could get away earlier.

"We'll be here to pick you up on Friday." Another kiss and they parted. Dani strode off to her plane and Hawke to his vehicle.

"Let's go load up Dot and head for Hat Point." It was light long enough that they could make it halfway down to the river before dark. That would give him more time tomorrow to search the river for Ford and Harry.

Chapter Twenty-five

The sun was barely coming over the top of the canyon on the east side of the river when Hawke swung up on Dot's back. They'd made camp last night just as the moon rose high enough to give him light to see the flat surface he used to roll out his sleeping bag. Dot had stood with his back legs downhill and his front uphill munching on grass all night.

Now they made their way down to the area at Sluice Creek where they'd found the professor's bones. Dog loped ahead and then circled back several times. It was almost as if he was trying to hurry Dot along. The horse was picking his way down the steep slope with care.

While Hawke was anxious to get down along the river to look for the men, he understood the need to be careful descending the canyon. As they drew closer and he could see the airstrip on the flat above the river, he noticed all the tents from the dig site were gone. There were marks in the ground that revealed there had been multiple tents and traffic paths were smashed in the grass. If no one knew about the discovery of bones here it would just look like several different parties had camped in that location.

Moving down the canyon wall, Hawke scanned up and down the river and the canyon to see if anyone was in the area. That's when he spotted a camouflage tent tucked into the edge of the brush and trees on the south side of Sluice Creek.

Why would anyone put their tent in with poison ivy and hawthorn trees? He veered to the left, heading toward the tent.

Dog stopped, his tail quivered, and he peered up the canyon.

Hawke drew Dot to a stop and stared. "What do you see, Dog?" he asked quietly. "Is it that cougar?"

Scanning the side of the canyon, Hawke studied all the places a cougar might be hiding. He didn't see any sign of the tawny-colored animal. But he saw a flash of blue in the green of the bushes. "Is someone up there?" he asked Dog. The animal's hackles were up and quivering.

"Let's go investigate." Not wanting to leave Dot alone for someone to ride away on, he dismounted and led the animal uphill in the direction he'd seen the movement of blue clothing.

It took fifteen minutes to get up to the area. He found the spot where the person had entered the brush. The limbs were bent inward and the ground revealed the print of a boot. He continued through the trees and brush, avoiding the poison ivy that the person they were following plowed right through. Using the broken limbs and smashed grass and plants, Hawke followed the person's trail to the other side of the creek.

Once on the other side, he spotted a man hurrying down the side of the canyon toward the river. He had no idea who it could be but it was evident the person had been trying to not be seen. Hawke swung up into the saddle and they trotted after the man.

Dog caught up to the man first. He snarled and the man spun from where he was scratching at his legs.

Hawke had never seen the man before. "Morning," he said.

The man's face was full of whiskers and dirty. His fingers were crooked with large joints. "Could be morning. What you doin' sneakin' up of a person like that?"

"I wasn't sneaking. Is that tent in the trees yours?" Hawke asked.

"What's it to you?" The man scratched and then pulled a jar out of his pocket and started slathering its contents onto his legs.

"Just wondered why you were hanging around where there had been a dig going on less than a week ago." Hawke dismounted, pulled out a bottle of water, and took a drink.

"I don't know nothin' about a dig. I'm up here spending some alone time. Don't get enough of it at home." The man's eyes darted in all directions as he talked.

"Did you happen to see a couple of men dressed like cowboys down here fishing?" Hawke asked.

"Maybe, why?" The man studied him.

"They're friends and they told me I might catch up with them. Are they upriver or down?" Hawke swept his gaze up and down the river, then back to the man.

"They were downriver."

"Thanks," Hawke said, squeezing with his knees to urge Dot to start walking.

"But one of them was up here yesterday digging around like there might be something worthwhile here. Don't know if he found anything or not."

Hawke swung Dot around and faced the man. "What did he look like?"

"I stayed away and watched. Didn't see his face. I watched him and followed him back to where the two were camped."

"Was he tall, short, thin, fat?" Hawke asked.

"Built like a basketball player. But not nearly as athletic." The man nodded at his last statement.

"Thanks. What's your name?" Hawke wasn't going to pull his notebook out. He knew if this man thought he was law enforcement, he'd clam up.

The man squinted. "Ain't none of your business."

"Okay. Thanks." He wasn't going to push it. Just knowing Harry Croft had been interested in something along Sluice Creek gave him information that fell into what he'd been thinking.

Where the ground wasn't too rocky or steep, Hawke would urge Dot into a jog to cover more ground quicker. He only had today to catch up to the men and ask them questions. He had to be back to work tomorrow.

About a mile downriver, he found the men sitting on rocks fishing in a calm inlet just below a rapid. As he rode up, Ford watched him. The man's eyes were shaded by the brim of his hat. He said something to Harry and the man stood, facing Hawke's approach.

"Hey, you're the guy who got me arrested!" Harry

exclaimed. "Why are you following me?"

Hawke let his gaze travel to Ford. "I was curious why the two of you picked this of all places to go fishing."

"What does it matter to you where we go fishing?" Harry asked, clearly keeping the attention on himself.

From the corner of his eye, Hawke watched Ford reel in his pole. "Surely you know that this is where Christa's first husband was killed."

Harry swung toward Ford. "What is he talking about? Evan's death was an accident."

"No, it wasn't. We found another body from the same time as Evan's death. With the bones was an undeveloped roll of film. It shows someone hitting Evan in the head and tossing his body in the river." Hawke glanced back and forth between the two men.

"Are you here harassing us because you think one of us killed him?" Harry asked.

Hawke shrugged. "I just find it a bit of a coincidence that you two would come here of all places to fish and one of you was looking for something up Sluice Creek yesterday."

Ford stood up. "How the hell did you know that? Have you been following us this whole time?"

Hawke smiled. "I have my ways. Does this mean you aren't going to deny it?"

"I was just curious about where they dug and what they were looking for." Ford picked up a creel and motioned to Harry. "Grab the cooler. We might as well go back. The fish haven't been biting."

"Need help getting out of here?" Hawke asked, wondering how they got down in the canyon. There hadn't been a ranch vehicle parked at Hat Point.

"We're good," Harry said, picking up the cooler and a lever action rifle.

The gun had the well-worn wood stock of a much-used and loved weapon. The thought this could be the rifle that was used to strike Evan ran through Hawke's mind. But he couldn't take the gun. He'd need a warrant and some kind of evidence.

Hawke sat on Dot watching the men walk downstream. When they were out of sight around a bend in the river, he turned Dot and headed back the way he'd come. He knew Harry owned a rifle unless it belonged to Ford or the ranch. He'd have to come up with evidence to get a warrant. As he rode, he thought about the conversation. It sounded as if Ford were the one looking around Sluice Creek. But the man had said the person looked like a basketball player. That would have been Harry. Had they both been there and only Ford confessed to being there?

None of this was making any sense. Hawke tumbled everything he knew around in his head as he, Dot, and Dog headed out of the canyon and back to Hat Point.

《》《》《》

Tuesday morning, Hawke went into the office in Winslow and opened up his computer to add in the information he found over the weekend and to see if any new reports had come back from forensics. As he sat down at the computer his phone buzzed. The number was familiar but he couldn't remember who it was.

"Hawke," he answered.

"It's Fanny Pinson. Remember our discussion about my DNA not matching Ford and wondering if I am Evan Nestor's child?"

"Yes."

"I contacted the people who matched my DNA and I'm not related to him either. But they did match me to someone else I've never heard of. I wondered if it would help your investigation into Evan's death."

"You're saying that neither of the men your mother has been married to is your father?" Hawke wanted to make sure he was clear on that subject.

"Correct. Unless she had a marriage in between the two. I couldn't find that out." She sounded disappointed.

"But you did match someone else? Give me the name and I'll see what I can find out."

"Weston Haston. When I Google him, it comes up some wealthy man in Portland. I can't believe if he was wealthy that mom wouldn't have gone after him for child support."

"That sounds like you think your mom is money-hungry?" Hawke posed it as a question.

"She would do anything to be rich and keep all her horses." The woman didn't sound bitter only disappointed.

"Let me do some digging. Have you brought this up to your mom?"

"No. I'm still trying to figure out when I was conceived and if Evan knew or if Ford thinks I'm Evan's." She paused and let out a breath. "I honestly don't know what to think given my mother has kept my biological father a secret from me. What else hasn't she told me? I'm ready to take Alicia and start over in another state."

"Can you do that? Start over? What about Alicia's

father?"

"He died in a car crash when Alicia was three. That's when we moved in with Ford and Mom. I wasn't ready to find a husband and the company I worked for was downsizing." There was a pause. "I wanted to get away from all the memories and I wasn't ready to find another husband. I don't care what my mom says or did, I wasn't ready to replace my husband with another one. I wanted the dead one back."

Hawke was learning a lot from this conversation and just let the woman go on.

"I loved my husband and had expected to spend the rest of my life with him and have more children with him. His lost devastated me for several months. Mom and Ford brought Alicia over here while I dealt with everything in Portland. However, unlike her and Uncle Harry, I believed in my marriage vows and loved my spouse."

Hawke sat up in his chair. "Did your uncle's marriage not last?"

"From what I've heard over the years, he got cold feet and didn't go through with the marriage."

Ideas started pinging around in Hawke's mind. There hadn't been a wedding. At least not one that Harry or most likely his sister attended the day Evan was killed.

Chapter Twenty-six

As soon as Hawke ended the call with Fanny, he looked up Weston Haston. He was indeed a rich man who owned one of the largest outdoor retail stores in the Pacific Northwest. Hawke then dug into DMV records to find an address and then a phone number for the man.

When he had that information written in his notebook, he looked up an address and phone number for Harry and Christa's parents. He would rather ask them about Harry's wedding than the siblings. It was apparent by their lack of saying the wedding never took place that they were hiding something.

"What are you banging away on the keyboard about?" Ivy asked as she sat down at the computer to his right.

"Some new leads in my cold cases." He glanced over. "What are you catching up on?"

"Reports from yesterday. I had a car theft and vandalism. Not together. But they were both done by

Paty Jager

teenagers. They really need to find something more for teenagers to do in this county. They get into mischief because they're bored."

Hawke agreed and directed his attention to the monitor when the Croft's information came up. The father had passed away twenty years earlier. However, the wife, Christa and Harry's mother, still remained in their home. He dialed the number and introduced himself.

"Why would a State Trooper need to know about Harry's wedding?" Mrs. Croft asked.

"We're just checking up on a cold case. The suspects say they were at his wedding." Hawke didn't want to implicate her children or he might not get the information.

"The date was June sixteenth. However, the wedding didn't happen. It was called off the night before at the rehearsal and we contacted everyone on the invitation list to let them know it wasn't happening. My husband went to the church and the few who turned up he sent home. If someone is using my son's wedding as an alibi, they are guilty."

Hawke smiled. "Thank you, Mrs. Croft. This is very helpful. Have a good day."

"Good news?" Ivy asked.

"Yeah, two of my suspects in the cold cases don't have alibis. At least not the one they gave me." He tapped a pen on the phone number for Weston Haston. Might as well see what he had to say.

Hawke dialed the number.

"This is the office of Haston Outdoor Wear. How may I help you?" a young man's voice asked.

"Hello. I'm Senior Trooper Hawke with the

Oregon State Police. I have some questions for Mr. Haston. How might I get a hold of him?"

"You need to contact his lawyer." He recited a legal firm and a phone number.

"It isn't anything that warrants a lawyer. I want to ask him about a person he knows. You know, to get some background on someone," he said before she hung up on him.

"What is the name of the person? I'll see if he is available to speak to you."

"I'd rather wait on the name and judge his reaction. Please, just ask if he will speak with me."

Violin music whined in his ear as he waited.

"Trooper Hawke, who is it you want to talk to me about?" a smooth, deep voice asked.

"Mr. Haston, do you remember Christa Croft, or she may have gone by her married name of Christa Nestor?" Hawke said.

"Of all the names from my past I hadn't expected to hear that one. She went by Christa Nestor when I met her. Her husband had died and she was a wreck. I gave her a job and she would have moved up the ladder quickly but she made the mistake of thinking she could become my wife. Don't get me wrong, I wasn't married at the time, but I wasn't looking for a wife. I was growing my business and knew I didn't have the time to give to a wife or children. But when she tried to blackmail me into marrying her—that was it. I fired her and told her she had better not try to get a cent out of me for sexual harassment or anything else or I'd have the police look into her husband's death."

Hawke had been writing down what the man said. His pen stopped and he asked, "What did you know about her husband's death?"

"Nothing concrete, but I had the money to have someone look into it and she knew that."

"You were astute to have thought she had something to do with his death. That's what I'm looking into. Her husband's death wasn't an accident. I've found evidence that proves it was murder. I'm trying to piece together if she was behind it."

"Ha! I knew my instincts were right about her."

The triumphant proclamation made Hawke smile. He liked the man. It wasn't his place but he wanted to ask. "Do you have a family now?"

"A wife and two boys. They're in college. Why?"

"Just curious."

"There was more in your asking than just being curious. Spit it out."

"While working on this case I've met someone who believes she is your daughter. And I believe you and she might get along. She has a daughter and needs to start a new life."

The man was quiet for several seconds before he asked, "Did Christa and I have a child?"

"Yes. Through DNA Fanny discovered that neither Evan Nestor nor Christa's current husband were her father. She is struggling right now and could use solid judgment to help her."

"Tell her to call me on this number." Haston recited a cell phone number. "I'd like to meet her and the daughter."

"I will let her know." Hawke ended the call feeling as if he'd made a major breakthrough for the case and Fanny.

"What was that all about?" Ivy asked.

"You'll know when it can come out. I'm going to get Spruel up to speed and see how I can get some warrants." Hawke stood and walked across the room and into Spruel's office.

"How goes the cold cases?" he asked.

"Getting warmer. The alibi for the brother and sister doesn't hold up. There wasn't a wedding. Harry backed out the night before. And someone in Christa's past felt she had something to do with her husband's death. She appears to have been a widow who wanted to marry rich. From the description of the person the boy saw sneaking into Six Pines the night Lucas Brazo died, I think it was Christa. From the photos found with Professor Chang, we know it was a man who struck Nestor on the head and fired the rifle at the professor. I'd like to get a warrant for the Pinson financial records to see if Christa has been paying her brother all these years for killing her husband. But then we have Ford. I'm pretty sure the hair I found in the window sash in Brazo's bedroom will come back as Ford's. Which would mean he was the person in the oilcloth duster that snuck into the mobile park and left the booze."

"Is the warrant for financials all you need?" Spruel asked.

"I'd like one for all the rifles on the ranch. See if we can find any with a trace of hair or anything that might help us establish if the person and the rifle came from that ranch."

"That's a long shot given the years and the fact the blow may not have penetrated the scalp to leave any blood or tissue." Spruel studied him. "Do you have any other evidence that could get the warrants?"

"I think Ford stole a vial of xylazine from Dr.

Ashley's vet clinic. But I don't have proof. One is missing and the Pinsons did have it administered to a horse. That's it." Hawke knew in his gut that Christa was behind all of the murders. But proving it would be hard.

"Did Dr. Ashley give you the video from her security system?" Spruel asked.

"What security system?" Hawke straightened from where he'd leaned against the door jamb.

"She asked me a while back when I took our dog in if I had a suggestion for a security system. I suggested an outfit out of Lewiston and I'm sure she had it installed."

Hawke straightened. "I'm headed there now. I wonder why she didn't mention it to me when I was asking about the xylazine before."

"Could have slipped her mind since she isn't used to having it. I'll see if Lange is available this afternoon for you to talk to him about the warrants. Go get your report all in order."

Hawke took that as an invitation to leave. He headed out to his vehicle. Once he was settled behind the steering wheel, he called in that he was on duty and drove toward Alder.

《》《》《》

At Dr. Ashley's Vet Clinic, Hawke parked and studied the entrance to the building. That's when he noticed the cameras at both corners of the eaves. He wasn't sure how cameras on the outside of the building would help but exited his vehicle and entered the office.

Brittney glanced up and then froze.

"Hi, Brittney. Is Dr. Ashley in?"

"No. She's out on a call," responded the

receptionist.

"Could one of you tell me if there are more security cameras around here than the two on the front of the building?" He glanced from the receptionist to Brittney and back to the receptionist.

"Dr. Ashley had them set up throughout the building." The receptionist stood. "Brittney, answer the phone if it rings."

Hawke followed the woman with graying hair and a stern demeanor into the back room where the supplies and drugs were kept. She pointed up at a camera in the corner of the room.

"That one is so we can see who goes near the drug cabinet, even though we keep it locked." She continued out into the area where they doctored the large animals. "There are two cameras out here. One at the entrance over there and one over this door we came out." She pointed to the entrance where the animals would be unloaded and moved into the covered area and turned to point at the camera above the door they'd just exited.

"Is there any chance I can look at the video from these two cameras the day the Pinsons brought a mare in?" Hawke studied the woman.

"I'd have to call Dr. Ashley and ask."

Hawke nodded. "Let's go call her."

They walked back into the office and the woman called her employer. Hawke listened to the one-sided conversation. It appeared that the video was stored by the company that had installed the equipment.

The receptionist put the phone down and swiveled her chair to face him. "Dr. Ashley is going to call the company and have them send that day's video to the State Police."

"Can you have her request they send it to the Winslow Office, please? Otherwise, it won't be to me until I can find it at one of the other offices."

"I'll text her. She wasn't going to make the call until she finished taking care of Mr. Deerling's sheep."

"That's fine. It will still get to me quicker than if she sends it just to the State Police. It's hard to say where it would end up. Thank you for all of your help." Hawke exited the veterinary office and settled behind the steering wheel. He couldn't confront or take warrants to the Pinson Ranch until he had more information. But he could have a chat with D.A. Lange and let him know what he'd found out and what he planned to do. That might help get the warrants he needed.

Chapter Twenty-seven

Entering the old Bowlby Stone courthouse always impressed Hawke. He liked that the building that had been standing here since 1909 was made from material in the valley. He walked up the long wide staircase and turned left down the hall to the District Attorney's office.

Terri, Lange's receptionist, smiled. "It's been a while since you've visited this office."

Hawke grinned and stopped in front of her desk. "How's things going for you and John?"

"He's busy at work and the kids are great." She reached for the phone. "I don't think you came here to ask about my family."

He nodded. "I need to discuss some things with Lange. Does he have time?"

"He's taking a deposition on the phone and should be finished in about an hour."

"Okay, I'll be back in an hour." He backtracked down the stairs and walked to the back of the building and outside to cross over to the sheriff's office that sat next door to the courthouse. He punched in the entry number on the keypad and walked through the jail, surprising the deputy on duty.

"Hey, I didn't get a call you were bringing anyone in." The young officer stood up, knocking paperwork onto the floor.

"That's because I didn't bring anyone in. I'm just passing through." Hawke smiled and let himself out through the double, locked doors. He walked by Rafe's office then spun around and walked into the room.

The sheriff looked up from the papers he was reading. "Hawke, what brings you unannounced into my office?" The man leaned back in his chair and pulled the glasses from his face.

"I wondered how the dig went and if you had anyone not authorized snooping around." He lowered onto the chair by the door.

"You're in here asking me that when we finished up there about a week ago? What have you found?" Rafe pressed his forearms on the desk and leaned forward.

"I can't go into detail. I have a meeting with Lange in an hour to request warrants. A short story…" Hawke went on to tell Rafe about his suspicions of the Pinsons and possibly her brother. He finished with, "I wondered if anyone came by asking questions about the dig or trying to find out what you were looking for."

"There was an older guy who showed up about the time we were wrapping up."

"Did he pitch a camo tent in the bushes on the south side of the creek?" Hawke had wondered about the man sneaking around Sluice Creek. But didn't see how he tied into the murders.

"Yeah. He would talk to people when they were alone. He stayed away from anyone in uniform. I think he was hoping it was an Indigenous burial ground and was looking for artifacts."

Hawke nodded. He'd had the same thought about the man. Who was going to be highly disappointed when he spent time there and realized there had been only one body and it was removed. And it wasn't Indigenous.

Standing, Hawke said, "I'm going to use the extra computer and check in on some of the reports that came in on my cold cases until I need to meet Lange."

"Help yourself." Rafe put his glasses back on and picked up a paper.

Hawke exited the office and walked down the hall to the extra room with a computer that was there for visiting law enforcement to use. He could have sat in his vehicle and used his laptop but if he wanted to print out information to help persuade Lange to give him the warrants, he could do that here.

Once he was settled in the room, he started up the computer and logged into his OSP account. As the site came up, he walked down the hall to the break room and poured a cup of coffee. He also grabbed a couple of cookies that one of the staff or a wife of the staff must have made.

Back in the room, he opened the first report. It was the hair on the window sash. It was male and since Fanny had put Ford's DNA in a system, it came up with a match for him. It made sense except for the description Dougie gave him of the person sneaking around the mobile park. He had said the person walked like his mom. That meant it was a woman. And Hawke believed that to be Christa.

His email dinged. Clicking on his email, he found the security footage from the vet clinic. Hawke opened the link and sat back sipping his coffee as he watched.

When Christa walked in leading the mare, he kept his eyes on her every movement. At the end, right before she and Dr. Ashley walked into the clinic, Christa walked past the cart that held all the utensils and the vial of xylazine. He didn't see her pick up the vial but it was missing from the cart before Ford helped Brittney. He made a clip of the video before Christa walked by the cart and after. He emailed the clip to himself.

Christa killed Lucas and planted her husband's hair in the sash to make it look like it was him. He wondered who had suggested Ford and Harry go fishing on the Snake near the crime scene. Hawke was beginning to believe the siblings might be working together to get control of the Pinson Ranch.

He glanced at his emails and saw one from Spruel. He'd come through with financial records for both the Pinsons and Harry. Spruel had even highlighted the matching amounts and where they came from and went. Before digging into that, Hawke looked up the marriage license for Ford and Christa. He wrote down the date and went back to the financials. The week after Christa married Ford, she sent a check for ten thousand dollars to Harry. Then every month after that five thousand was sent to him from the same account. The photocopy of the checks before they were sent to a routing number were signed by Ford with the words, to help parents in the FOR line on the check.

Hawke read the note written in Spruel's block letters. *The account number belongs to Harry Croft*.

It appeared Christa had her husband paying her brother, thinking he was paying to help his in-laws. Did he know that money was a payoff for his brother-in-law? Hawke shook his head. He had to admire a woman who began setting her new husband up from the start of the marriage and implicating her brother. The latest killing could easily be either or both of the men.

He printed out all the information he felt would be needed to get the warrants he wanted and headed to the courthouse and his visit with D.A. Lange.

《》《》《》

In the D.A.'s office, Hawke took a seat and studied a man he had thought was a crook several years earlier. As Hawke had tried to find a way to show the District Attorney was selling hunting tags, he'd discovered Lange was being set up and then someone was out to kill him. Now he and Lange were on good terms. Or as good as he could be when the man kept tossing laws at him of why he couldn't do what he wanted to do.

Hawke laid all the printouts in front of Lange and said, "I believe this is enough proof to get a warrant to look for the coat that a witness saw the night Lucas Brazo was drugged and confiscate all the rifles on the ranch to see if they have hair or blood on the stock."

Lange shook his head. "You have no proof there would be any trace of the victim on the stock. And because you were the person who called the city police on Harry Croft, he could sue us for harassment. Not to mention the fact half the ranchers in this county will have oil-cloth dusters. How could you even prove if that duster was the one seen?"

Hawke leaned forward, tapping the papers he'd spread out on the desk in front of the D.A. "From the checks, the hair in the sash, and the fact Harry took Ford to the river to snoop around, making him look guilty, not to mention the first and second murders were committed not far from Ford's land, I believe that Christa or Harry and Christa have set up Ford. If I can find the evidence that does point to him, they will think they got off and I can use his anger at them to find out what we need to convict them."

Lange picked up the bank records. His thin finger followed the highlighted lines. "You believe that Christa Pinson was paying off her brother to keep quiet by way of making it look like her husband was paying him off?"

"Yes."

Peering up at him, Lange asked, "How would she get Ford's signature on every check? Surely after some years, he would question the checks?" He moved his finger to one of the first checks with a photocopy of the back. "Right here, Harry endorsed the check. How would he not see that?"

Hawke ran a hand across the back of his neck. That same thought had been running through his head. "We'll have to pull him in and ask. But we need to make a show of finding all the evidence that points at him. Because we are going to need his help to catch the real killers." Hawke tapped the block calendar on the D.A.'s desk. "Especially since two of the murders were committed over thirty years ago."

"Write up the warrants and I'll sign them. But I want all of this done so I don't have to do any fancy footwork to cover up the fact you arrested them on false evidence." Lange narrowed his eyes staring at Hawke.

"I'll write up the warrants and send them over this afternoon. We'll do the search tomorrow. Christa is supposed to be back home from a horse show then." He stood and walked out of the room. His first plan of catching the killer was in motion. Now to write up the warrants and make a call.

《》《》《》

Hawke leaned back in his chair at the Winslow OSP office and stretched his arms above his head. He'd been at the computer over an hour making sure he covered everything they would be searching for at the Pinson Ranch and making sure the wording didn't leave any loopholes for a defense attorney to throw the case out.

His notebook was open to the page with Haston's number. He found the call from Fanny and pushed dial. It rang three times and she answered out of breath.

"Hello?"

"Fanny, it's Trooper Hawke. Do you have a minute to talk?"

"Ummm."

He could hear her walking.

"Just a minute." Then away from the phone, she said, "I have to use the restroom. Alicia, stay with grandma, I'll be right back." He heard the sound of boot heels on asphalt, a door squeaking, and then more walking only this sounded like on leaves and twigs. "Okay, I'm alone. What did you find out?"

"I wanted to give you a heads-up that you and Alicia should go to town tomorrow. I'll text you what time. We'll be arriving with a search warrant. You don't need to be there and I don't want Alicia to see us take away one of her family members."

"Her grandmother?" Fanny asked in a quiet voice.

"I can't tell you who. And if you want it, I have the phone number of your biological father. He said he would like you to call him."

A gasp and nervous laugh came through the phone. "Really? He wants to talk to me?"

"Yes. He knew nothing about you. He has a wife and two boys but he would like to connect with you. Not your mom," Hawke hastily added.

"I can understand that. I don't have anything to write with can you just send me the number, no name attached?"

"I'll do that as soon as we finish talking and I'll text you when we are headed that way tomorrow." Knowing he was helping Fanny who had been used as a means for her mother to be a rich wife, made him feel good.

"Thank you." The call ended.

Hawke smiled. He texted the number to Fanny and shoved his phone in his pocket. Time to go home and hang out with his horses and Dog. Tomorrow would be busy and he hoped it would bring out the truth about the cold cases and Lucas's death.

Chapter Twenty-eight

The phone rang early Wednesday morning. Hawke answered it as he walked out of the bedroom from dressing, "Hello?"

"It's Marion. Do you mind if Mom and I come over on Thursday? That way we can be down at the Powwow ground early on Friday to help."

"Good morning, *kskís yáka*." He used his childhood name for her, Small Bear. "I see you are up and full of energy as usual." Hawke smiled. They had gone too many years not talking. Now having her at Mission with his mom and talking usually once a week the scar on his heart had healed.

"Well, do you mind if we spend Thursday with you and Dani?"

"It will be just me—"

"Don't tell me Dani won't be able to attend, Mom has made her a ribbon skirt," Marion interrupted.

"If you had let me finish. Dani won't be coming out until Friday. That's when her guests need flown out.

You and Mom can come take over Thursday, Dog and I don't care." He would enjoy sharing his new home with his mother and sister.

"One more little change. I've been getting kind of serious with someone you know. Can he spend Saturday night at your house too?" The wheedling in her voice was something he remembered from when she was a child. He'd headed off to fight for this country when she was eight. He hadn't seen much of her in her teen years and even less as an adult. He'd talked to her on the phone but they had been short conversations.

"Who is this man you're getting serious with. Not a cop I hope." That was the only way he figured he could know who the person was, if he worked in law enforcement.

"Not exactly. It's Quinn Pierce."

"FBI! Marion are you crazy. What will everyone on the rez think of you marrying a Fed?" He had nothing against Pierce. They'd worked together on several cases, but he couldn't see her fitting in at the reservation if she were married to him. Her job was advocating for tribal members. They wouldn't trust her anymore.

"We aren't marrying. At least it hasn't been brought up formally yet. I'll worry about that when the time comes. Do you mind if he spends Saturday night there? You have enough room."

"If he is willing to sleep on the couch, we have enough room. Or if you and Mom share a room." Then it hit him. She wasn't asking so much if he could stay at the house as if he could stay in her room. He slapped his forehead with the palm of his hand. "How can I

258

okay him sleeping in your room with Mom in the house?"

"Gabriel, I'm a woman and Mom knows Quinn and I have been intimate. She really doesn't care as long as he puts a ring on my finger soon. She keeps talking about grandkids and knows you will never give her any." Marion's voice softened. "I'm sorry. I didn't mean to- you know- make it sound like you wouldn't like to have kids. But unless you marry someone younger than Dani or you two adopt, Mom won't have grandchildren from you."

"I understand. We'll just play it by ear on Saturday night. I'm looking forward to having all of my family together. I have to run. See you Thursday." He ended the call with a smile on his face. It would be good to have family in the house. Even if one of them turns out to be a Fed.

《》《》《》

Hawke took the courthouse stairs two at a time. Once he had the warrants in his hands, he'd gather up another Trooper and a couple of deputies to go with him to serve and search the Pinson Ranch.

Terri smiled at him. "Two days in a row. But I knew you were coming. The warrants are in this envelope. Mr. Lange said to look them over and make sure he or you didn't miss anything."

Hawke took the envelope and sat in a chair. He pulled the documents out and read through them. "They look good," he said, stuffing them back in the envelope. "Thanks."

"Any time," Terri said before picking up the ringing phone.

Hawke walked slower down to his vehicle. He

called Spruel to request the trooper and then Rafe to get the deputies. "I'll be at the Imnaha store waiting for them," he told both men.

Out in his vehicle, Hawke texted Fanny he was on his way. Driving to Imnaha, he went over all the scenarios they might come up against when he presented the warrants. He needed to have all three of his suspects in front of him when he showed them the warrants. He wanted to see their faces and reactions.

At the Imnaha store, Hawke parked and entered. He sat down at the counter and ordered coffee and a piece of pie.

"What are you doing out this way so soon after your last visit?" Tyler asked.

"Just cleaning up some old business." Hawke sipped his coffee as the owner placed a slice of peach pie in front of him.

"Old business. Like the two cold cases you came across?"

Hawke studied the man. "What do you know about those?"

"Only what everyone along this river has been saying. That at first, one was an accident until you found the other one and now they're linked." Tyler leaned on the counter. "Do you suspect someone from around here?"

Hawke shrugged and watched Fanny and Alicia drive past. He was glad they wouldn't be there during the search. As far as he was concerned, they were innocents in the events that happened before their births.

Chewing his last bite of pie, he glanced out the window as the two county vehicles came over the bridge and turned into the parking lot. He finished the rest of his coffee, put money on the counter, and stood. "Thanks for the coffee and pie."

"You have reinforcements. Do I need to worry about Mandy and the kids?"

"No. We're just doing a search. No one should get trigger-happy." He walked out of the store as the two deputies walked toward the entrance.

"Ready to go?" Hawke asked as Ivy pulled into the parking lot. The deputies returned to their cars and Hawke leaned down to tell Ivy to follow them.

He slid behind the steering wheel of his vehicle and led the way to the Pinson Ranch. All the hands in and around the barn, house, and arena stopped and watched the four law enforcement vehicles park in front of the house.

Hawke, followed by the rest, walked up to the front door and knocked.

Ford answered the door. His eyes widened as his gaze drifted down the line of officers.

"I'd like you to gather your wife and brother-in-law in the great room where I can tell you all what is about to happen." Hawke waved a hand for the man to walk ahead of him.

Ford studied him for several seconds before walking to the great room calling out, "Christa, Harry, come to the great room!"

Hawke, Ivy, and the deputies all stopped at the entrance to the room.

Christa walked in, her eyes widened before her gaze landed on the floor, hiding her emotions. Harry strode in behind her and stopped, staring at them, his jaw dropped a fraction before his lips clamped shut.

"Have a seat," Hawke said, motioning for the three to sit. Harry and Christa sat on the couch and Ford sat in a chair to the side.

"I have a warrant to search all of the buildings." Hawke handed Ford the warrants. "And I'd like you three to remain here until we finish. Trooper Bisset will be here watching you."

"I don't understand. What are you looking for?" Christa asked.

Ford held up the warrants. "Their taking all of our rifles and looking for a duster and vial for xylazine." He glared at Hawke. "I hope you have enough boxes to carry all of those items back to wherever you're taking them."

Hawke had his gaze on the woman as Ford pronounced the items they were looking for. He witnessed a slight flicker at the corners of Christa's lips. He would bet money that she used Ford's duster and possibly left the vial in the pocket.

"Trooper Bisset, make sure none of these people leave this room until we've finished our search." Hawke walked closer to Ivy and whispered, "And pay attention to who talks to who and what they say if you can hear it." She nodded.

He led the deputies back to the front door. "Calvin, you search the barn. Dave, you search the arena. You heard the warrants are for rifles, particularly ones that would have been around over thirty years ago, dusters, particularly ones made out of oilcloth, and if you find any kind of medicine vial. I'm going to go through the house."

The two headed off in the direction of the outbuildings and Hawke began searching the first floor.

262

He found a locked gun cabinet and asked Ford to unlock it.

"I don't understand, why are you here looking for a rifle and duster? What do they have to do with Evan's or Lucas's death?" It was clear by the confusion on his face, he didn't have a clue what had happened to the two men. Hawke was more than ever sure that Christa had masterminded the two deaths.

"I can't divulge that at this time."

Ford opened the door of the cabinet, and Hawke spotted the lever action rifle that Harry had been so quick to pick up at the river. He reached out and plucked it from the safe. "Is this your rifle?"

"Yeah. It was my father's and he gave it to me when I turned thirteen. I'd hoped to have a boy to hand it down. Guess I should have given it to Fanny when she turned thirteen but she only carries a pistol in case she comes across an angry rattler. She couldn't kill anything unless it was going to hurt someone."

Hawke had that impression of the woman. "What about Christa?"

Ford pointed out two rifles. "That's her hunting rifle and that one is her bird hunting gun. She keeps a rifle in the sheath on her saddle for rattlers."

"Thank you. Go back with the others now." Once the man left the room, Hawke tagged all the rifles and carried them out to his vehicle. As he passed by the great room, he made sure to capture the expressions on Christa and Harry's faces. Christa had a slight smile. Harry looked a bit worried.

Continuing through the house, he came to the back porch. Several coats, dusters, hats, and sweatshirts hung from hooks. Boots of different sizes and states of wear stood under the outerwear.

Hawke took the first duster he came to down and examined it. It was made of canvas. He searched the pockets and came up with a horse hoof pick and a couple of nails. The next duster was oilcloth. There were a couple of fence staples in the pocket and a crumpled piece of paper. He unfolded what looked like a receipt. It turned out to be a receipt from the gas station in Winslow dated the night of Lucas's death. His heart started racing. This would be the duster the person had on that night. He could ask whoever was working if it was Christa or Ford who purchased gas that night.

He slipped the paper back in the pocket and rolled up the coat, placing it in a large evidence bag. He wrote on the bag and set it by the door. Even though he was pretty sure it was the evidence they needed, he bagged another oilcloth duster. It was smaller, most likely Fanny's. After searching the room for the vial and any other rifles, he carried those out to his vehicle. Back in the house he went through the garbage and trash cans, and looked in every cupboard and drawer. It was nearing noon.

When he walked into the great room to head upstairs, Harry asked, "Can we get something to eat?"

Hawke glanced at Ivy. He could tell by the set of her jaw and the spark in her eyes, she was waiting for him to tell her to go make the three lunch.

"Christa, come with me," he said and led her into the kitchen. "Make sandwiches for you, Ford, Harry, and Trooper Bisset."

She crossed her arms and stared at him. "I don't like to be ordered around in my own home."

"Fine. Then go back to the other room and you can

all eat when we finish with our search." Hawke motioned for her to turn around and head back to the great room.

She didn't move. "Fine! I'll make sandwiches." She marched over to a cupboard and pulled out a loaf of bread, then she stomped over to the refrigerator and pulled out condiments, meat, and cheese. "But you have to answer my questions." She placed everything next to the bread and started dealing out eight slices of what looked like whole wheat.

"Only if they don't hinder the investigation." He leaned his butt against the counter across from where she worked.

"Why are you looking for a rifle?" She spread mayonnaise on the slices of bread.

"It could be important to your first husband's murder."

She glanced up, studied him, and put pieces of lunch meat on the bread. "And the coat?"

"It's important to Lucas Brazo's murder."

Her eyebrows went up, but she didn't look up from where she was putting cheese on each slice. "And the vial?"

"Also important to Lucas's murder."

She flipped the sandwiches together and put them all on one plate. "What about drinks?" she asked.

Hawke opened the fridge and grabbed four bottles of water. "Got it."

Christa offered a sandwich to Ivy. She glanced at Hawke, he nodded, and she took it.

Then Christa offered the plate to her husband and then sat it on the coffee table in front of the couch. Harry grabbed a sandwich. Hawke handed them each a bottle of water.

"I'm going to finish my search upstairs." Hawke climbed the log staircase and began going through the cupboards and closets in each room. When he opened the door to what appeared to be Alicia's room, he started to back out but then decided that might be what the murderer would hope for. He opened all the drawers, felt through them, and looked at every box in the closet. Nothing. He started to walk out of the room and realized he hadn't looked in the wooden box at the end of the bed.

Raising the lid, he looked in and found stuffed animals, dolls, and horses. He pulled each one out and at the bottom of the box lay a vial. He took a photo, pulled on a glove, and put the vial in an evidence bag. All the while his anger built that an adult in this house would hide something lethal in the child's room.

He finished his search of the upstairs and returned to the great room to find Calvin and Dave waiting. "Thank you for your cooperation. Anything we took today will be returned to you after it has been evaluated at our lab. He took the copy of the list of items each deputy had confiscated, added his list copy, and handed them over to Ford.

"We'll be in touch."

Ford shot to his feet. "Aren't you at least going to tell us why you took the items you did?"

Hawke stared at Christa. "The guilty party knows why."

He motioned for the deputies and Ivy to follow him out of the house. When they stood by his vehicle he asked, "What did you do with the items you found?"

"Put them in my car," they both said.

"Put them in my vehicle. I'm taking the lot to Pendleton today." As the two deputies transferred the items they seized, he told Ivy, "Stop at the store and you can tell me what all went on while I was searching the house."

She nodded and walked to her vehicle.

"Thank you for your help," he said to Dave and Calvin.

"How do you plan to find the murder weapon from a thirty-plus-year homicide?" Calvin asked.

"We might get lucky or we might not. My guess is if the rifle that was used to incapacitate Evan was here, it was in the barn or arena. Most likely it hasn't been used for years. The duster, I'm sure is one I found on the back porch. It was there to be found. The vial." He clenched his jaw and said, "I found it in the granddaughter's toy box. I'm not sure if they thought no one would look there or if they are trying to also set up the daughter. But whoever put that dangerous vial in a child's room, needs to go to jail just for that."

"I hope you can get the evidence you need to get this person. If they aren't stopped think of what could happen to anyone who gets in their way?" Calvin said.

"I know, that's what worries me. Now that they know we have this evidence, will they think they fooled us into believing someone else did it or will they kill again to hide their tracks." Hawke blew out a breath. "All the more reason to get this to the lab. I'll let you know what they find."

"Thanks, appreciate that," Dave said, walking to his vehicle.

Hawke followed the deputies down the road and pulled up alongside Ivy's vehicle at the store. He found her sitting at the counter with a soda and a piece of pie.

"Tyler, I'll take a burger." He tapped Ivy on the shoulder. "Let's go to that table in the corner."

She nodded and carried her plate and drink to the table. It was situated close to the doors to the restrooms, but far from the counter and kitchen where Tyler was busy cooking his burger.

"What did you witness?" Hawke asked, sitting down.

"When you took Ford in to unlock the gun cabinet, Christa and Harry whispered a lot. It looked like they were arguing. As soon as Ford entered the room they quit talking. The three barely said anything to each other otherwise. But from the expressions on their faces, Ford looked worried, Christa was the most relaxed, and Harry was jumpy and nervous."

Hawke smiled. "Good observations."

"Thanks. I've gotta run. I promised Steve I'd be on when he had to go to an appointment." She stood and walked to the door. She stopped and said to Tyler, "Put mine on his tab." Ivy smiled at Hawke over her shoulder and walked out, leaving the bell above the door tinkling.

Tyler chuckled as he crossed the room to deliver Hawke's burger and drink. "She got you."

Hawke smiled. "Yeah, but it's worth it. She's turning into a good law enforcement officer."

"Did you take care of what you came for?" Tyler asked.

"Yes." He pulled out his phone and texted Fanny they were done at the house.

Thank you was her reply.

He wanted to ask her who would have put the vial

in her daughter's toy box but didn't want anyone to know he'd found it. However, if they read the list of items taken, they would know.

He finished the burger, paid, and slipped into his vehicle. As he headed out of Imnaha, he called dispatch to let them know he was headed to the lab in Pendleton.

Chapter Twenty-nine

Hawke called Darlene Thursday morning to see if she could run over during the day and do a little house cleaning. Their bi-weekly house cleaner wasn't due until the following week.

"I thought you weren't having company until Friday," Darlene said.

"Marion called yesterday and said they'd be here today. I don't want Mom cleaning the house when she gets here. She'll be busy finishing up things for the giveaways at the powwow." Hawke patted Dog on the head. "I'm going to try to get off early but it will depend on what happens."

"I'll get the house clean and air out the guest rooms. Don't worry about it."

"Thanks. I'm going to owe you more than I already do," Hawke said.

"This is what neighbors do. We'll need you and Dani to help us now and then. Don't worry about it."

Hawke ended the call and finished getting ready

for work. He and Dog had already fed the horses and mule. He'd returned home late last night after driving the evidence they procured at the Pinson Ranch to Pendleton. The staff had said they'd get right on it. Hawke had little faith they would find anything on a rifle but he was positive one of the dusters, the one with the receipt, had been worn to kill Lucas. And he was positive the vial would have xylazine in it, and most likely have been wiped of prints.

He'd decided to have breakfast at The Rusty Nail in Winslow and ask at the gas station about the receipt. He had the lab give him a copy of the receipt.

"Darlene is coming over to clean house this morning and you'll have company shortly after lunch. I'm sure you won't be lonely," Hawke told Dog as they walked out to his work vehicle.

Dog sat down and wagged his tail as if he understood. Hawke patted him on the head one more time and climbed into his work rig. He backed up and headed down the driveway with thoughts of breakfast.

He'd only gone three miles on the highway when he spotted a car off the side of the road. He pulled in behind and put his flashers on. As he called in 'vehicle needing a tow' he recognized the car. Stepping out of his vehicle, he walked to the driver's side.

Olive Good Fox looked up at him, tears in her eyes.

Hawke opened the door. "What's wrong Olive?" He crouched so he didn't have to lean over.

"I'm supposed to be at Eagle helping prepare the long house and my stupid car took today to finally die." She wiped at the tears on her cheeks.

"I can give you a ride to Eagle. And I'm sure you

can find a ride home and back tomorrow from someone going that way." He stood and held out a hand. "Leave the keys in the car. I've called a tow truck."

"I can't afford a tow truck and buying a new car." She crossed her arms and glared at him.

"Let's get the car towed and see if you need a new car or if it can be fixed." He called on the mic to have the car towed to Jerry's Automotive. He knew the mechanics were good there and Jerry didn't charge over what a person could afford.

He led Olive to the back door of his vehicle. "Sorry, but you'll have to ride in the back."

"A ride is a ride," Olive said, pulling herself up into the back seat.

Hawke's stomach grumbled as he settled behind the steering wheel.

"Didn't you eat breakfast this morning?" Olive asked.

"I plan to get some at The Rusty Nail."

"You can stop now if you want. I'm late now, so it doesn't matter."

"I'll get you to Eagle and come back. I have to go into the office today too."

"Okay, but I don't want to listen to your stomach all the way to Eagle." She sat back and stared out the window.

Hawke chuckled to himself and pulled onto the highway.

An hour later he'd dropped off Olive and was sitting at the Rusty Nail ordering his breakfast.

"How are your cold cases going?" Justine asked.

"Slow but sure." He ordered his usual and sipped his coffee while Justine put the order up.

She returned. "Are you excited about this weekend?"

Hawke studied her. "Not as excited as you seem to be."

Her cheeks flushed. "I know it's silly I'm so excited. All these years I've lived here and haven't attended the powwow, but now that I'm going, I can't wait."

Hawke shrugged. "I'm excited to be hanging out all weekend with my family. I haven't done that since I joined the Army."

The door jingled. Hawke turned his attention to the door.

Wendy walked over to a table and sat. She scanned the room, spotted him, and held his gaze.

Was this the day she usually came in? He was trying to remember. It was much later than the last time he saw her here.

Justine set his food in front of him, breaking his gaze with the other woman. "You got a thing for her?" Justine asked quietly and chuckled.

Hawke shook himself and cringed. "No. Is this her usual day to come in?"

"Not usually. But she does pop in now and then when she isn't cleaning houses in this area."

He grunted and ate his food. When he finished, Hawke paid and walked by Wendy's table. "Do you have a house to clean here today?"

"No. I'm just enjoying Merrilee's tasty pancakes on my way to do some shopping in Alder."

"Have a good day," Hawke walked out of the café and crossed the road over to the gas station. He asked who was working the night of July 6th and was told the owner, who happened to be in the back working on the books.

Hawke knocked on the office door.

"Come in!" called Harvey Amund.

Hawke opened the door and Harvey glanced at the door.

He stood up and stared. "What can I do for you, Hawke?"

"I have this receipt from July sixth. I wondered if you could remember who purchased the gas. Was it Ford or Christa Pinson?" Hawke held out the copy of the receipt.

"Eight at night. We rarely get a vehicle from the Pinson Ranch here. They usually fuel up in Prairie Creek or Alder. But Mrs. Pinson does drive to Eagle at least once a month and would sometimes stop here."

"Do you know if it was her that night?" Hawke pointed to the receipt.

"Yeah. She was driving her SUV and I wondered why she had a duster in the passenger seat."

Hawke pulled out his notebook and wrote the information down. "I'm going to give you a call to come to the office later today and sign a statement that you sold her gas on this date and that you saw a duster in her passenger seat."

Harvey stared at him. "What do I need to do that for?"

"She's a suspect in a murder investigation."

The man's mouth dropped open and his eyes grew round before he said, "Not that nice woman."

Hawke nodded. "But keep this to yourself. I'm still gathering all the evidence."

"I wouldn't want to speak ill of the Pinsons. I'll

keep my mouth shut. And I'll come in when I get off work at five and sign the statement."

"Thank you."

Hawke crossed the road as Wendy pulled out of the parking lot. She was on her phone and he could have pulled her over but he was more interested in who she was talking to. He didn't trust her. Mostly because she never got back to him with information from Dougie. He had to go to the boy and collect the information. It was a sign she didn't want to help him find Lucas's killer. While he had confirmation that Christa had been driving around that night with a duster, it didn't rule out the fact that he'd given Wendy a chance to give Lucas the bottle laced with xylazine. The person in the duster could be a way to take suspicion off of Wendy.

But the vial was found hidden in Christa's granddaughter's toy box. Or was that the vial that had been stolen for the purpose of killing Lucas?

Hawke went straight to the OSP office. He stopped at Spruel's office.

"Can you get me the phone records for Christa Pinson and Wendy Fielding?" Hawke asked, sticking his head in the door of the sergeant's office.

"I doubt I can get them today but I can put in a request and have it here for you after this weekend."

"That's fine."

"When do your mom and sister arrive?" Spruel asked.

"Today. They're helping with setup, dances, and gifts and need to be there early in the morning."

"Enjoy your time with your family."

"I plan on it." Hawke wandered over to his desk and started typing up Harvey's statement and then adding what he'd learned the day before. Leafing through the notes, he read that Christa had told Fanny she was helping a horse north of Alder on the night Lucas was killed. North of Alder was a long way from Winslow where she purchased gas. He checked his emails for any updates on all the items he'd sent to the lab in Pendleton and Clackamas.

His phone buzzed. A glance revealed D.A. Lange. "Hawke."

"It's Lange. Did you find anything from the search yesterday?"

"A vial labeled xylazine. A duster that had a gas receipt the night of Brazo's death. I followed up on the receipt and was told it was Christa Pinson who purchased the gas. We confiscated eight rifles that I took to the Pendleton lab." Hawke leaned back in his chair, waiting to hear what Lange was going to say.

"The drug can be linked to the household. And the receipt to Mrs. Pinson. Did you ask her about the duster?"

"No. I gave them the warrant that stated what we were looking for and the list of what we took."

"I'll start drafting the evidence we do know together and see if we have enough for a case against Mrs. Pinson." He paused. "That is who you believe killed Lucas Brazo, isn't it?"

"Either her or Wendy Fielding."

"Who is she?"

Hawke explained how she was the most obvious to have poisoned Lucas. But he didn't see how she fit in with anything other than that. "I requested Sergeant Spruel get phone records for the two women to see if they have been in contact."

"Good call. Keep me informed."

"I will."

Hawke finished making a list of the results so far at the lab. It was close to five and he had company waiting for him at home. He turned off his computer and headed out to his vehicle. He hoped he could forget about the cold cases and homicide and enjoy the weekend.

Chapter Thirty

Friday morning, Hawke stayed home taking care of his animals and waiting to pick up Dani at the airport. His mom and sister went on to Eagle to get things rolling at Tamkaliks.

Hawke spent the morning going over all the evidence and statements he'd gathered for the cold cases and Lucas Brazo's death. The evidence of the photo showed that a man with a rifle struck Evan's head and tossed him into the Snake River. That person also shot at Professor Chang who died of that gunshot wound.

An email popped into his inbox. It was from Professor Galler. Hawke opened it.

Trooper Hawke, I and a forensic pathologist have discerned that the body we dug up was shot in the chest. There was a hole in a scapula that could have only been made by a bullet going through it. We measured the hole and given the years and possible shrinkage of the dry bone, it was most likely a .44 caliber. I hope that

helps you with your investigation. I've attached the
pathologist's report to this email.

Professor Phillip Galler

Hawke immediately opened the report, read
through it, and then forwarded it on to the lab so they
knew to only check that caliber of rifle.

He received an email right back thanking him for
the information.

Then he forwarded the information to Lange.

A glance at the clock said he and Dog needed to get
to the airport and pick up Dani. She normally left her
SUV at the airport but it had been in the shop since her
visit two weeks earlier to get the engine worked on.
She'd refused to purchase another vehicle when the
repairs on hers would be less money.

"Come on, Dog. We need to get going," He called.

The clatter of toenails on the wood flooring echoed
down the hall.

"Where were you?" Hawke asked, wandering back
up the hall to see what the dog had been doing. The
covers in the middle of the guest bed where Marion
slept were wrinkled and looked like a nest. "I see. You
like her better than me, now?"

Dog pressed against his leg.

"Buttering me up isn't going to change my feelings
of betrayal." Hawke headed to the front door and Dog
beat him there. "Maybe you just miss Dani and are
using Marion as a substitute?"

They both settled in the pickup and headed to the
airport.

They were early enough to watch her land and help
tie the aircraft down in her usual spot. Then they carried
her bag of dirty clothes to the pickup and headed home.

"What are your mom and sister doing?" Dani asked.

"They've been at Eagle all day. I'm sure Marion has been dancing and helping with events. Mom was anxious to see some of her friends from other areas. We'll take your stuff home, let you get a shower and start your laundry, then go to the grounds for dinner and watch the dancing."

"That's a good way to slowly work your way up to joining in," Dani said.

《》《》《》

At five o'clock they drove into the grassy parking lot at the edge of Eagle that was half filled with vehicles. As he stepped out of the pickup the drum beat coming from the dance arbor entered his chest and started his heart beating with the drums. It had been a long time since he'd been at an event with drumming and dancing.

He met Dani at the front of his vehicle. They clasped hands and walked toward the arbor where people in regalia stood around talking and adjusting their colorful adornment. Visitors sat on the thick wood bleachers under cover from the sun. Tribal members sat in camp chairs between the bleachers and the grassy dance floor in the center of the arbor.

"Oh, I love this!" Dani whispered, clutching his arm.

He glanced down at the sparkle in her eyes and awe on her face. "It's the shawl dance or butterfly dance. Haven't you seen it before?" He led her to an empty place on a bleacher where she could see better.

"No. I told you. When my father married my mom, we walked away from our culture. My father was tired of being put down and treated poorly. As a member of my mother's Anglo family, he was treated as their equals. I don't ever remember anyone calling my father a name. If they had, I'm sure my grandfather would have fired them. He believed in my father and it took him far in the company." She sighed. "But this. It calls to my heart."

Hawke understood what she meant. Sitting among their people, hearing the drums and voices, and seeing the fluid movement of the dancers waving their shawls like butterfly wings and placing their feet with the beat of the music, he felt another piece of what had been missing in his life slowly moving into place.

"Gabriel, Dani!" His mom stood up from where she sat in a camp chair a good thirty feet away from them.

"How did she see us with her back in this direction?" Hawke asked, waving back.

Then she made a motion with her arms for them to come to her.

"We've been summoned," he said, taking Dani's hand and leading her off the bleachers and down to where his mom sat.

She motioned to the two empty chairs beside her. "These are for you."

"I think we can see better up in the bleachers," Hawke said, but sat when the woman behind him told him to sit. He pulled Dani down into the seat beside him.

"Nonsense. You want to be here to watch your sister dance. It will be the third time today she's been out there." His mom's voice held a note of pride. He knew she'd missed watching her daughter at powwows ever since Marion went off to college and then took a job in Texas.

The music ended and the dancers moved off the dance floor. The emcee called out for another drum group to take over the next dance. He talked about some of the dancers leaving the floor and then told the story of the jingle dance. How a medicine man in the 1920s whose granddaughter was sick had a dream that told him to make a dance that was pleasing to the ear. He rolled up snuff can lids and baking powder lids and sewed them to a dress with ribbon. The soft jingle as the girl danced made her heart happy and she became healthy. The jingle dance was thought of as a healing dance.

The emcee asked the Jingle dancers to enter the arbor. They entered youngest to oldest. The drumming and the jingle of the dresses, as the girls and women danced, lightened Hawke's heart. However, what brought him the greatest joy was seeing the happiness on his sister's face as she danced past.

"She's beautiful!" Dani exclaimed.

"My daughter. See how she radiates the goodness of this dance," said his mom.

Hawke just nodded and watched his sister. Eventually, his gaze wandered and he noticed many people with their eyes only on Marion. His mom had said she had that effect when she was a teenager and it seemed to still be with her.

The dance ended much too soon.

"That was lovely," Dani said. Then she faced Hawke. "Where's the dinner you promised?"

"Come, I know where you will get a good meal for a good price." Mom rose and he and Dani followed her out of the arbor and around to where the food vendor trailers and tents were set up. One of the tents had a sign *NDN Tacos*. Mom led them to it and had a conversation with the woman behind the table.

She smiled at Hawke and Dani and then turned to the woman behind her. She dropped a round of fry bread dough into the hot oil. Then another round into another fryer. Hawke watched as she turned them and pulled them out.

Then they were topped with beans, taco meat, lettuce, chopped onions, tomatoes, and topped with shredded cheese. She placed the two plates on the table and Hawke paid for the food and two iced teas.

"Why didn't you get one, Mom," Hawke asked, as they walked over to a picnic table to eat.

"I had something to eat with Marion an hour before you arrived. We hadn't eaten since leaving your house and were hungry." She pulled a water bottle out of her purse and drank.

"Did you get everything set up and ready that you were worried about?" he asked.

"Yes, everything is set up." She smiled and he wondered what that was about.

Marion strode over to where they were sitting. She was wearing an event t-shirt and tight-fitting pants, that Dani told him were called jogging pants. She plopped down on the bench beside their mom and then pulled a piece off of Hawke's fry bread.

"Hey!" he slapped her hand. "This is my dinner."

She laughed and popped the piece in her mouth.

Mom just smiled.

Dani laughed.

"If hanging around with you means I have to share

my food, I'll stay home tomorrow," Hawke said.

"No, you can't!" his mom said, her eyes wide and her voice high-pitched.

He narrowed his eyes and studied her. "Why can't I stay home?"

"Because I have something special I want you to see," Marion said, grasping their mom's hand and holding it.

Hawke didn't believe what she said, but he didn't say anything more because he saw it was something that meant a lot to his mom. He and Dani finished their food and stood.

"Let's go look around at the vendors," Dani said.

"That sounds like fun." Marion and Mom stood and they all walked around looking at the booths of jewelry, crafts, knives, and memorabilia.

Dancing and drumming continued as the sun set and the night grew cooler. They watched the conclusion of the dances and wandered back to their vehicles along with the other attendees. Many families had set up tents and teepees for the weekend. They now visited with their neighbors and put families to bed.

Hawke and Dani drove home with Marion and his mom following them.

Dog greeted them when they drove up to the house. Hawke was surprised the dog hadn't come running from Herb's place or the barn with the horses.

As they walked up to the house, his phone buzzed. A quick look had him slowing down. "Go on in," he said and walked out toward the barn answering his phone.

"Hawke."

"Trooper Hawke this is Gary at the Pendleton lab.

After receiving your email with the caliber of the rifle to check, we took the three rifles of that caliber completely apart. We found hairs caught between the butt pad and stock on a corner as if the butt of the rifle had been slammed into a head. They've been there a long time and I'm not sure if we can get a DNA match but we sent them off to Clackamas to see if they can. There wasn't any sign of blood. I did test it with Luminol and didn't find anything. There were also hairs found inside the barrel that we believe are horse hairs."

"What color of horse hair?" Hawke asked, trying to remember if he knew what horse was Christa's.

"It looks like red so a sorrel or a bay. I'd say it's darker in color more like a bay."

"Thanks. This is all good. Do you know if the vial I sent had xylazine in it?" The label had said that but labels could be removed.

"It was xylazine."

"Thanks."

"Are you coming in or hanging out here at the barn all night?" Marion walked toward him carrying two mugs.

"What do you have?"

"Hot chocolate. Mom insists it brings good dreams if one has it before bed." Marion smiled and handed him a mug.

"How's living with Mom going?" he asked, walking over to a bale sitting next to the barn. He sat and Marion sank onto the bale.

"Not as bad as I'd thought. She's doing her best to not be pushy or nosey but you know how badly she wants more family. She's tried to set me up with several men. Even when she knows I am seeing Quinn."

"He's not a tribal member," Hawke said.

"I know and as much as I love mom and my culture, I'm not going to marry someone just to make her happy. I'm the one who has to be happy with my life. And Quinn makes me happy. When I lost Aiden, I didn't think I would ever want another man in my life. But I was working with a woman who was trying to find her missing daughter and was given Quinn's name as a person to contact for information. The first time we started talking I had that spark that I'd felt with Aiden."

"I'm glad. Quinn's a good guy. A bit intense at times, but I'm sure he'll do good by you." Hawke drank his chocolate. "What does Mom have planned for me tomorrow?"

Marion spit out chocolate and peered at him. "What do you mean?"

Hawke shook his head. "Don't play innocent. I can tell she's set me up for something tomorrow. Tell me she didn't sign me up to dance. Do you know how long it's been since I danced? Over forty years. I'm not dancing."

"She didn't sign you up to dance. She knows you're rusty." Marion's lips curled into a smug smile.

"Good. She didn't sign Dani up, did she? Dani has never danced."

"No, she didn't sign either of you up to dance." Marion finished off her drink and stood. "Don't you tell her I told you, but she signed you up to carry the flag at the opening flag ceremony in the morning, and Dani to walk with the veterans." Marion strode toward the house.

Hawke thought about what Marion said. Carrying the flag at the opening ceremonies wouldn't be that bad.

He had fought for this country and he was proud to be Indigenous. He threw the rest of his hot chocolate into the bushes and walked to the house. They would need to be at the grounds before the horse procession at nine.

Chapter Thirty-one

The following morning, they took two vehicles to Eagle arriving at eight-thirty to have plenty of time to watch the horse procession and let the organizers know that Hawke and Dani were there.

Dani looked pretty in the ribbon skirt his mom had made for her. She'd even given Dani a deer hide belt with silver conchos to wear at her waist. The shirt Dani had paired with the skirt had a more feminine look than he'd seen her wear before. He'd commented on how pretty she looked several times until she became mad and told him not to expect her to wear a dress just to make him tell her she was pretty.

However, she had also said he looked handsome in his ribbon shirt. Just not as many times as he'd mentioned how pretty she looked. The colorful ribbons ran across the chest of the shirt and had streamers of the same ribbon hanging down the front and back. The ribbons matched the colors on Dani's skirt.

As they walked toward the arbor, they received

many compliments on their clothing. Marion was dressed in a ribbon skirt and concho belt. Topped with the event t-shirt.

His mom's head was held high. Her pride in her family showed on her face. He put an arm around her shoulders and squeezed. She looked up at him and smiled, a tear in the corner of her eye.

"Gabriel, Mimi!" a voice called.

Hawke and his mom turned and watched as his Auntie Flo walked toward them. He felt his mom shudder under his arm. He glanced down and saw tears sliding down her cheeks.

"If you don't want to talk to her, I'll keep her busy and you and Marion can go on," he said.

"No, I want to talk to her. It's just. I've missed her so." She stepped out from under his arm and into the arms of Flo. The two held each other and cried.

"Who's that?" Dani asked.

Hawke explained the family dynamic and how the two had lost touch when his father dropped them at Mission and never came back.

She put an arm around his and squeezed. "That must have been hard."

"I got over it." He glanced down into her concerned eyes. "But I didn't realize how much Mom missed being part of the Hawke family."

They waited for the two women to finish crying and hugging before Hawke led Marion and Dani over to them.

"Flo, this is my sister, Marion, and my partner, Dani Singer." Hawke kept his arm around Dani as she greeted Flo.

His Auntie studied the two of them and nodded her

head. "I take it you don't have a business partnership?"

"No. It's a partnership of the souls," Dani said.

Hawke's gaze flitted from his aunt to Dani. She smiled up at him and he shrugged. "What she said."

The women all laughed, and Hawke scanned the area to see if anyone was watching. He didn't see anyone watching but he saw Dr. Ashley talking to Wendy over by the horses. How did the two know one another? Did Wendy take her dog to the vet?

"Who are you watching now?" Dani asked, as he drew his attention back to the women. His mom, Marion, and Flo were wandering over to the tents.

"One of my possible suspects." He grinned at her. "Don't worry I won't leave you here. I plan to spend the whole day with you and my family."

"That's good. Your aunt said there are a dozen of your Lapwai relatives here and also half a dozen of mine."

Hawke studied her. "Is that good news or bad that you have relatives here?"

"It depends on whether or not they feel I've rejected our culture." She shrugged.

Hawke glanced over his shoulder and saw Dr. Ashley taking a look at one of the horses in regalia. He figured it would be ridden in the Horse Procession. "I want to talk to Dr. Ashley. You want to come or find everyone else."

"I'll come with you." Dani fell into step beside Hawke.

He stood back from where the veterinarian was flexing the horse's leg.

"If he is the riderless horse for the procession, he'll be fine. But I wouldn't put any weight on him for at least a week," she told the man in a breechcloth and ribbon shirt.

"We will make this the riderless horse. Thank you for looking at him." The man led the horse away and Hawke walked forward.

"Dr. Ashley, how do you know Wendy Fielding?" Hawke asked without making any introductions or small talk.

"Hi, Hawke. Wendy? She cleans my house. Why?"

"Do you keep any drugs you use on animals in your house?" he asked.

"No. Why would I do that? I have kids at home." She studied him. "Do you think Wendy stole drugs from me?"

"Do you drive your work vehicle home every night?" Hawke asked.

"Yes, but they are locked in my truck."

"Has Wendy ever been at your house when your truck is there? And possibly your keys were left out?" Hawke wasn't going to let this go. He had to know if the person who had the easiest access to drugging Lucas had access to the drug that killed him.

"Yes, there have been a couple of times that my truck was at the house while I was at a school event with my husband and Wendy was cleaning the house. But the keys to the truck were in my purse."

"Can I see the keys?" He held out a hand, palm up. She handed the keys over.

Hawke pulled out the knife in the sheath of his left boot and ran the pointed end down the indentions of the key. When he held the blade up there was wax on the tip. "She made a copy of your key at some time while she was cleaning."

Dr. Ashley's face darkened in color. "I trusted her!"

"Don't say anything to her. I'm trying to build a case against her for Lucas Brazo's death. But I'll need you to come by the office on Monday and give me a statement about the times she was left at your home when your truck was parked there and you need to think about when the keys would be out for her to make a wax copy." He held up a hand. "Don't confront her. She's dangerous. Let me deal with her."

Dr. Ashley nodded.

"Thank you for all the information." Hawke drew Dani away from the angry veterinarian.

"I'd be pissed too if someone I trusted did something like that," Dani said.

Hawke nodded. "She's a sly one. Acts like she plans to help but she only does as much as will make her look innocent."

"Are you going after her?" Dani stopped and grasped his arm. She peered into his eyes. "You have to keep her from killing someone else."

"I agree, but I don't see her killing anyone today. She doesn't know we're onto her. Let's enjoy today."

By the time they found his mom and sister, it was time for him and Dani to stand by the entrance to the arbor and watch the Horse Procession. The announcer told how the riderless horse was in memory of all the ancestors who were no longer with them. Whether it was someone who died recently or the brave warriors and women who gave their lives to protect their people and land.

Then they called together the Grand Entry and handed Hawke the MIA/POW flag. He held it proudly as they walked around the center of the arbor as the flag song was sung. Pride expanded his chest as he carried the flag and followed the other flag bearers. His name was mentioned and there were a few cheers. He didn't want to peer around to see who made the noise. His gaze remained front and center just as he'd been taught in the Army. They all stopped and an elder offered a prayer. When the elder finished, the victory song was sung and the flags were placed in the standards on the platform where the emcee sat.

Then they asked the veterans to form a line. He and Dani walked out to the line. There were twenty-three people in the line. The emcee went down the line asking when they served and for how long. Dani had the longest service. When the man walked up to Hawke, he said, "I understand you are serving in the State Police now."

"I am."

"It's time we had someone to speak up for us there." He put a hand on Hawke's shoulder and moved on to the next person.

When they finished with the veterans, Hawke grasped Dani's hand and they went looking for his mom and sister. Just as they were sighted, his phone buzzed.

Dani gave him a look that said, he should have left it at home. But he glanced at the name and saw it was Sergeant Spruel. He wouldn't have called if it wasn't important. "I'll catch up," he said and answered. "Hawke."

"Hey, I was going through some of the current financial records for the Pinsons and they paid Wendy Fielding two payments of one-hundred-and-twenty dollars in the last month. Once specifically after the Brazo homicide."

Hawke stared at Tick Hill rising on the north side of the powwow grounds. "I'll call Fanny and see what she can tell me. I don't want Christa to know we are looking into Wendy if they are working together. I just found out that Wendy cleaned Dr. Ashley's house and that she probably made a wax impression of the doctor's key for the drug box on her vehicle."

"That's a huge break in this case. Keep me up to date on what you discover. And sorry to call you when you're spending time with your family."

"It's all good. Thanks." Hawke spotted his family heading toward the arbor as they called for the Friendship dance.

He quickly dialed Fanny.

"Hello. I didn't expect to hear from you again," Fanny answered.

"I have a question I want you to answer and not tell anyone else I asked you. Why would your mom pay Wendy Fielding a hundred and twenty dollars several times?"

"She cleans when our regular lady is visiting her family," Fanny said. "Is that a problem?"

"Do your mom and Wendy act as if they've known each other before?" Hawke asked, seeing his family all going into the arbor for the dance. His mom was searching the outside of the arbor. Her gaze locked on his and he knew he better get in there.

"No. I thought she was recommended by our housekeeper. Do you want me to ask?"

"No. Don't say anything to anyone. Thank you for the information." Hawke ended the call and strode to the arbor. He entered through a side opening and stepped into the line of people stepping to their left, going clockwise around the edge of the dance floor, stepping to the beat of the drums. His mom, Marion, Dani, and Flo were directly across from him. He smiled at them and drifted into the beat of the drums. The beginning of the line broke free and began moving in the opposite direction, shaking hands down the line. When his family came to him, he received a reproachful glare from his mom and amused smiles from the other women.

When the dance ended, he found his family and was drawn over to a group sitting in camp chairs not far from one of the drum groups. He was introduced to cousins, aunts, and uncles whom he had never met before. As they sat around talking, he relaxed and felt a part of something he hadn't known had been missing. The men joked and the women talked about regalia and family members his mom had known during her brief marriage to his father.

The naming ceremonies went on as he visited with his family.

Dani pulled on his sleeve. "I'm thirsty. Do you want to go with me to get something to drink?"

He nodded. "We're going to get something to drink. Anyone else want anything?"

They all said they were fine.

As he and Dani wove their way through the spectators out to the food vendors, his phone buzzed. He glanced at the caller and handed Dani a twenty. "Get me an iced tea. I need to take this."

She nodded and disappeared.

"Fanny, what else did you learn?" he answered.

"Nothing. But Wendy called here asking to talk to Mom. She told me to go back to what I was doing but I

295

listened around the corner since you'd asked me about Wendy this morning. From her side of the conversation, it sounded like Wendy asked her something that upset her and then asked Mom to meet her somewhere."

"Did you hear anything about where they were going to meet?"

"No. When I asked Mom where she was going, she said none of my business. I didn't know what else to do but call you."

Hawke wondered where Wendy would meet up with Christa. "How long ago did this happen?"

"About thirty minutes ago. I couldn't get on the phone because Dad was on it as soon as Mom hung up." Fanny sucked in air. "What is happening? Do you think Dad and Wendy are going to hurt Mom?"

"Why do you say that?" Hawke went on alert that the daughter would jump to this conclusion not knowing about Wendy and Ford's past.

"Because I heard Dad saying she doesn't know anything. You're going to ruin things." Fanny's voice was rising to a higher pitch as she talked.

"Calm down. Is your dad still there? Or did he take off, too?" Hawke asked.

"He went out to the barn. That's what he does when he's upset. He goes out and cleans stalls."

"Go get him and call me back. We need to find out where Wendy is meeting your mom. But don't let on that we know he talked to Wendy, if that was who he was talking to."

"Who are you talking to?" Harry demanded.

"Hey!" Fanny cried out.

"Who is this?" Harry demanded again, this time in the phone.

"It's State Trooper Hawke. Do you know where your sister went when she left?"

"Why would I keep tabs on my older sister. She can take care of herself."

"I don't think so. We need to know where she went. I think she's walking into a trap." Hawke hoped the man didn't go running to Ford. Because it sounded like he knew what was about to happen.

"You're kidding me, right?" Harry said.

"No, I'm not. Do you have any idea how to find out where she is?"

"Ford has tracking on her phone. I'll go get his phone. Fanny, keep him on the line."

Hawke heard running steps echoing in the house. "Fanny. Follow him."

He heard heavy breathing and the sound of smaller feet running.

"Oh, no!" Fanny exclaimed.

"What is it?" Hawke asked.

"Uncle Harry punched Dad and he's pulling the phone out of his pocket."

"From what I see on this phone, she just entered Eagle." Harry's voice boomed in the phone.

Hawke ran toward his pickup. "Tell me if she turns down Fourth Street. If so, I know where she's going."

He started the vehicle and maneuvered through the parked cars and out to Whiskey Creek Road and then onto the main road through Eagle.

"She is on Fourth Street and it looks like she's stopped," Harry said.

"Hang up and call the county police and ask them to pick up Ford for Trooper Hawke to question." He didn't wait for Harry to acknowledge what he'd said.

He ended the call and concentrated on getting to Lucas Brazo's mobile home before it was too late.

Chapter Thirty-two

Hawke parked at the Six Pines entrance and didn't even hide as he walked straight for Lucas's mobile home.

"Hawke, why are you dressed like that?" Dougie called from his yard.

Changing his direction, Hawke walked over to the boy. "I'm busy at the moment. But you could help me out if you'd go in the house and use this phone to call," he scrolled to Sergeant Spruel's number, "this number and tell him Hawke needs backup."

Dougie studied him. "You need backup to talk to two ladies?"

It was Hawke's turn to study the boy. "What two ladies?"

"Wendy and another lady I've seen talking to Lucas are in his house. I thought maybe they were cleaning it out."

"They aren't. Make that call for me, please."

Hawke gave the boy a little push toward the door of the house and spun around, moving quickly and quietly toward the mobile home with the crime scene tape flapping in the wind.

He moved carefully up to a window and peeked in. Christa was sitting at the kitchen table, a pen in her hand and paper in front of her. Wendy stood with her back to the window.

"I want you to write down that you couldn't live with the guilt any more. And sign your name," Wendy said.

"What guilt? I don't have any guilt." Christa glared at her.

"The fact you paid someone to kill your first husband so you could marry Ford and then killing Lucas when you realized he'd figure out you were the killer." Wendy's tone held a note of the wildness Hawke had thought was on the periphery of her too staid personality.

"But I didn't do any of that."

"Are you sure? I know you and that brother of yours weren't at a wedding the weekend your first husband died. And the police know. They think the two of you killed him. So, therefore, you did. And the vial of the drug used to kill Lucas was found in your granddaughter's toy box. You hid it there thinking no one would ever find it."

"Why would I put a drug in my granddaughter's toy box? That's insane."

"Exactly. You've cracked and now you're going to end your life as you did Lucas's." Wendy stepped forward and Hawke saw the syringe in her hand.

He didn't know how to get in the house without

Wendy seeing or hearing him. But he needed to get in there before she gave Christa a lethal dose.

Sirens shrieked, growing louder as his backup arrived.

Wendy spun to the door. Hawke placed his hands on the window, shove it up, and motioned for Christa to dive for the window. She did just as Wendy turned back to the room. Hawke pulled Christa to safety. "Go to the front and tell whoever just showed up that there is a hysterical woman inside."

Christa nodded and ran to the front of the house.

Hawke faced the window to make sure Wendy didn't try to get out through him.

She walked back into the kitchen, her eyes wild with fright. She spotted him, glanced over her shoulder at the front door, and jabbed the syringe into her neck, pressing on the plunger with the flat of her hand.

He ran around to the front, barging through the deputies who were cautiously entering, and found Wendy writhing on the floor. He knew it was too late to try to save her.

«»«»«»

Hawke ran a hand across the back of his neck and called Dani. "Hey, I'm not going to make it back to the powwow. I can't talk about it yet. Just go home with Mom and Marion when they're ready to leave. I'll get home as soon as I can."

"Is everything okay? Or are you going after someone?" Dani asked, a hint of worry in her tone.

"I'm not going after anyone. It just turned messy. I have interviews to do and reports to file. See you at home." He ended the call and glanced over at Christa. She was visibly shaken. Her arms were wrapped around her body and her face was pale.

Before approaching her, he walked over to Deputy Alden and Trooper Shoberg who arrived while Hawke was talking to Dani. "I'll leave you two to wait for the medical examiner and the morgue. She stabbed herself in the neck with the drug. I saw it from outside the window and couldn't stop her." He tipped his head toward Christa. "I want to know if any of the things I heard the victim say to her were true. And a lot of other unanswered questions. Then I'll write up my report on the incident. Could you call Spruel and let him know I'm bringing her to the Winslow office?"

Shoberg nodded. "Sorry this happened on your weekend off." His gaze scanned Hawke's clothing.

"Yeah, me too." Hawke left them and walked over to Christa. "Come on. We're going to the Winslow Office. I want to ask you some things." He took her by the elbow and led her over to his vehicle.

Once they were headed out of Eagle, she asked, "Why are you dressed like that?"

"I was attending the powwow with my family." He regretted he'd left them all there as if the event meant nothing to him when he was sad to have missed Marion's dance competition.

"How did you know I was at Lucas's?" She sat against the passenger door as if she would be ready to run as soon as he stopped the vehicle.

"Fanny called me. She was worried you were in trouble." He glanced over. The information seemed to shock her.

"Fanny? Why would she think I was in trouble and why would she call you?"

"Because I had talked to her earlier to find out if

Wendy had ever been to your house and discovered she had cleaned it since Lucas's death. That's how she put the vial of xylazine in your granddaughter's toy chest. But we'll discuss that at the station."

He slowed as they entered Winslow. Driving straight to the OSP office, he was happy to see that Sergeant Spruel's vehicle was in the parking lot. He didn't want to be alone with the woman. She had a cunningness to her that made him suspicious of any actions she might take to keep him from learning what he wanted to know.

"Why do I need to be interviewed? I was the victim."

"Which is why we need your statement to clarify why Wendy killed herself." Hawke parked and Spruel and Ivy walked out of the office.

Christa drew in a breath, and Ivy walked to the passenger side of the vehicle and opened the door.

"Mrs. Pinson, if you'll come with me, I'll get you settled with a cup of coffee in the breakroom." Ivy stood back, letting the woman slide off the pickup seat, and then led her into the building.

"Good call having Ivy here. I could see Christa trying to say I sexually harassed her to keep from telling me what I wanted to know."

"When Shoberg called and said you wanted me here, I figured there was a reason." Spruel waved Hawke into the building. "You want to go home and change before you do the interview?"

"No. It will waste time. I want to get this over with so I can get back to my family." Hawke stopped at Spruel's office. "You might call County and ask if they can bring Ford here."

Spruel's eyebrows raised. "County?"

"I asked Harry to call the Sheriff's office and have Ford picked up when I discovered where Christa had gone."

Spruel smiled. "You just want to see what he'll say and do."

"Yeah, don't say anything about Wendy. We'll see what he has to say and what he does when he gets here."

"Will do."

Hawke walked into the breakroom. Ivy placed Christa with her back to the door. She had a cup of coffee between her hands on the table. He walked around the table where Ivy had placed a cup of coffee, notepad, and pen. Along with a small recording device.

He smiled at the younger trooper. "Thank you for setting everything up."

She nodded and stood by the door.

"Why is she guarding the door? I thought this was just a statement about what happened to me?" Christa said.

"It is. She's only staying in the room because I wouldn't want you to feel vulnerable alone with me." Hawke moved the recorder to the middle of the table. "I'm going to record this so it will be easier for me to type up the report."

He pressed the button, stated the date and time, and his name. "I'm taking a statement from—" he nodded toward Christa.

"Christa Pinson," she said.

"Mrs. Pinson, why were you at Lucas Brazo's house? A place that was clearly marked as a crime scene."

"I received a call from Wendy Fielding. She cleans house for us. She said when she was at our house last, she found incriminating evidence in my granddaughter's room and if I wanted her to keep quiet, I needed to meet her at her house."

"What was the incriminating evidence?" Hawke asked, when what he really wanted to know was if you were innocent, why did you meet her?

"I'm guessing the vial of some drug she said she saw in my granddaughter's toy box." Christa picked up her drink and sipped.

"Why did you go? If you're innocent and didn't hide the vial, why would you agree to meet her?" Hawke asked.

She set the cup down and folded her hands in front of it. "I wanted to find out what she was talking about. You've been sniffing around my brother and my husband as if you think they killed Evan. I wanted to find out what she knew or thought she knew."

"Do you know if your husband or brother killed Evan and Lucas to hide the fact?" Hawke asked.

A nervous giggle escaped before she clamped her lips together.

"You do believe one of them killed Evan. Which one? You said you were with your brother at his wedding, but we learned the wedding didn't happen. Did the two of you decide to join your husband on the Snake River and instead of making it a happy family weekend, you had your brother kill him?"

"No! I didn't have anything to do with Evan's death, other than telling Harry he was lucky he backed out before he got caught up in a loveless relationship." Her eyes widened. "Do you think he killed Evan to get me out of my marriage?"

Hawke caught the theatrics in her question. He wondered what Harry would say if he knew his sister was practically saying he killed Evan. "You're saying your brother killed your first husband as a gift to you and you didn't realize it until right now?"

"That could have been what happened. Now that I think about it. I left Harry sitting at a bar the night he called off his wedding. I went to my room and then left for home the next morning. I don't know where he went."

Hawke jotted down *find out where Harry was after he canceled his wedding.* "What about the drug in Alicia's toy box? Why would Harry put it there? If indeed he is the one who drugged Lucas?"

"Who knows? He has never liked Fanny or Alicia. He sees them as competition."

"For what?"

"My money. I've been paying him five thousand dollars a month. At first, it was to help with my mom and dad, but when dad passed, she told him to stop giving her money. He needed it. You see, he didn't tell her it was coming from me."

Hawke could tell that angered her. Her cheeks flushed and her eyes sparked.

"Have you and Harry been competing for your mom's affection your whole lives?"

Her chin came up. "I can't help it I was a daddy's girl and Harry could never do anything right by him. But mom, she hated me because of my relationship with dad. But she didn't dote on Harry."

They'd strayed from what Hawke wanted to know. "Why did you meet with Lucas once a month?"

She stared at him, picked up the cup, acted like it was empty and set it back down. "He was Evan's friend."

"And he was looking into Evan's death. He never believed it was an accident. Did he keep asking you questions that were getting close to the truth? Is that why you took the xylazine bottle from Dr. Ashley's cart and put it in a bottle of booze that you knew Lucas would drink because he'd become an alcoholic."

"Who said I took a vial at the vet's?" She narrowed her eyes.

"No one. I saw it on a video." Hawke pulled out his phone, found the video he'd copied, and slid the phone across to her. "That was taken about a week before Lucas died from ingesting that drug with whiskey."

She shrugged. "I took the vial so I wouldn't have to put Shadow through an extra trip to town for another injection. She's old and riding in the trailer hurts her."

"Are you sure you didn't take that drug to get rid of the person who was getting too close to the truth about your first husband's death?"

She slammed a hand down on the table. "I thought I was giving a statement about why I drove to Wendy's when she called, not being interrogated like I am the killer."

Hawke settled back in the chair. "Then tell me why you went and what happened when you arrived?"

"I got the call, and being curious, I drove to Eagle and knocked on Wendy's door. She said she wanted to show me something she'd found at Lucas's. So we walked over there, and when we got in the house, she shoved that syringe in my face and told me to sit at the table. There was a piece of paper and a pen sitting on the table. Then she wanted me to write a note that I was sorry for killing Lucas and Evan and that I couldn't live with the guilt. I knew she planned to kill me and make it look like a suicide, but I didn't know what to do. Then I saw you through the window and heard the sirens. She went to look out the door and you opened the window and pulled me out. I did as you asked and told the cops in front what you said." She crossed her arms and leaned back. "That's my statement."

"Did Wendy say why she was going to kill you? Why she wanted the deaths pinned on you?" Hawke asked.

"She killed herself, she was nuts. I don't know why she wanted to pin the deaths on me. I know she's hated me ever since I married Ford."

"Why was that?" Hawke asked.

"Because he has been in love with me since our college days. He brought Wendy to my wedding to Evan. I don't know if he thought that would make me jealous and not go through with the wedding or what. But she was definitely hanging on to him like an octopus to a rock."

"Didn't you find it awkward to have her cleaning your house since she had a thing for your husband?" Hawke asked, never sure he'd ever understand women.

"She was recommended when our housekeeper had to visit a relative. I was a little unsure but Ford told me he didn't have any feelings for her and never had. He'd only used her. Which I thought was funny since we were using her to clean our house." Christa barked an edgy laugh.

"I want to know where my wife is?" came a shout from outside of the room.

The deputy must have arrived.

"Mr. Pinson, she's giving a statement. Why don't you wait in here," Spruel's voice carried into the room.

"Ford! I'm in here!" Christa called out.

Ivy moved just before the door burst open.

Ford stood in the doorway. His nose was red as well as the whites of his eyes. It was pretty clear he'd been drinking before the deputy picked him up.

"Mr. Pinson, I'm just about finished taking your wife's statement. If you could, take a seat outside," Hawke said.

"No! I want to know why you have her in here? And why you sent a deputy to pick me up?" Ford stood in the doorway, his legs spread and his hands on the door jamb.

"That crazy Wendy tried to make me write a suicide note and kill me!" Christa flew out of her chair and landed against Ford, nearly toppling him over.

"Wendy? Why would she do something like that?" He stared at Christa before his gaze landed on Hawke. "Why the hell are you dressed like an Injun?"

Spruel moved Ford and Christa into the room and Ivy closed the door. "Why don't you both sit down until we conclude this interview." Spruel sat the couple together.

"Mr. Pinson, were you aware your wife took a vial of xylazine from the vet clinic the day you two brought her mare to be injected?" Hawke asked.

The man studied his wife. "You took the medicine? Why?"

"She said to give the mare a shot herself." Hawke studied the man's features.

Ford shook his head. "You didn't give her a shot. I

know, you need me to help hold her when you give her shots."

Christa grasped his hand. "That's because it hasn't been long enough to give her a shot yet."

"If that's the truth, then where can we find the vial you took from the vet clinic?" Hawke asked. "There should be a dose left in it."

She chewed on the tip of her upper lip and stared at Ford's hand that she clasped. "I'm not sure where it is."

"Could it be the empty vial I found in your granddaughter's toy box?" Hawke asked.

"You put a vial of a lethal drug in our granddaughter's room?" Ford drew away from his wife.

"She never plays with the toys in there anymore." Christa shrugged.

"Does this mean you are saying that you used the drug in that syringe to kill Lucas Brazo?" Hawke asked.

Christa sat back, pressing her lips into a firm line.

"What?" Ford stared at his wife. "You killed Lucas? Why?" He grabbed at her arm.

Ivy stepped between the two chairs, keeping the couple apart.

"You have pretty much told us you killed Lucas, you might as well tell Ford why since I'm pretty sure, you had hoped to make it look like he'd killed Lucas and your first husband." Hawke held back a triumphant smile when Christa's gaze bore into him with enough hatred to theoretically knock him out of his chair.

"You planned to pin Evan and Lucas's deaths on me?" Ford shot out of his chair and paced the room.

"Don't forget, whoever killed Evan also killed Professor Chang for taking a photo of Evan's murder," Hawke added.

Ford sat in a chair away from his wife and leaned toward Hawke. "I don't understand. If you had a photo, you would know I didn't do it and should know who did."

"The film was over thirty years old. We could see the actions the person did but we couldn't make out the face." Hawke held his hands out palms up. "We knew Evan had been struck and rolled into the river and the person had shot the man who took the photos but we have been piecing information together to find out who did those two killings." He tapped the pen on the notepad. "Lucas had also been piecing information together. After his death, we found a flash drive with information he'd gathered, but he hadn't made it any farther than we had. Then we used your financials and phone records to put your wife and Wendy together. That's when Fanny called and said Christa had received a call from Wendy and Fanny was worried. I was in Eagle at the powwow and popped over to the trailer park to check things out and found Wendy wielding a syringe and telling Christa to write a suicide note. I think she realized who had killed Lucas and Evan and just wanted you and knew the only way you'd turn to her was if Christa was dead and guilty of the crimes she'd committed. When I rescued Christa, Wendy knew she'd never have you and killed herself."

Ford stared at his wife. "You have killed four people. Not with your own hands but with your manipulation." He stood and headed for the door. He stopped. "And I've always known Fanny wasn't mine. You told me a long time ago that I didn't have the right lines to give you a child but you sure as hell liked my money. I knew that one night we spent together you didn't become pregnant. But I was so in love with you that I didn't care." He threw his hands in the air. "I'm through with you, and I'll make sure your daughter and granddaughter aren't caught up in your deceit." He walked out the door.

"Ford! Come back! I need you!" Christa wailed as Ivy put handcuffs on her.

"Take her to the jail," Spruel said.

When the women had left the building, Hawke pressed the button on the recorder and released a long sigh. "I'll get the paperwork written up. You might want to send someone to the ranch to pick up Harry." Hawke studied Spruel. "She didn't say it outright but she alluded to the fact she gave Harry the idea to kill Evan."

"What a mess. Just write up the paperwork to get her locked up and finish the rest on Monday. She won't be going anywhere until Lange reads the report and presses charges."

"If he's smart, he won't let her out on bail. She's a flight risk." Hawke stood, stretched, and walked out to his computer. He sat down and processed the arrest record and sent it to the county jail where Christa would be held until Lange pressed charges.

Hawke walked out to his vehicle, knowing he wouldn't be disturbed tomorrow at the powwow.

Chapter Thirty-three

Hawke smiled at Dani as they side stepped during the friendship dance on Sunday morning. He glanced across the circle at his mom, sister, and Quinn. When the FBI agent walked out of Marion's room that morning and Mom just smiled at him, Hawke decided he didn't care as long as Marion was happy.

His heart beat with the drums and his mind emptied of worry. He looked forward to watching Marion during the jingle dance later in the day. Today was all about family and connecting with his roots. Something he'd thought about and hadn't pursued.

Dani bumped him with an elbow.

He glanced over at her.

"You're smiling." She smiled back at him.

"I'm content and glad to be spending this day with you and my family."

Dani raised her chin, and Hawke glanced across the circle. "Even if it means spending the day with Quinn?"

He smiled. "Yes, even if it means spending the day

313

with him. He's not so bad. I think my sister brings out the best in him."

"I've heard a good woman can do that to a man."

He glanced over and noted the curve of her lips. "Has someone been saying something to you?"

The beginning of the line doubled back and everyone started shaking hands as they went by.

When the dance finished, Dani led him over to where the family had set up their chairs. "Your mom was telling me yesterday how she is so glad I've given you a reason to not work all the time."

Hawke sat in a chair and patted the one next to him. When Dani sat, he put a hand on her knee and said, "I think so too."

A boy of about six pulled a wagon toward them. Four furry puppies had their heads hanging over the edge.

Hawke stopped the wagon. "What breed are they?"

The boy smiled, showing off that his two front teeth were missing. "The mom is a mix of little dogs. Mom thinks poodle, terrier, and something else. The dad was a mutt down the street. They're only twenty dollars."

Hawke thought of Dougie and how much help he'd been to the investigation. "Which one of them follows you around the most? I want it for a boy so I'd like a dog that would be his friend."

"This one would be the best. He likes me and follows me everywhere, but mom said we can't keep any of them." He smiled. "I would like to see him go to another boy."

Hawke pulled out a twenty-dollar bill and handed it to the boy. "Thank you." He picked up the puppy the boy had indicated as liking him and set her on Dani's lap.

"Did you really get this for a boy?" she asked, petting the puppy.

"I did. Do you want to sit here with her or go with me to find a collar and leash?" He stood and took the puppy from her arms.

"I'll go with you. That is a girl so you can't be giving her some macho collar." Dani rose and they walked out of the arbor. "Who are you giving this puppy to?"

"A boy who lives at Six Pines. He was a big help in discovering information. He wants a dog but his mom said they couldn't afford the food."

"Then you shouldn't be giving them a dog." Dani stopped, placing her hands on her hips.

"I plan on setting up something with Mr. Barnes at the grocery here in Eagle. I'll pay him monthly for them to get the food for the dog and I'll tell the mom, I'll pay to have the dog spayed when she's old enough."

Dani wrapped her arm around his. "You are a big softy."

"Don't tell anyone. I have a reputation to keep up."

《》《》《》

Thank you for reading *Cougar's Cache.* I enjoyed writing this book and learning more about the job of an Oregon State Trooper in Wallowa County. I hope you enjoyed Hawke's latest adventure. Please leave a review where you purchased the book. You can also leave them at Goodreads and Bookbub. Reviews are how an author's book gets seen.

If you would like to stay in contact with me or know more about my books you can go to my website: https://www.patyjager.net or get my newsletter https://bit.ly/2IhmWcm

Murder of Ravens
Book 1
Print ISBN 978-1-947983-82-3
Mouse Trail Ends
Book 2
Print ISBN 978-1-947983-96-0
Rattlesnake Brother
Book 3
Print ISBN 978-1-950387-06-9
Chattering Blue Jay
Book 4
Print ISBN 978-1-950387-64-9
Fox Goes Hunting
Book 5
Print ISBN 978-1-952447-07-5
Turkey's Fiery Demise
Book 6
Print ISBN 978-1-952447-48-8
Stolen Butterfly
Book 7
Print ISBN 978-1-952447-77-8
Churlish Badger
Book 8
Print ISBN 978-1-952447-96-9
Owl's Silent Strike
Book 9
Print ISBN 978-1-957638-19-5
Bear Stalker
Book 10
Print ISBN 978-1-957638-64-5
Damning Firefly
Book 11
Print ISBN 978-1-957638-82-9

While you're waiting for the next Hawke book, check out my Shandra Higheagle Mystery series or my Spotted Pony Casino Mystery series.

About the Author

Paty Jager grew up in Wallowa County and has always been amazed by its beauty, history, and ruralness. After doing a ride-along with a Fish and Wildlife State Trooper in Wallowa County, she knew this was where she had to set the Gabriel Hawke series.

Paty is an award-winning author of 54 novels of murder mystery and western romance. All her work has Western or Native American elements in them along with hints of humor and engaging characters. She and her husband raise alfalfa hay in rural eastern Oregon. Riding horses and battling rattlesnakes, she not only writes the western lifestyle, she lives it.

By following me at one of these places you will always know when the next book is releasing and if I'm having any giveaways:

Website: http://www.patyjager.net
Blog: https://writingintothesunset.net/
FB Page: https://www.facebook.com/PatyJagerAuthor/
Pinterest: https://www.pinterest.com/patyjag/
Goodreads:
http://www.goodreads.com/author/show/1005334.Paty_Jager
Bookbub - https://www.bookbub.com/authors/paty-jager

Windtree
Press

Thank you for purchasing this Windtree Press
publication. For other books of the heart, please visit
our website at www.windtreepress.com.

For questions or more information contact us
at info@windtreepress.com.

Windtree Press
www.windtreepress.com
Corvallis, OR

Printed in the USA
CPSIA information can be obtained
at www.ICGtesting.com
LVHW090015030624
782054LV00002B/393